ALL THE BEAUTIFUL BRIDES

GRAVEYARD FALLS

ALL THE BEAUTIFUL BRIDES

GRAVEYARD FALLS

RITA HERRON

Montlake
Romance

Published by Montlake Romance, Seattle

www.apub.com

Amazon, the Amazon logo, and Montlake Romance are trademarks of Amazon.com, Inc., or its affiliates.

ISBN-13: 9781503945500
ISBN-10: 1503945502

Cover design by Marc J. Cohen

Printed in the United States of America

To Mother
For all your loving support—you'll always have my heart.

CHAPTER ONE

"There's been a murder in Graveyard Falls."

Special Agent Cal Coulter pinched the bridge of his nose as his director's words sank in. He'd been summoned to his boss's office first thing for a new assignment on the task force he was spearheading to hunt down the most wanted criminals across the Southeast.

But Graveyard Falls? That was the little town Mona had moved to after Brent had died.

Brent, his best friend.

And Mona, the only woman he'd ever wanted.

When Brent had become romantic with her, Cal had honored their friendship by stepping out of the picture.

"I want you to head up the investigation," Director Hiram Vance said, oblivious to his turmoil.

"Why are the Feds on this case?" Cal asked.

"You don't know the history of that town," Director Vance said. "For starters, it's named after a big waterfall in the mountains. Thirty years ago, three teenage girls were murdered there, pushed off the falls and left in the elements with a rose stem jammed down their throats. They called the perp the 'Thorn Ripper' because the girls' tongues and throats were bloody from the thorns." Director Vance paused. "Each year the town holds a memorial service. That service is being held today."

"So a murder occurred on the anniversary of the memorial," Cal said, understanding dawning.

"Exactly."

"The Thorn Ripper killer was never apprehended?"

"Yes, he was." Director Vance flipped his laptop around to show Cal the screen. "This man, Johnny Pike, was convicted of the crimes. But he's up for parole next week."

"How's that?"

"He was only eighteen at the time of his arrest. Due to his age and the controversy surrounding the case, the judge gave him life with the chance of parole after he served thirty years. That thirty years is up."

Cal considered the timing. "You think this latest murder is connected to the Thorn Ripper?"

Director Vance ran a hand over his balding head. "That's one thing I want you to find out. There are already protestors lining up to rally against Pike's parole."

"So someone could have killed the girl to cast doubt on Pike's guilt? Are the MOs even the same?"

"All questions I want you to find the answers to."

Now he understood. "All right. But odds are it's just some local domestic. Girlfriend-boyfriend fight gone bad."

"Could be," Vance said. "But the Thorn Ripper case attracted a lot of publicity at the time. Pike could have developed a protégé or attracted a copycat. I need you to go to the town. Get the background on the MO, the victim. Talk to the locals. Find out if there is a connection to Pike."

Cal stood. Any one of the theories was possible.

And if they didn't solve the case soon, he could imagine the panic in Graveyard Falls.

Mona Monroe had moved to the small town of Graveyard Falls on a mission.

To find her birth mother.

She twisted the silver baby bootie charm on the chain around her neck, her stomach knotting. She wished she had more information.

But all she had was the envelope her parents' lawyer had given her after their death. The letter explained that her birth mother had lived in this town. Inside, she also found a yellowed sales slip from a gift store in Graveyard Falls where the charm had been bought. It was dated the same year as the Thorn Ripper murders.

She still couldn't believe it. Her whole life had been a lie.

But she was determined to unearth the truth.

She parked at the Baptist church, which was holding the memorial service for the Thorn Ripper victims. Every March the town honored the girls.

She'd heard the story. Three pretty, popular girls who were loved by everyone had been killed shortly before their senior prom and graduation. Just as winter barreled on with frigid temperatures and snowstorms this year, it had refused to leave the mountains back then. Outside it felt more like January than two weeks before spring.

The football star Johnny Pike had been convicted of the murders. Although Mona had never heard anyone say he had a clear motive. Just that he was a psychopath.

Apparently her mother had given birth to her months after the murders occurred. She also could have known Johnny Pike and the victims.

Whether she'd stayed in Graveyard Falls or moved away was the question.

But if she had stayed, she might be attending this memorial.

Would Mona recognize her if she saw her? See some family resemblance?

Probably not. But it was worth a shot.

If she got to know some of the locals, maybe she'd find out exactly who she was.

She pressed a hand to her stomach, feeling the loss of her own child deep down in her bones. She'd wanted that baby so badly, but a miscarriage had stolen it from her.

She would never have given up her child.

She had to know the reason her own mother had.

Cal pulled up a summary of the Thorn Ripper case to study it before he got on the road.

He had his job cut out for him just to keep this recent murder out of the press before he could absorb the details. He wanted to avoid panic and sensationalism, and he needed time to analyze the situation before the reporters starting dogging him.

Information about the Thorn Ripper filled his computer screen: three girls, all homecoming royalty, murdered, found at the base of the waterfall, the stem of a blood-red rose jammed down their throats.

Johnny Pike, football star and voted "Most Likely to Succeed," arrested by local sheriff Ned Buckley. A well of circumstantial evidence had been found implicating the young man, who was now serving his sentence in a maximum-security prison.

Although Pike had pleaded not guilty and claimed he was framed, at the last minute he'd accepted a controversial plea bargain to be eligible for parole in thirty years.

The serial killer had torn the town apart years ago. Was this homicide related?

Cal closed his laptop, then carried it to his vehicle and started the drive toward Graveyard Falls. The sun fought to shine through the gray clouds hovering above, giving the mountains a gloomy feel.

On his way out of Knoxville, he drove past the cemetery where Brent was buried.

But Cal couldn't bring himself to stop.

Because the secrets he'd harbored for his buddy were eating him up.

It had only been three months since Brent had been in that fatal car accident. Cal had attended the funeral. How could he not?

They had been like brothers. He'd known Brent since they were kids in foster care together. Brent had taken beatings for him when they were little.

He'd owed him . . .

But things had changed the last few years. Now Cal's grief was mixed with animosity.

And resentment that Brent had married Mona.

Dark clouds rolled in, threatening sleet as he turned on the country road toward the small town. Dead leaves swirled across the highway, broken and crumbling like ashes against the snowy ground.

The mountain roads were treacherous, and his tires skated on the black ice from the last storm. Trees stood so close together and thick on the ridges that they looked ominous, like soldiers guarding the dark secrets in their depths.

Some said the devil lived inside these mountain walls. That the mountain men were his followers.

Ten minutes later, Cal was still trying to shake off his bad mood as he parked at the clearing for tourists who came to hike the falls.

Tugging his coat around him, he yanked on gloves and started through the path, grateful he'd worn boots. Spring should be coming soon with budding trees and flowers, but just as the groundhog had predicted, winter had relentlessly stayed.

He'd thought the gossip about hearing the dead girls' screams echoing off the mountain was just local folklore. But dammit, the screech of the wind sounded exactly like a woman crying.

Hemlocks, oaks, and white pines covered acres, magnolias and rhododendrons surrounding the base of the falls, where the water formed a deep pool. It was a good two-mile hike to the top with the 250-foot waterfalls creating 20-foot cascades, and a dramatic 130-foot drop-off at the lowest base.

Voices sounded ahead.

He spotted a dark-haired man in a deputy's uniform talking to a young guy, probably college aged, dressed in hiking gear. North Face jacket, custom boots, and an insulated backpack—the kid came from money. He also had a high-tech camera slung around his neck.

Cal parted the limbs, fresh snow pelting him from the branches. He came to a halt, his stomach knotting as he spotted the victim.

A young woman lay at the edge of the falls, her head positioned on a jagged rock as if it were a pillow, her dress in folds around her legs, the lace wet from the water.

But it was the wedding gown and red rose that made him go cold.

The white dress was torn, marred in mud now, and a lacy garter was around her neck.

Even more disturbing—the flower petals of the rose were torn off, lying nearby, the end of the stem extending from her mouth, the rest likely crammed down her throat just like the Thorn Ripper had done thirty years ago.

CHAPTER TWO

Mona searched the crowd at the memorial service for a familiar face just as she'd searched shopping malls, grocery stores, and parks, almost everywhere she went these days, for someone who might resemble her.

Could one of the women at the service be her birth mother?

If not, where was she? And what had she been doing the past thirty years? Did she ever think about her? Miss her? Wonder what she looked like or what she'd done with her life?

A stiff wind whistled through the hemlocks and swirled dead leaves across the tombstones, nearly drowning out the pastor's words. Sniffles echoed through the crowd, the women and men hunched together against the cold and the horror that still shrouded this town from the teenage deaths that had left everyone in shock.

No one had wanted to believe high school girls were in danger. Not in a small town where everyone knew everyone else. Where neighbors watched your back and people left their cars and doors unlocked.

Or that the resident popular football player Johnny Pike would take anyone's life.

After all, why would he push the teenagers to their deaths? All the girls liked him . . .

According to the articles she'd read, gossip and paranoia led to different theories. Some said he was a closet narcissist. A psychopath.

But his parents had denied the allegations.

"Today we're here to honor three girls who will forever stand in a special place in all our hearts," the pastor began. "Tiffany Levinson. Candy Yonkers. And Brittany Burgess."

As he named each girl, a representative of her family stepped forward to light a candle in her honor. Sara, Tiffany's mother, Mona heard someone say. Candy's brother, Doyle Yonkers. And Brittany's father.

Mona's heart squeezed for the families. She'd lost her baby in utero. She couldn't imagine holding that child, watching it grow to be a young man or woman, then losing him or her so violently.

The service ended, and Mona strolled through the crowd and introduced herself to a few locals, but she felt like an outsider, as if she was intruding on their grief.

Now probably wasn't the best time to ask them if they remembered a pregnant classmate. Still, she was here and she barely knew anyone in town, so she joined a group of women huddled by the photographs, candles, and flowers arranged in memoriam to the girls. One of them was Sara Levinson.

She introduced herself. "My name is Mona Monroe. I just moved here and wanted to offer my condolences."

Sara gestured toward a woman working the crowd. "This day is hard enough without reporters like that Carol Little poking their noses in our past," Sara said. "We've been through enough."

Mona dug her hands in her pockets. She hated that the press invaded people's grief just to get a story.

"I heard Johnny Pike might be paroled," another woman said.

"Oh, God," Sara said. "They can't let that maniac back on the streets."

"I've already written a letter to the Board of Pardons and Parole voicing my opinion," a woman with dark, thinning hair said.

Mona noticed Candy Yonkers's brother, Doyle, watching them with a frown. He must have been, what? Ten or so when his sister was murdered?

Sara cleared her throat. "Sheriff Buckley said he'll go to the hearing and make sure the judge knows how dangerous that boy was."

"I thought Ned retired," another woman said.

"He did, but that doesn't mean he can't testify."

Mona spotted the man they were talking about standing close by with the preacher—Sheriff Ned Buckley. He appeared to be in his late sixties with a craggy face and wore khaki pants and a hat.

He was talking to a woman wearing a big black hat and long skirt. The two of them looked serious, deep in conversation, then the woman wiped her eyes with a handkerchief.

"Don't worry, Felicity, Pike will never get released," Sheriff Buckley said.

The woman looked worried, her eyes darting about, then she suddenly dashed away through the tombstones.

She must have known the victims and obviously didn't want Pike paroled.

"Sheriff Buckley made the arrest, didn't he?" Mona asked.

Sara nodded. "If it hadn't been for him, there would have been more murders."

"His daughter, Anna, dated Johnny," the woman with the thinning hair whispered. "Some of us thought she knew what he was up to. I heard her daddy covered up for her. That's why she left town."

The reporter Carol Little approached the sheriff. "Sheriff, can I get a statement from you about the Thorn Ripper?"

"Leave us the hell alone." Sheriff Buckley started to walk away, but Carol followed on his heels and caught his arm.

"But isn't it true that you're going to attend Johnny Pike's parole hearing?"

Sheriff Buckley jerked around and glared at her. "Yes, it is. As long as I'm alive, that boy won't see the light of day."

"But it's been thirty years," Carol said. "Don't you think he's redeemed himself?"

The sheriff's nostrils flared. "How can you redeem yourself for stealing the lives of three young women?"

But Carol didn't back down. "Mr. Pike claims that he was framed," she said. "With new technology, shouldn't the evidence be reviewed? Now they could run DNA tests—"

"Listen to me, lady," Sheriff Buckley said with a dark scowl. "Don't stir up trouble. We make it through this ceremony every year, then we try to forget it for a while."

Buckley glanced over the reporter's shoulder at Mona, and for just a moment, his gaze latched with hers. His eyes darkened, his scowl growing more intense.

Then he pushed past the reporter. "Now, leave the past buried where it belongs and get out of town."

Mona shivered. His cutting look chilled her to the bone. He'd been talking to the reporter, but he was looking at her as he said it.

◆ ◆ ◆

The rain and sleet slashing the sharp mountain ridges looked like a river spilling over the ledge as he drove around the switchbacks.

Just as the locals claimed, he'd heard the cries of the dead girls echoing through the hills. Especially the one he'd just left behind at Graveyard Falls.

He'd honored her by staying with her last night. Because she had been so beautiful and he'd wanted her.

But she hadn't returned his love.

He could still see her begging him to stop. To save her.

She'd promised to do anything if he let her go.

But she hadn't been worth saving.

Not to worry, though.

He would find another.

CHAPTER THREE

Cal introduced himself to the deputy, a tall, broad-shouldered man named Ian Kimball, then knelt to examine the victim's body.

He estimated her age to be early twenties. Damn. She'd had her whole life in front of her.

Judging from the wedding gown, marriage had been part of her plans.

He glanced up at the mountain and around the woods. Questions assailed him. Was the killer trying to draw attention to the old case and Pike's upcoming parole hearing? Did he have some kind of hero worship for Pike and want the same kind of attention he'd received?

Or had the killer simply dumped the victim here thinking no one would find her? That the elements would destroy DNA or forensics? That the animals in the wilderness would ravage her body, making identification more difficult?

He touched her arm. Her skin was as cold as ice. Her brown hair was choppy, wet, and tangled, the long white wedding dress splattered with mud. Her oval face was devoid of makeup except for the stark red lipstick on her mouth.

Her green eyes stared at him as if in shock that someone would do this to her.

Crystals of frozen water had settled on her lashes, sand and limestone particles mingling with leaves and twigs from the falls on her hands and clothing.

He surveyed the deserted clearing, a sick knot in the pit of his stomach. Was she on the way to her wedding when she was attacked? Had she just gotten married?

He examined her hand. No engagement or wedding ring. Had the killer taken it?

The garter was wound so tightly around her neck that purple marks darkened her pale skin. Scratches marred her neck where she'd fought to keep from choking.

Hopefully she'd scratched her attacker, and they'd find DNA beneath her fingernails.

But the thorns in her mouth made his stomach clench.

The fact that she was dressed in a wedding gown suggested she probably knew her killer. Her fiancé? Husband? Lover? Someone who didn't want her to get married? A jealous woman?

And if she was engaged, where was her fiancé?

Confusion clouded Mona's mind as she left the memorial service. She understood how painful it was for victims and their families to discuss crimes against them.

After all, her parents had died during a break-in at their house.

Apparently the robbers, who'd been casing the neighborhood for weeks, had thought her parents were out of town for the holidays. But her mother had had a migraine that day and they'd postponed their vacation.

At least the police had caught the men, but that hadn't brought her parents back.

Fortunately, she'd met Brent during the investigation. He'd tracked down the culprits and put them away.

After that, she'd decided to add criminology studies to her counseling degree and had spent a year learning about the minds of criminals.

Then she'd accepted a job with the courts as a victim's advocate. She'd counseled victims, sat with them during court trials and hearings, and mediated between them and the attorneys. She'd even assisted the prosecutor and detectives a few times. She had a knack for understanding criminal behavior, and helping others had aided her in working through her own grief.

But when she'd moved here, she'd decided to take a break to research her past so she'd set up a part-time private counseling office. Shortly after she opened her practice, a man named Chance Dyer had approached her and asked her to do a radio talk show, and she'd agreed.

She parked in front of the radio station, forcing herself to move forward. One day at a time. Her boots sank into the snow and ice, the freezing wind ripping at her, nearly knocking her over. The wind banged the shutters against the wood frame of the older colonial house where the station was located. She battled against the force of it and ran through the slush until she reached the door.

Chance, the producer of the radio station, a hippie-looking guy in his thirties, greeted her with a smile. He was handsome in a throwback kind of way, and an interesting DJ with a charismatic, honey-slick voice.

He'd asked her out for coffee once, but she'd gently turned him down. She wasn't interested in hooking up or opening her heart to a man and getting hurt again.

She settled into the chair, while Chance went to the sound room connected to the studio by a glass partition, where he would screen calls and cue up intro and outro music, then motioned for her to begin.

So far, the show had gotten off to a good start. People called in to discuss anything from work-related issues to marital and family problems. Today she expected callers who wanted to discuss the memorial service.

Mona slipped on her headphones. "This is Mona Monroe coming to you live with *Ask Mona*. The lines are open."

Chance pointed to the board as it began to light up with calls.

"Hello, this is Mona. And you are?"

"Josie."

"What's on your mind tonight, Josie?"

"It's my mother. She grew up in Graveyard Falls but moved away. Last week we came back to town to take care of my grandfather, who has health issues, only she acts like she hates him. They had a big falling out before I was born, and have hardly spoken since."

"Did she tell you what went wrong between them?"

"No. But it all happened the same year those girls died."

The hair on the back of Mona's neck prickled. "She lived here then?"

"Yes. But she won't talk about the past. I think she might have known some of those girls. I guess it was hard to see her classmates murdered."

"Yes. That obviously was a difficult time for everyone," Mona said. "People are still grieving."

"I get that. But she especially won't talk about my father. She told me he died. But I don't think that's true."

Mona could certainly relate to being lied to. Her adoptive parents had done that all her life. "Have you tried talking to her?"

"Yes, but she clams up." Josie paused. "I found a diary she kept in high school. I think my father's name might be in it. But she became livid when I tried to look at it."

Mona took a deep breath. She didn't want to encourage the young woman to violate her mother's privacy, but she understood her need to know the truth. "I suggest you have a heart-to-heart and explain how you feel."

A voice sounded in the background, and Josie muttered she had to go. Mona hoped she'd call back.

Another call was waiting, so Chance connected it. The caller immediately launched into her suspicions that her husband was cheating on her.

Mona suggested she confront her husband and then encouraged her to ask him to attend counseling.

To her, trust was the most important thing in a marriage.

At least Brent had been faithful.

No one could take that away from her now.

◆ ◆ ◆

Cal catalogued the details of the MO—wedding dress, red lipstick, the rose, the thorns that had bloodied the woman's mouth and throat . . .

The location and the rose stems were similar to the Thorn Ripper case. But there were also differences.

The wedding dress, the garter, the lipstick, the stun gun markings.

The wind whipped the trees into a frenzy, sending icy pellets from their branches and twigs falling to the ground. Cal stepped sideways to avoid getting pummeled by the deluge.

Identifying the victim was the first step in uncovering what had brought her to this point—and who had left her here dead.

Cal turned to the deputy. "Have you received any missing-persons reports in the past week?"

The deputy shook his head, a dark glint in his eyes. Adrenaline, excitement, he was wired to work this case.

"First murder, Deputy Kimball?" Cal asked.

The deputy nodded. "Yeah, things have been calm since I took over for Sheriff Buckley. Sometimes I wonder if we even need the two assistant deputies in town. Although now they're coming in handy."

"What's going on with Sheriff Buckley?"

"He has a brain tumor, inoperable," Deputy Kimball said. "Although he's adamant about attending Pike's parole hearing." Kimball cleared his throat. "I called a forensic unit from the county. They oughta be here soon."

"Good. Do you know this woman?"

"No. But I just moved here a couple of months ago. And I didn't find a purse or wallet."

The hiker looked up at Cal, his color pasty gray. In spite of the cold, a fine coat of sweat beaded his skin. "Can I go now?"

The deputy glanced at Cal. "His name is Joey Lamb. I got his statement and contact information."

Cal crossed his arms. "Do you mind running through what happened again?"

Joey jiggled his leg up and down. "I was hiking and found her like that." He pointed to the poor woman. "What kind of sick creep does such a thing?"

"That's what we intend to find out," Cal said. "Did you touch her?"

"Hell, no. I mean, I could tell she was dead, so I called nine-one-one."

"You come hiking in weather like this a lot?"

Joey's shaggy, dark hair brushed the collar of his insulated jacket as he shook his head. "I'm taking a photography class, and the teacher's running a contest. I came to take some pictures of the falls and the woods—you know, the ice and snow on the mountains." He dug his boot into the sludge at his feet. "Thought maybe I'd capture the image of the dead girls' faces they say you can see on the side of the ridge, but I didn't see 'em." He coughed into his gloves as if he realized the implications as he looked at the victim. "I never expected to find an actual dead girl."

"You camped here last night?"

Joey pointed to the hills. "Up the mountain a few miles. Brought a night lens hoping to see the water turn red like some of the locals claim. They say it's the girls' tears turning to blood. That's why they nicknamed this mountain 'Teardrop Mountain.' It's supposed to show up at dawn and sunset. Figured I could win the contest with a shot like that. Winner gets a thousand bucks."

Cal picked up the travel backpack. "Mind if I look in here?"

Joey muttered something under his breath but shrugged, and Cal unzipped the bag. He rummaged through it but found nothing suspicious. An extra camera lens and memory card. Snack bars, a water bottle, tarp, sleeping bag. There was a pocketknife, but it had no blood on it.

Cal shoved the backpack toward the kid. "Did you see or hear anyone else around?"

"No. Spotted a few deer and thought I saw a coyote. But no people."

The deputy's phone buzzed, and he answered the call. "Yeah, come on up." He pocketed the phone and looked at Cal. "Crime team and medical examiner are here."

"Good, maybe the ME can establish time of death." Cal turned back to the boy. "One more thing, Joey. Did you take pictures of the woman?"

A guilty look flashed across the young man's face. "I . . . just a couple. For my class."

Damn Internet-crazed generation. Probably took a selfie posed beside her. "Let me see your camera and phone."

Joey handed over the camera, then his cell phone.

"You text or email the pics to anyone?" Cal asked.

"No, not yet."

"And you aren't going to. These might be evidence." Cal texted the pictures from the guy's phone to his, then deleted them. Next, he removed the memory card from the camera.

"I need those other pictures on the card, man," Joey said.

"I'll get them back to you as soon as CSI processes them."

Joey didn't look happy, but he gave a resigned nod.

"And don't leave town. We might need to talk to you again."

That comment brought alarm to the young man's face, and he snatched his camera. "Can I go now?"

Cal nodded, and the boy headed down the trail just as the medical examiner and crime team appeared.

CHAPTER FOUR

The scent of death swirled in the air, the wind raging off the mountain screeching a reminder that winter could kill with its brutal force.

While the investigators combed the woods and falls for forensic evidence, the medical examiner, Dr. David Wheeland, stooped down to examine the body. "Judging from rigor and the liver-temp test, I'd estimate TOD around midnight last night, give or take a couple of hours. The freezing temperature and temperature of the water probably slowed down decomp."

"No wedding or engagement ring, so she either didn't have one, hadn't gone through with the ceremony, or the killer took it." Cal gestured toward the woman's hands. "Her fingernails are broken and jagged. Looks like she fought. Think you can get DNA?"

"I'll try." Dr. Wheeland eased the garter slightly to the side and indicated the bruises on her throat. "Appears she died of strangulation, but I'll know for certain after the autopsy."

"Do you see any other injuries?"

Dr. Wheeland pointed to her wrists. "She was tied up, but she fought back. There's also stun gun burns on her neck." He lifted the bottom of the tattered wedding gown and muttered a sound of disgust. "Some bruises on her legs and thighs, but I don't see fluids. I'll let you know about sexual assault once I've completed my report."

Cal scanned the area. "No evidence the falls was the kill spot, although the wind and snow drifts could have covered the tracks. My guess is he killed her somewhere else, then brought her body to the falls and dumped it." She was petite, probably five-three, 115 pounds. A lightweight, but a dead body was heavier than a live one, and the conditions would have made it difficult to walk. Rafting in seemed unlikely—the current ran away from the falls, not toward them, which would have meant paddling upstream.

"Probably thought it would be days, maybe weeks or months, before she was found, what with the park being closed for winter." Dr. Wheeland lifted his head. "You know, this is odd. It looks like the killer might have cut her hair."

"What?"

"The ends are jagged."

Cal bent over, grimacing. Why cut her hair?

He snapped close-ups of the jagged ends and the bruises on her arms and legs, then turned to look across the mountain into the woods. CSI was searching for campsites, an RV, an abandoned cabin, any indication that the killer had kept her out in the woods or somewhere on the mountain.

He scanned the area again, looking for evidence indicating which direction the killer had come from. It was at least a mile to the nearest clearing. Two to the spot where he'd parked. Four to the nearest campground.

Although it wasn't camping season, some hunters still liked to brave the elements.

And there were the occasional tourists traveling through who wanted to see the much-gossiped-about Graveyard Falls, where the Thorn Ripper had created havoc.

Remote cabins were scattered through the hills, some so far off the grid that Cal wondered who the hell would live there.

Someone mentally deranged or hiding from the law? The few true mountain people he'd met were . . . strange.

They lived off the land, fished in the streams, were antisocial, and didn't appreciate visitors. Some were paranoid about the government, hoarding food and weapons in case of a nuclear bomb. A few suffered from mental problems.

Others were running from the law.

One of the CSIs had knelt by a clump of bushes to examine the ground. Blowing on his hands to warm them, Cal walked over to join him.

"Did you find something?"

The CSI pointed out a partial boot print. "Might be from the killer. Looks like a man's."

"Take a photo and cast of it," Cal said. He studied the angle of the boot print and noticed it was headed east. "Did you find any other prints?" Cal asked. "The woman's?" Not that the heels she was wearing would have made much of a print.

"None as small as the victim's. We did find one partial print a few feet up, but there's not enough to tell us much."

Though not surprised, Cal gritted his teeth in frustration.

Identifying the victim might lead him to a fiancé or husband.

Or someone who could have wanted to stop the woman's wedding enough to kill her before she said *I do.*

♦ ♦ ♦

Mona adjusted her mic. "Yes, this is Mona. What would you like to talk about tonight?"

A breath echoed over the line, then a moment of silence stretched between them, awkward and unsettling. She reminded herself that some people were reluctant to spill their personal problems to a stranger, especially on air. Men usually balked at counseling anyway.

"You think you can help me?"

"I hope so," Mona said, forcing herself to remain calm, professional. Confident.

"What's your name?"

More breathing. "You can call me Will because I will get what I want. I will obey God. I will take care of my family as I should."

A shiver rippled up her spine. His words and the sinister ring to his voice made her uncomfortable.

"I want a family. Tell me how to find the perfect wife."

Mona made a note on her pad, her first impressions of the caller. When she'd accepted the job, she'd insisted that all the calls be recorded for safety and legal reasons. "Why don't you start by telling me about yourself. What do you do for a living?"

"Is that all women care about?" Will asked, defensive. "How much money a man makes?"

Mona tapped her fingers along her thigh. One rule of counseling was not to get personally involved or bring one's own opinions into the situation. She needed to guide him to make choices, not tell him what to do.

"No, but your job or career choice reflects your interests. For instance, you'll have more in common with a lady you work with or someone who shares a similar hobby."

His tone softened. "I see your point."

"What are some of your interests?" Mona asked.

"I go to church," Will said. "I believe in family, in taking care of your loved ones." He paused. "I want a home, a wife, children. The same things most people want."

"Those are admirable values," Mona said. "Have you been in a relationship lately?"

"Why do you want to know that?"

Again with the attitude. "Because we can learn from prior relationships. If they were good ones, we try to re-create that relationship. Look for someone with similar traits. By the same token, if we've had a failed relationship, we can learn from our mistakes."

"I just ended a bad one," he admitted.

21

Mona toyed with a paper clip on the desk. "I'm sorry to hear that. What happened?"

"All she wanted was a fun night. She didn't care about family or making a good house or pleasing a man."

Mona's concern about the stability of the caller mounted. He was exhibiting signs of narcissistic behavior.

"Where did you two meet?"

The sound of something thumping echoed. Maybe his foot? A nervous habit?

"A bar. But Mama says only tramps go to bars."

Mona swallowed. "Perhaps you should try other places. How about your church or your workplace? Maybe your office."

"I don't work in an office."

He obviously didn't want to divulge his occupation. "Then you might join a singles group at your church or a club like a running or hiking club."

He heaved a breath. "Maybe."

"You mentioned that this woman wasn't interested in pleasing a man. A healthy relationship is a give-and-take on both parts."

"Are you implying that I did something wrong?" he asked, his voice rising in pitch.

"Do you think you did something wrong?"

"No, she did. She failed."

Mona tensed and waited for him to say more, but the phone went silent.

"Time for a word from our sponsors," she said, eager to take a breather.

She motioned for Chance to go to a commercial break, then joined him. "Who made that call, Chance?"

He shrugged. "No idea, it was an Unknown, but he was insistent about talking to you."

The fact that the number hadn't shown up added to her uneasy feeling. Will not only sounded narcissistic, but he seemed demented.

Dangerous, even.

♦ ♦ ♦

That fucking bitch Mona. How dare she ask him what he did for a living? A man didn't have to earn a million dollars a year to make a woman happy.

His mother's pain-filled snore rent the air, and he pulled the quilt up over her, tucking it tightly around her thin, frail shoulders to keep her warm.

Then he walked over to the jewelry box on her vanity, slid onto the stool, and opened it. Mama's gleaming necklaces, earrings, and bracelets twinkled in the dim light. He picked them up, watching the silver chains slide through his fingers, smiling as he remembered Mama wearing them to Sunday church.

He added the new charm bracelet to the mix. He would show it to her tomorrow when she felt better.

Except . . . Mama said she wasn't going to get better.

Panicked at the thought, he took the bracelet to her. "Look, Mama, I brought you a gift."

She stirred, her eyes sparkling. "Oh, how pretty! You're such a good boy." She held out her wrist. He slipped the bracelet around it and fastened the clasp. "That looks wonderful, son."

He kissed her cheek, glad he'd thought to bring her a token of his love. That radio lady's voice echoed in his ear.

She'd suggested other places to meet women.

It wouldn't hurt to widen his hunting ground.

Except he did have that one secret place where he looked. Mama had always kept him away from the computer. Said it was evil, that talking to strangers online wasn't normal. That only sinful women posted pictures of themselves there to lure men into their whore beds.

But Mama didn't have to know everything about him.

He wasn't as stupid as she thought. And there were so many more women online to pick from than in Graveyard Falls.

Sometimes he clammed up and started stuttering when he met a girl in person. Then she thought he was stupid, too.

But online he could be smooth and charismatic.

He lit a cigarette, stepped outside on the back porch, and took a drag.

For a long moment, he watched the wind hurl leaves and twigs across the woods. Branches snapped and twigs crackled with the weight of the snow. The white-capped mountains rose to form sharp ridges against the night sky. Somewhere in those dark woods an animal scavenged for food.

This was where he belonged. Where he thrived.

Where he would bring his lover and keep her as his.

He noticed a deer at the edge of the woods, grabbed his rifle from the rack in the kitchen, and stepped back outside.

For a long minute he watched the animal in its natural habitat. Watched it pause to graze, glide gracefully through the woods, stop, and perk its ears at the sound of another animal nearby.

So beautiful.

But it was meant to die.

He lifted the rifle and tracked it as it darted to the right. One. Two. Three.

The animal paused again, head lifted toward the sky. Neck, long and sleek. Its eyes looking his way. Daring him to let it go. Daring him to fire.

It was a game of cat and mouse just like the game women played with men.

But they needed to learn in the end that men were in charge.

He smiled and pulled the trigger, catching the animal between the eyes. It fell onto the ground, as its blood painted the snow a dark crimson.

CHAPTER FIVE

Mona tugged on her coat, anxious to leave the station. Another storm warning was in effect, and she didn't want to get stranded. Her car was ancient and lacked traction—something she and Brent had planned to remedy with a new vehicle. But when he died, those funds had paid for his funeral.

Wind battered the old house, shaking windowpanes and adding to her nerves. The call from Will still disturbed her.

In her previous work, she'd met numerous women victimized by men who shared Will's attitude.

The last situation had ended in a woman's death.

She had to be careful when he called again. And she had no doubt he would.

He sounded needy . . . desperate.

She jumped in her car, turned on the heater and defroster. On autopilot, she flipped on the radio, tensing when she heard a late-breaking story on the news.

"We have just received word that a woman's body has been found at the base of Graveyard Falls. Police haven't identified her yet, but the FBI is at the scene. With local sheriff Ned Buckley's recent retirement, Deputy Ian Kimball says FBI Special Agent Cal Coulter will be leading the investigation into the woman's death."

Mona clutched the steering wheel in a white-knuckle grip. A woman had been murdered at Graveyard Falls? Found on the very day of the memorial service for the other three girls?

That was eerie.

And Cal had been called in to work the case? It had been three months since she'd seen him. Three months since Brent's funeral.

That hurt.

She'd thought they were friends. That he cared about her. In fact, she'd met both Brent and Cal during her parents' murder investigation. She'd thought she and Cal had connected. But Brent had flirted outrageously with her and asked her out. And Cal hadn't shown any interest after that.

She rubbed the charm at her neck. She'd been so lonely since she'd lost her parents, even more so after losing Brent and the baby.

But Cal was in Graveyard Falls now working this new case. Maybe they could reconnect.

♦ ♦ ♦

Cal paced outside the autopsy room, hoping the medical examiner worked quickly. The stench of formaldehyde, death, and body wastes permeated the area, permanently infused in the faded walls of the basement room in the hospital.

Before he'd left the falls, one of the investigators had sent photos of the victim to the tech team at the Bureau, along with the woman's fingerprints.

Cal also wanted to know more about the wedding dress and lipstick.

His phone buzzed. Peyton Duke from the tech team at the Bureau.

He punched Connect. "Agent Coulter."

"Coulter, I have an ID on the victim." The sound of keys clicking on her keyboard echoed in the background.

Cal's pulse spiked. "That was fast. What's her name?"

"Gwyneth Toyton. She's twenty-five, a student at TCAT–Knoxville."

The Tennessee College of Applied Technology. "Do you have an address for her and contact information for next of kin?"

"I'll text you both addresses. She rents an apartment near the campus. Father deceased. Mother is on disability and lives in a rental house a few streets from her apartment."

"I'll have the deputy make the notification to the mother, while I check out her apartment."

Cal disconnected the phone, called the deputy, then stepped into the autopsy room, pausing to adjust to the strong odors.

"Dr. Wheeland, the victim's name is Gwyneth Toyton. I'm on my way to her apartment. Do you have anything yet?"

A frown marred the doctor's face. "Cause of death was asphyxiation due to strangulation."

Just as he expected. "Rape?"

The doctor pushed his goggles onto the top of his head. "No. No vaginal bruising or fluids."

So sex wasn't part of the motive. "Any DNA?"

"I scraped under her nails and combed through her hair, although I think the particles beneath her nails are coat or glove fibers, not skin. I'll let you know once we analyze it."

Cal told Wheeland to call him if he learned anything else, then headed down the long hallway in the basement to the elevator. The frigid temperature took his breath away as he stepped from the building, making him sprint to his car.

The wedding dress and garter disturbed him. But those thorns in the woman's throat seemed especially sinister and mimicked the Thorn Ripper's MO.

Mona would probably be able to give him insight. She'd helped the police on cases in Knoxville. At one time Brent had suggested to her that she become a criminal profiler.

But she had wanted a family.

A family with Brent.

He struggled to banish the resentment that that fact stirred. Mona had deserved better.

Gwyneth Toyton's face flashed in his mind. So had she.

He couldn't turn the clock back and prevent her death. But he could get justice for her.

◆ ◆ ◆

Mona fought a case of nerves as she parked at the antiques gift store in town. The fact that a girl had been murdered and left at the falls where three murders had occurred thirty years ago, and on the very day of the yearly memorial, seemed too coincidental.

Cal would find the truth, though.

Meanwhile, she had her own answers to find.

She stroked the baby bootie charm again. The receipt had come from a gift store here in town. That store was gone now, though, and this one stood in its place.

As she entered, the scent of candle wax assailed her. Timeless Treasures overflowed with antiques, old books, vintage jewelry, and an assortment of gift items. She maneuvered through the customers to the counter.

An older woman wearing a feathered hat and gold cape looked down at her from a stool where she was dusting a Tiffany-inspired lamp. For a moment, Mona studied the woman, looking for any family resemblance. But this lady wouldn't have been the right age to have given birth to her.

"Can I help you?"

"I hope so." Mona introduced herself and learned the owner's name was Aretha Cummings. "I received this charm from the woman who gave birth to me thirty years ago. The receipt showed that it was purchased here . . . well, at the store that was here back then, Garage Sale Finds. Would you know who owned that store, or how I could find them?"

Aretha tilted her head and studied her. "I'm afraid that was Ms. Hazel, but she passed away last year."

Disappointment filled Mona. Although she knew coming here had been a long shot. "Does she have family whom I could speak with?"

"Not Ms. Hazel. She lived and died alone." Aretha descended the steps and took a closer look at the charm. "That is pretty. But you know, whoever bought it might not have been living here. It could have been a tourist passing through."

Mona nodded. That was true. "Did you live here thirty years ago?"

Aretha shook her head. "No, my husband and I retired here three years ago."

Mona thanked her and left. She'd visit the local hospital or county office and search their birth records.

Maybe she'd find answers there.

♦ ♦ ♦

Sheriff Ned Buckley rubbed his head with a groan. If only he could quiet the damn voices. What a shitty way to go. This fucking brain tumor was not only sucking the life from him, it was also robbing him of his mind. But he knew enough to realize there was talk about that Pike boy getting parole.

He couldn't let him be released. And he sure as hell didn't want anyone digging around too much.

Not with his daughter, Anna, back in town.

She hated him enough already.

Although some days it was good that his memory went and the awful years eluded him.

Then he was back in the time when Anna was a little girl, and she sat on his knee and he bounced her up and down, and she'd laugh and hug him and tell him she loved him.

She'd stopped telling him she loved him when she'd turned seventeen. Then she'd turned her affection toward that Pike boy.

And now another girl's body had been found at the falls.

He went to his desk, pulled out the folder on the Thorn Ripper case, and spread the pictures of the dead girls across the desk. The thorny rose stems in the girls' mouths still made his skin crawl. And he never had figured out why Pike had whacked their damn hair.

Those young ladies had gone to the falls expecting to receive a rose as an invitation to prom. Hell, that tradition had started when he was in school.

Instead they'd been lured to their deaths.

He limped to the window and looked out at the mountains, his vision blurring. Today was a good day. The details of the arrest and the evidence stacked against Pike was as clear as it had been back then.

But some days it wasn't so clear. He had flashes of himself at the falls. Of setting things up to make the Pike boy look guilty.

Or was that just the accusation Anna had screamed at him?

Hell, it was all a blurry damn mess. He just prayed this recent murder didn't make people start asking questions about how he'd handled the case.

♦ ♦ ♦

Nervous over the fact that a girl had been murdered, Mona rushed up the steps to the small house she'd rented on the outskirts of town. The shadows from the woods suddenly looked ominous, the thick trees a perfect place for a predator to hide.

Icicles clung to the awning, breaking off in the wind and crackling like glass. She kicked snow from her boots and unlocked her door, the blustery wind rolling off the mountain confirming another storm was imminent.

The house was cold, the furnace grumbling as it tried to warm the interior, the windows rattling with such force she thought the panes might explode.

She turned on the gas logs, the silence in the house making her ache with loneliness, a reminder that Brent was gone and would never walk through the door again.

The wedding photo of her and Brent on the mantel drew her eye, and she blinked back tears. They'd been so happy that day.

With her parents gone and Brent's family deceased as well, they'd decided on a simple ceremony at a little chapel in the woods that overlooked the valley below.

Cal had been Brent's best man, but he'd looked nervous at the ceremony. Then she'd heard Cal and Brent arguing. When she'd asked what they were fighting about, both had clammed up.

It must have been important because after that, the two men had barely spoken.

Why she was remembering that argument now she didn't know.

Maybe because Cal was in town and she hadn't heard from him. Maybe because he was working a murder case, and she worried about him just as she'd always worried about Brent when he'd been on assignment.

She'd been terrified that he'd be killed on the job.

Ironic that he'd died from a car accident on a mountain road in the middle of nowhere instead of in the line of duty.

The gas logs slowly warmed the den, and she brushed away fresh tears and poured herself a glass of chardonnay.

A noise sounded out back, and she walked to the kitchen and glanced out the window. The woods backed up to her property, the night dark with clouds, shadows hovering everywhere she looked.

Maybe she should call Cal and ask him about the case. He might drop by to visit, talk to her, assure her she was safe.

Assure her *he* was safe.

She'd lost Brent already. She didn't want to think about Cal falling prey to the dangers of his job.

Remembering the commendation Brent had earned for bravery and courage, she went to the desk in the corner of the kitchen.

She removed the keepsake box where she'd stored the medal, opened it, and ran her fingers over the carving. She'd been so proud of her husband the day he'd received it, although Brent had been humble, had shaken off the praise, saying he didn't deserve it.

She studied the photograph of the award ceremony. His face was stoic, eyes cast downward. Cal stood beside him, ramrod straight, not looking at Brent as Brent shook hands with the mayor, who'd called him a hero. Brent had not only busted up a big gang, but he'd saved two lives during the takedown.

Later at dinner, though, neither Brent nor Cal had wanted to talk about the actual arrests. She'd heard Cal mention something about losing a CI and suspected there was more to the story. But she hadn't pushed Brent.

She found Cal's number in her phone and punched Dial, but the phone rolled to voice mail.

"Cal, this is Mona. I need to see you. There's something of Brent's I want to give you."

Maybe Cal would finally tell her what had happened that day, why neither of them wanted to talk any more about it. Why Brent being heralded a hero had made them both so uneasy.

She'd also find out what he knew about the murder in Graveyard Falls.

Cal's phone dinged that he had a message, and he checked it, surprised to hear Mona's soft voice.

His gut clenched as he listened. She needed to see him. Was something wrong?

Had she learned more about her husband since his death, something that had upset her?

Of course it would upset her . . .

Sweat broke out on his neck. How could he tell her that he didn't want anything that had belonged to his best friend?

Anything except *her.*

But he would never confess that. Not with the lies and secrets he'd kept for Brent.

Damn his friend. He'd owed him, but never expected the price to be so high.

He'd postpone that call as long as possible. He had a case to work. He needed to get to Knoxville and find out more about the victim.

Solving this murder was all that mattered at the moment.

He smiled at the young woman with the blonde hair. She'd been eyeing him all night. Flirting in a shy-like way that was even more appealing than the blatant perusal from some of the women he'd met at the bar.

Of course their interest had turned him on. But he reminded himself what Mama said about slutty girls. They didn't make good wives.

Every now and then, she lifted her head from the book she was reading to let him know she was interested.

Yep, she was the one he'd met online. Constance Gilroy. And she looked just like her picture.

Of course he looked nothing like his, but that was all right. He had to be careful.

She had a stack of child development books on the table.

Excitement zinged through him. She must like children. Maybe she'd want to have a baby right away.

Mama would like that. A grandchild would make the perfect Mother's Day present.

Even better, the idea of being a grandmother might spark some life back into her. Give her a reason to live.

He pictured his mama cuddling his son like she'd held him when he was little and suffered from nightmares. She always kissed his scrapes and made them better.

She'd cradled him in the bed with her when he heard monsters outside, held him close, and he'd felt her big, warm, soft bosoms against him. Then she'd rubbed his back and shoulders and kissed him until he'd fallen asleep next to her.

When he and his wife had a little boy, she'd do the same for him.

A smile split his face. Yes, his son would grow up to be a good man just like him.

The blonde shifted, fiddling with her hair again, and heat shot through his body. But he jabbed his palm with the angel pin he carried to remind himself to take it slow, to stay calm. Just like the hunt in the wild, he had to be patient. Eye his prize. Watch it. Study it. Not make any sudden moves to frighten her.

He closed his book and laid his hands on top of it. A drop of blood seeped from his palm from the pinprick. Another reminder to stay focused. He stood, approached her, and asked if she wanted to get coffee.

"Have we met?"

"On Facebook," he said with a smile.

She narrowed her eyes as if trying to place him.

"My friend put up an old picture. I guess I've changed since then. In fact, you know him. Doug, he's in one of your classes."

Constance stood. "Oh, right. I like Doug." She hesitated, and for a moment he thought she was going to turn him down. Then she smiled. "All right. I'll meet you at the coffee shop."

He followed her to the door, sniffing her feminine scent like a bloodhound following a trail. As soon as they stepped outside into the cold, she looked up at him with glowing pink cheeks and a smile that made her look like an angel.

He struggled to find his voice. "It's cold. Let's take my truck."

She pulled her keys from her purse. "No, thanks. I'll drive."

He gritted his teeth. She was being cautious.

Or was she afraid of him?

Either way, he couldn't let her get away.

She headed toward a small sedan, and he hurried up behind her, then slipped his stun gun from his jacket and zapped her. Her body shook and convulsed, her legs shaking as she flopped against him.

She was such a pretty thing. He really wanted her to be the one.

But if she gave him trouble, she'd have to go bye-bye just like Gwyneth.

CHAPTER SIX

Cal parked at Rock Ridge Apartments, an affordable option for students commuting to colleges in the area, and situated on a hill with the mountain peaks soaring behind it.

He'd phoned ahead to ask the manager of the complex to meet him at Gwyneth Toyton's apartment.

The nondescript cement building was dingy and needed paint, but the parking lot held dozens of cars, indicating that many of the units were occupied.

He battled a gust of wind as he hurried up the sidewalk and found 13A. A gray-haired man with small wire-rimmed glasses stood by the door hunched in a tattered wool coat.

Cal flashed his badge. "Agent Cal Coulter. Thanks for meeting me here, sir."

"Walt Clancy." Keys jangled as he jammed one in the lock and twisted it. "You say the girl Gwyneth is dead?"

"I'm afraid so."

The man's eyebrows climbed his wrinkled forehead. "What happened?"

Cal didn't want to divulge details, although the news, which was already reporting that a body had been found, would quickly pick up that it wasn't an accident. "She was murdered," he said matter-of-factly.

"Lord help us." Clancy staggered back, his eyes bulging. "How? Who killed her?"

"We're investigating that now," Cal said. "That's why I need to get inside."

Quickly recovering, Clancy pushed open the door. "You want me to show you around?"

"No, sir, this could be a crime scene. It's important that no one else enters the apartment or touches anything. Do you understand?"

The older man bobbed his head up and down, but he still looked shaken.

"What can you tell me about Gwyneth? Did you know her well?"

"Barely knew her at all. She signed the lease and moved in the next day, a couple of months ago. Said she was getting some kind of computer degree, but her mama's health was failing so she wanted to stay close by."

"Did she have a roommate?"

"No, lived by herself. Hers is an efficiency, pretty small, but she insisted it was fine for her."

"Did she have friends over? Anyone you remember?"

"Listen, Mr. . . . I mean, Agent Coulter. I manage the units, but I mind my own business."

"But you must know if she was a party girl. Any complaints from anyone about her?"

He shook his head.

"How about her fiancé?"

Clancy's eyes narrowed, accentuating the wrinkles on his forehead. "Didn't know she was engaged."

"You didn't see her with a steady guy?"

"No."

"Did she ever complain about another tenant?"

"No, nothing like that."

"How about strangers lurking around? Someone who might have been bothering her or watching her?"

The man shook his head. "I don't keep up with everyone's goings on. Long as they pay the rent and don't cause trouble, I leave the tenants alone."

Cal nodded. "Thanks. If you think of anything, no matter how small, please give me a call."

Clancy accepted the business card Cal offered. "You need me to stay around?"

"No, sir, I'll lock up when I'm finished. Thanks."

The old man rubbed his chin as he hobbled back toward the stairs. Cal turned back to the apartment and stepped inside.

Hopefully he'd find something to lead him to Gwyneth's killer.

Graveyard Falls was the last place on earth Anna Buckley DuKane wanted to be.

But here she was, back in the same little house where she'd grown up. Back in the town where the murders had occurred thirty years ago. Where the secrets had nearly destroyed her.

She'd had to come home, hadn't she?

Her father needed her.

Except how could she help him when the two of them hadn't spoken in years? When he'd forced her out of town with his hatred and determination to drive a wedge between her and the boy she loved?

When he'd arrested Johnny . . .

Even worse, her daughter Josie had insisted on coming with her. On her twenty-ninth birthday this year, Josie had announced that she wanted to be a true-crime writer. She was intrigued by the Thorn Ripper case.

Which meant that she might be asking her grandfather questions.

Thankfully his memory was shoddy. And he didn't want to discuss the past any more than Anna did.

It was almost as if Josie knew that Anna had once been involved with a killer. But she'd never told her daughter about Johnny.

And she didn't want to now.

Would people in town still point at her and gossip behind her back?

Would Josie discover the truth?

No . . . she couldn't let her.

Although she'd heard whispers today at the ceremony that Johnny might get paroled. Was there new evidence? Something to prove he was innocent?

Hope budded in her chest, but she tamped it down as she remembered the last time she'd seen him. She'd gone to the jail to visit him, but he'd told her to leave. That the only way she'd be safe was if he was locked up.

The cold way he'd said it had terrified her.

Locals thought she'd known about Johnny's psychotic behavior back then, but she'd been in love with him.

All the girls at school had wanted him. In fact, she'd heard that Tiffany, Candy, and Brittany had made a secret pact, that they all intended to sleep with him before graduation. And all three were vying to be his prom date.

Oddly, plain Anna Jane Buckley had landed the prize after she was assigned to tutor him, and their connection blossomed.

Then he'd been arrested and she'd wondered if everything he'd said was a lie.

She tiptoed to her father's room and peeked inside. He was sleeping. Thank God.

The nights and days were hard for him now. The brain tumor was destroying his mind and affecting his moods. But maybe it was God's way of helping him forget the shame she'd brought on the family.

He'd never forgiven her for loving Johnny.

She'd never forgiven herself for loving him either.

So she'd married another man, one she didn't love, because she'd vowed never to let her heart be broken again. In the end, her husband had known that, and he'd left, too. Then he'd been killed.

Now here she was, back in Graveyard Falls, in the house with a father who hated her one day and didn't recognize her the next. In a town where her name had been etched in the minds of the locals like that folk legend about the falls had been.

Back in the house where she'd scribbled in her diary about falling in love, about her first kiss with a serial killer who'd made the town famous by murdering three teenage girls.

◆　◆　◆

Cal yanked on gloves as he entered Gwyneth's apartment. He flipped on the light and surveyed the interior.

He could see the entire space at one glance. A tiny kitchen connected to a living room/bedroom, which consisted of a couch, chair, small desk, and television, and an adjoining bathroom. One window in the living space, another small one in the bath. The couch was faded blue, the desk scarred, but Gwyneth had obviously tried to punch up the place with bright throw pillows, a multicolored rug in fuchsia and blue, and a lamp with a bright blue shade.

At first glance, he saw no signs of a break-in or a confrontation, or any blood.

Had the killer been inside Gwyneth's place? Was it a fiancé? Or was it possible a stranger had abducted and killed her on her wedding day?

Instincts on alert, he scanned the room once again before he moved forward. No photos of Gwyneth and a boyfriend on the wall. No signs of a man living here, but he'd have to check the closet and the bathroom.

He examined the kitchen first. No dirty dishes in the sink, no wineglasses or beer mugs either, so she hadn't been entertaining before she'd been killed.

Or if she had, the killer had cleaned up.

He leaned forward to sniff the sink and counters, but didn't detect bleach. A crime team would be able to tell more with their chemicals and lights, but her apartment didn't appear to be the crime scene.

He opened the fridge. Milk, eggs, cheese, salad fixings, a veggie lasagna, a bunch of kale. Definitely food for a woman living alone. Although he did find a couple of steaks, burgers, and a six-pack of beer in the fridge.

He closed the refrigerator and searched the basket on the counter for bills and notes. Everything was neatly organized, no late bills. All the mail was addressed to her.

Nothing to indicate she lived with a man.

The desk in the living room held a laptop, which he'd have to send to the lab for further study. He also found books on computer programming, brochures on the grad school programs at various colleges, and a ticket stub to a movie at the local theater. One ticket, not two.

He searched for notes regarding wedding planning, a copy of an invitation, tickets for a honeymoon, but found nothing. He glanced at the day calendar on the desk, but all he saw noted were dates when school projects were due.

A picture of Gwyneth and a woman he assumed was her mother sat on the mantel. In the photograph, Gwyneth's hair was long, not chopped off above her shoulders.

Odd. If she had been involved with a man, why no pictures of the two of them?

Maybe they were all stored on her phone or computer.

He checked the bathroom cabinet but found no second toothbrush or male toiletries. No shaving kit.

The bed was made, the pillow on the right side flat as if it had been slept on, while the left one was still plump.

Maybe she was an anomaly and the boyfriend didn't stay over. Or maybe they spent the night at his place.

He glanced in the closet, frowning at the bare interior. A few pairs of jeans and shirts, tennis shoes, and boots.

Gwyneth was either not into shopping, had little money for frivolities, or . . . she'd moved some of her things to the place she and her fiancé planned to share. Hell, maybe they'd bought a house.

Hopefully the girl's mother would know.

He sat down at the desk, opened the laptop, and scanned Gwyneth's browser history. Mostly research sites for a paper she was writing. She had a Facebook account, but there were few posts, again mostly about school projects.

She did have several male friends, including a couple of men who'd suggested meeting up in a bar, both seeking a long-term relationship.

He made a note to have Peyton check out the names and find out where the guys lived so he could question them. Maybe one of them had become interested and had killed her because she'd chosen another man over him.

But there were no pictures of her and her lover in her Facebook profile. No posts about a wedding date or plans.

Now that *was* odd.

He skimmed emails and found several to a girl named Rosalyn, but they were comments about school, meeting for coffee, and a bar date at Blues and Brews.

Same bar as the men who'd Facebooked her had suggested.

He made a note to talk to Rosalyn.

His cell phone buzzed, and he pressed Answer. "Agent Coulter."

"It's Deputy Kimball. I'm at Gwyneth Toyton's mother's house. You need to get over here now."

He carried Constance into the cabin, hating that he'd had to subdue her. But she'd looked as if she might run, and he couldn't let her leave him.

They were soul mates.

Or at least he'd thought they were when he'd seen her smiling at him over those books on children.

The tests would tell, though, if she would be the one.

He brushed snow from her hair as he laid her on the sofa by the fire. Mama sat hunched in her wheelchair watching him, the afghan over her legs slipping slightly.

He hurried to tug the blanket around her legs—Mama did get so cold. The circulation in her legs had gone downhill fast with the sugar, and she was always freezing. He poked the fire to stir it up again, then set the poker on the hearth.

Constance lay like an angel on the sofa, her long hair spilling across her shoulders, her lips parted slightly in sleep.

"What do you think, Mama?" he asked. "Isn't she beautiful?"

"She's pretty, all right," his mama said. "Where did you meet her?"

"In the library." He didn't tell her he'd actually found her online. Mama didn't know everything he did in his spare time.

He lifted Constance's hand in his. Her skin felt cold to the touch, and her face was pale now, her hair tangled from the wind.

An image of her holding that blood-red rose flashed behind his eyes, and he smiled. She would look so beautiful in white.

"Cut that whore hair off of her," Mama said.

He nodded obediently, then grabbed the scissors from the kitchen and began to hack it off.

♦ ♦ ♦

Johnny Pike's gut knotted as he listened to the guards talking in the walkway between the cellblocks.

When that lawyer had contacted him a few weeks ago about the parole hearing, he'd tried not to get his hopes up.

"Did you hear about that girl murdered at Graveyard Falls?" one guard asked.

"Yeah. Found her the same day they held the memorial for the girls Pike killed."

Johnny curled his fingers around the bars. Another murder? Jesus. At least they couldn't pin this one on him.

Except . . . hell, Sheriff Buckley would if he could. He'd do anything to keep Johnny in prison.

When he'd first been locked up, he'd shouted and screamed his innocence to everyone in this godforsaken place. But not a soul had believed him. Every inmate in this hellhole claimed they'd been set up.

He'd stopped shouting long ago.

Hell, the evidence had been so stacked against him that he'd had to take that plea.

Besides, guilt smothered him. It was his fault those girls had died.

The dreams . . . the nightmares of the murders kept him awake every night. He heard the girls' screams in his sleep. Saw their eyes pleading to let them live.

Saw his parents', and sweet Anna's, faces staring at him with disbelief and shock.

Then their backs as they turned away from him.

"Think the Thorn Ripper has a copycat?" the guard asked.

Footsteps pounded as they walked down the block nearer him, and Johnny dropped back onto his cot, closed his eyes, and pretended to be asleep.

He didn't have to see them to know they'd stopped by his cell and were watching him with those condemning eyes as if he were some kind of monster. He should be used to those looks by now.

"Maybe Pike has a protégé," the guard mumbled. "Some creep who looked up to the sick son of a bitch."

Johnny thought about pictures of the dead girls the sheriff had found beneath his bed.

The pictures of those damn roses crammed down their throats . . . Panic seized him, making his stomach churn.

He had received hate mail over the years. And other letters from admirers who wanted to make a name for themselves as he had done.

Was some sick bastard using the Thorn Ripper's MO now to make himself famous?

CHAPTER SEVEN

Mona combed the house, too antsy to sleep. Ever since Brent had died, she'd become an insomniac.

Most nights she tossed and turned, only to finally fall asleep in the wee hours of the morning. Even then, she was plagued by nightmares.

First of the miscarriage. Then of Brent's death.

She brewed a cup of hot tea, then paced to the sunroom that overlooked the woods and curled up on the glider. The snowy mountains looked majestic in the moonlight, the ancient trees swaying with the wind, the sharp ridges jutting out, creating cliffs and overhangs.

So beautiful yet so dangerous.

Brent had died on one of the mountain roads outside Knoxville. She closed her eyes, willing the image of his mangled car from her mind. He'd flown over the edge on a switchback and nose-dived into the stretch called Devil's Canyon.

Tears burned the backs of her eyes. If only she hadn't pushed him about trying to get pregnant again, he might not have left the house that night. If she'd let it go, given him more time, he might still be alive . . .

Too frustrated to sleep, she retrieved the yearbook from Graveyard Falls High as she had done so many times before, the one from the year of the Thorn Ripper.

The girls had been killed a few months before she was born. Which meant that her mother's picture might be inside this album.

She'd looked through it several times, painstakingly, page by page, but maybe this time she'd see something she'd missed.

Settling back on the glider, she opened the book and began to search the faces of the girls in the senior class. Granted, her mother could have been younger, in a different grade, but she had to start somewhere.

Maybe she'd see something familiar in one of their eyes, a similarity to herself at that age, and she'd instantly know.

◆ ◆ ◆

Cal phoned Peyton and asked her to check out Gwyneth's Facebook account, especially the two men who'd suggested meeting her at the bar.

Then he headed to Mrs. Toyton's house.

He parked, noting most of the house lights in the neighborhood were off.

He doubted Gwyneth's mother would sleep at all tonight.

The deputy met him at the front door. "She's calmed down a little now that her neighbor came over."

Cal hated this part of the job, dealing with the families. Questioning them at the worst times of their lives.

Deputy Kimball led him inside through a small foyer with a side table showcasing various photos of Gwyneth, chronicling her childhood and high school years, including a prom photo.

Again, no engagement picture.

He squared his shoulders as he entered the kitchen, where two women sat around a pine table, sipping tea. Even if he hadn't recognized the mother from the photographs, he would have known her from the swollen, tear-stained eyes; glazed, anguished expression; and the wad of tissues she clenched in her hands.

Deputy Kimball introduced him to the women.

"Call me Linnea," Gwyneth's mother said in a voice that trembled with grief.

"Linnea, I'm so sorry for your loss," Cal said, feeling helpless at the phrase, but compelled to say it anyway.

"I don't understand why anyone would want to hurt Gwyneth," she said brokenly. "The deputy said she was . . . strangled. Why would anyone do that?"

"I don't know, ma'am," Cal said gently. "But that's what I intend to find out."

"She was a good girl," Linnea blubbered through another round of tears. "She worked hard to get through school, she was on a good path."

The other woman rubbed Linnea's back. "She was, Linnea. Everybody at church knew that."

Cal claimed a chair beside her, hesitant, but knowing he had to push forward. This woman was grief stricken, but she would want answers. Would want her daughter's killer caught.

And every second that passed counted.

"I know this is difficult, but anything you can tell me about her, no matter how small or insignificant, might help," Cal said. "Who was she involved with?"

Linnea frowned. "You mean, did she have a steady boyfriend?"

Cal nodded. "We need to talk to everyone she was close to. Boyfriend, fiancé, girlfriends."

Linnea's brows knitted together. "Gwyn wasn't seriously involved with any man."

Cal felt the creeping dread that he was on the wrong track. Her apartment had certainly made him question the engagement. "She wasn't engaged?"

"No." Linnea blew her nose. "Why do you think she was?"

"I don't know how to tell you this, so I'll just come out with it. She was wearing a wedding gown when we found her."

"What?" Her face blanched. "That's crazy. My daughter didn't even have a serious boyfriend."

"I'm sorry," Cal said. "And I will get to the bottom of this. Was she dating anyone in particular? Maybe some man wanted to marry her and she turned him down?"

"I'm telling you that she wasn't seeing anyone regularly. She would have told me."

Cal gave her a sympathetic look. If Gwyneth had some special guy or had been hooking up with a man, she obviously hadn't shared that with her mother.

And if she wasn't seeing anyone in particular, then the killer could have chosen her randomly.

Which would make him more difficult to catch. And it made the wedding dress even more bizarre.

Hell, the unidentified subject—or unsub, as they were called—could be anyone. He could have spotted Gwyneth in a crowd or on campus or in the damn grocery store.

Which meant he'd strangled her for the simple pleasure of watching her die.

And that he would kill again.

◆　◆　◆

The next morning Mona's eyes were still glazed over from scouring the yearbook. Unfortunately no specific face stuck out, no one who resembled her as a teenager.

She'd already called the hospital, but they didn't keep birth records dating back thirty years. She'd have to comb through files at the county records department.

Cal still hadn't returned her call, so on the way to the county office, she phoned him again.

"Hello?"

She heaved a breath. Something about Cal's deep drawl had always turned her inside out with longing. The ache felt deeper now, making emotions well in her throat.

"Cal, it's me, Mona. Did you get my message last night?"

A hesitant second passed. "Yeah, but I was busy with the case."

Of course. The case. "Do you have any idea who killed the woman?"

Another tense pause. "Not yet."

She rolled her shoulders to relieve the tension. At one time, both Brent and Cal had respected her opinion, had asked her advice about criminal behavior and profiling. "Is there anything I can do to help?"

"I . . . don't think so. I've questioned the mother and searched the girl's apartment. I'm going to talk with her friend this morning. Maybe she can shed some light on it."

"Good luck. And stop by tonight for dinner after you get through." He started to argue, but Mona shushed him. "I won't take no for an answer."

He reluctantly agreed, and Mona hung up.

She needed to see Cal's face again. Hear his voice. Know that he still cared about her, at least as a friend.

That he didn't blame her for Brent's death.

The sign for the county records department slid into view, and she turned into the parking lot. Determined to find the truth, she battled the cold to the front door.

She introduced herself to the woman in charge, a white-haired lady named Thelma with a sweet smile, who immediately told her that she'd lived in Graveyard Falls all her life.

"I know who you are," Thelma continued. "I heard your show last night."

"Thanks for listening." Mona explained that she wanted to look at birth records from thirty years ago.

Thelma raised a brow. "You looking for anyone in particular, dear?"

Mona debated how much to tell her. But she was never going to get any information if she didn't talk to someone. And since Thelma had lived here for years, she might have some answers.

"Actually, I was adopted and I'm looking for my birth mother. I have reason to believe she was from Graveyard Falls."

Thelma's eyes widened. "You don't know her name, hon?"

Mona shook her head. "I thought if I looked at birth records, I might find something."

"Of course." Thelma patted her hand and led her to another room. "We tried to get all the records entered into the computer, but we haven't made it back that far." She gestured toward a wall of filing cabinets. "They're labeled by years. You probably want to check those two on the end."

The task looked daunting, but Mona thanked her and Thelma left the room.

If her birth record was in there, maybe she'd find her mother's name.

That damn reporter Carol Little was driving Cal crazy by calling him, wanting the story. He'd phoned Deputy Kimball and told him to give her a brief statement, but to withhold details for now.

He clenched the steering wheel with a white-knuckle grip as he drove toward Rosalyn Nix's apartment. Dammit, Mona would want to talk about Brent, maybe rehash memories, and he would have to pretend he wasn't harboring secrets from her. That Brent was the wonderful, heroic cop she'd thought he was.

And he'd have to keep his hands off her.

Difficult to do when every night he fantasized about holding her, touching her, making her his.

A car beeped at him, and he realized he needed to focus on traffic. It had been minimal in Graveyard Falls, but grew thick with early-morning commuters when he turned onto the freeway.

It was midmorning by the time he reached Knoxville. Rosalyn lived outside the city in a small apartment complex. He veered into the parking lot, noting the nondescript buildings. Before he'd left his rental cabin, he'd done some research. She was twenty-six, working on a master's in communication, and had a waitressing job at a local diner. He'd also called and asked her if he could come by and talk to her.

He parked, yanked on his bomber jacket, and headed toward Rosalyn's building.

Wind beat at him as he climbed the stairs, and he knocked on the door. Seconds later, it swung open, and a young woman with red hair stood on the other side, coffee in hand.

"Rosalyn Nix?"

She nodded, eyes narrowed behind her rectangular glasses. Eyes that looked red-rimmed as if she'd been crying. "Yes?"

Cal flashed his identification. "I called earlier. I'm investigating the death of your friend Gwyneth."

Her lower lip quivered, and she gestured for him to come inside. He followed her to a tiny kitchen adjoining the living area by a breakfast bar. She set her coffee cup on the bar, and he noticed her computer was open to the news. "I . . . didn't know until I read about it this morning . . ."

"I know it's a bad time, but I need to ask you some questions."

A second passed, then Rosalyn burst into tears. "It's all my fault," she cried. "Gwyneth is dead because of me."

He had the skull ready to bleach in his workshop, but decided he'd better check on his mother. She needed her shot.

He helped her out of bed and into her wheelchair, then pushed her to the kitchen for breakfast. He'd hated to tie Constance to the chair, but a man had to do what a man had to do. And the sedative he'd given her had worked nicely.

After all, he didn't want her keeping Mama awake. She needed her rest.

"You need to go about your schedule as normal today," Mama said. "You don't want anyone asking questions."

"But it's Constance's first day here, Mama," he said. "I don't want to leave her."

Mama squeezed his hand. "I know, but don't worry. I have a lot to teach her while you're gone."

That was true. And she was right. He didn't need anyone nosing around.

"Please let me go," Constance said as she stirred. "I won't tell anyone about last night."

"No, you won't." He brushed her ear with his lips. "Listen and pay close attention today. When I get home from work, you can show me what you've learned."

Terror filled her eyes, and she tried to hit him with her bound hands. Will tsked at her. "The first lesson is to respect your husband."

She screamed and kicked at him, rattling the chair. He picked up a knife, one he used to carve out the eyes of the bobcat he'd worked on the day before, and waved it in front of her face.

"What did I say rule number one was?"

She went stone still, although her body trembled. He hated to frighten her. He really did.

But she had to learn.

"What is the rule?"

"Respect your husband," she whispered.

He kissed her cheek. "That's right." He angled his mother's wheelchair to face her. "Now, watch and listen to Mama today." He grabbed his coat and headed toward the door.

"Don't leave me here with her!" Constance screamed. "Please, don't leave me."

He smiled to himself as he stepped outside and locked the door. Constance's cries echoed through the window, but the wind choked out the noise as its shrill sound bounced off the ridges.

Mama had taught him how to be a good son. She would teach Constance how to be a good wife.

He whistled as he plowed through the snow to his truck and drove down the mountain.

CHAPTER EIGHT

Mona tried not to think about seeing Cal as she studied the birth records. It seemed eerie to her that she'd been born soon after the horrific crimes that had occurred in this town. Everyone had been so busy worrying about their daughters' safety with a serial killer on the loose that, for once, they probably hadn't noticed a pregnant teen.

Two hours of digging and she finally found the names of three female births to teen mothers around the time she was born.

Kay Marlin had delivered a baby girl at Graveyard Falls Hospital. May Willis had given birth to a little girl at her home using a midwife. And Felicity Hacker had brought a baby girl into the world on her parents' farm.

She scribbled down the addresses from the forms, hoping she'd find the women still in town, but thirty years had passed. No telling where they might be by now.

Still hopeful, she thanked Thelma, then checked her calendar. With a couple of hours to spare until her first appointment, she stopped in at Cocoa's Café for coffee, booted up her laptop, and punched in the names of the women on her list.

May Willis had died in a car accident ten years ago, but apparently her daughter owned a bakery in town. So May had kept her baby.

Felicity Hacker lived outside town and owned a plant nursery. There was no mention of her daughter.

A possibility.

Kay Marlin was more interesting. She had an arrest record for prostitution.

Mona gulped. Was her father one of Kay's johns?

She twisted the charm at her neck. No, surely not. Except . . . it would make sense. A hooker wouldn't have been able to care for a baby.

Needing to know the truth, she searched for an address.

A few minutes later, she discovered that Kay lived in the county's low-income housing.

She'd talk to Felicity first. Maybe she'd have some answers. And if she didn't, Mona would track down Kay.

Anxiety needled her as she drove through town, squinting as the sun glinted off the snow. By the time she reached the nursery, her hands were strained from gripping the steering wheel to stay on the road.

The sign for Felicity's Flowers and Garden stood tall against an oak and was painted bright yellow and orange. Mona parked and slogged through the snow to the rustic building.

Heat assaulted her when she entered the greenhouse, where a woman in her late forties wearing a big straw hat was tending a cluster of rosebushes. Although they hadn't talked, Mona recognized her from the memorial service.

"Excuse me," Mona said. "I'm looking for Felicity."

The woman spun around, her hand flying up in surprise. "Yes, that's me. But we don't get many customers in this kind of weather."

"Actually, I'm not here for flowers or plants," Mona said. "I just want some information."

The woman instantly looked suspicious. "What kind of information?"

Mona touched the charm. Maybe she should have invented a cover story, but she believed in honesty and wanted to see the woman's gut reaction. "A few months ago I discovered I was adopted. The only clue

I have is this charm." She lifted the baby bootie to show her. "I think I was born in this town, or at least that my mother lived here. And I know you had a child thirty years ago. A little girl."

Felicity's face paled, and she pricked her finger on a thorn. She instantly brought her finger to her lips, but a drop of blood seeped from the prick.

"I did have a little girl . . . but she died."

Mona sucked in a sharp breath, then opened her mouth to apologize.

But Felicity took her arm and ushered her toward the door. "Please go. Now."

"I'm sorry," Mona said. "I—"

"Just leave me alone and stop asking questions," Felicity said in a raw whisper.

Mona stumbled outside, hating that she'd upset the woman. But when she turned to go back and apologize, Felicity had disappeared. She glanced at the attached house and saw the curtains being drawn.

Shaken, she slid in her car and started down the drive. She paused at the highway and pulled over to check the address for the low-income housing development.

Suddenly Felicity's dark-green Tahoe careened past her and swung onto the highway as if she was running from something.

♦ ♦ ♦

Cal followed Rosalyn to her den and leaned against the big club chair by the window, giving the young lady time to calm down.

"Why do you say it's your fault?" he asked quietly.

Rosalyn wiped her eyes with a tissue, then tossed it on the coffee table and snatched another one from the box. "Because I talked her into going out with me the other night, then I left her at the bar alone."

Now he understood the guilt.

Cal chewed the inside of his cheek, waiting for her to elaborate. Instead, she began to shred the tissue into pieces, her fingers working nervously.

"What bar was this?"

Rosalyn sniffled. "Blues and Brews. Gwyn was so sweet, but she didn't get out much, so I convinced her to go with me."

"She wasn't dating anyone?"

"Gosh, no," Rosalyn said. "She was too busy taking care of her mother. Frankly, I thought she used her mother as an excuse not to date, because she was so shy, so I encouraged her to go out. To even meet people online."

"Did you meet some friends at the bar?"

Rosalyn bit down on her lip. "Two friends from my programming class came, but their boyfriends were with them."

Cal sensed this conversation could go on forever. "Did Gwyneth hook up with anyone?"

Rosalyn grabbed another tissue and began to mutilate it. "A couple of men asked her to dance, but she turned them down. Then Eddie showed up."

"Who is Eddie?"

"A guy I dated for a couple of years. We broke up last year, but he wanted to talk and said he'd made a mistake and . . ." Her voice cracked. "And I left with him." She released a pain-filled sigh. "I didn't think I'd be gone long. Eddie and I just stepped outside to talk, but then . . . things got hot . . ."

"And you two argued?"

Rosalyn shook her head, her cheeks flushing.

"You had sex?"

She nodded. "It had been a long time, and we were always good that way, so we ducked into the car—"

"You don't have to justify it to me," Cal said, trying to steer her back on track. "Then what happened?"

"By the time we went back inside, Gwyn was gone. I thought she was in the ladies' room, but she wasn't, then I called her cell but it went to voice mail, so I figured she caught a cab." Rosalyn brushed at more tears. "I tried again the next morning and she still didn't answer, then she didn't show up in class and I got worried." Rosalyn choked on another sob. "Then this morning I read in the news that she was dead."

So she'd only been gone one night. Not enough time for anyone to realize she was missing and file a report.

It also meant that the killer hadn't kept her very long.

Cal gave her a sympathetic look. "Was there anyone in the bar who stuck out to you? A man who asked Gwyneth to dance and got angry with her?"

She shook her head. "Not really. Both the men she turned down wound up with other girls."

"Do you know if she'd talked to these men before? Had she met them online?"

Rosalyn bit her lower lip. "She didn't say."

"Was anyone watching her that night? Maybe a guy who looked creepy or kept staring at the two of you?"

Rosalyn rubbed her forehead. "I didn't notice anyone."

"Would Gwyneth have left with a man if she'd met up with someone she liked?"

Rosalyn shook her head vigorously. "No. She didn't do one-night stands."

So if she had left with a man, it was possible he'd coerced her or drugged her.

He stood, jamming his hands in his pockets. "I'm going to talk to the bartender. Maybe he saw something."

Hopefully they had security cameras and he could get a glimpse of the person she'd left with.

◆ ◆ ◆

Mona drove to the county housing project, still disturbed about Felicity's reaction. Even thirty years later, it was obviously difficult for her to talk about the baby she'd lost.

Although Mona hadn't carried her baby to term, she understood the grief of losing a child.

Dark-gray clouds hung heavy over the sky, threatening another storm as she parked at the development. Brent had told her about this complex, that the town had built it ten years ago to help residents who couldn't afford housing. The brick units were sturdy against the stiff winds and close enough to town for the tenants to work in Graveyard Falls or the neighboring clothing factory.

She parked in front of the unit where Kay lived, cut the engine, and hurried through the sludge up to the door. The curtains were drawn, making it seem no one was home, or they wanted to be left alone. But she knocked anyway.

A young woman carrying a baby exited a unit and paused to stare at her. For a moment, Mona sensed the woman was upset, and she wanted to go to her, but suddenly the woman rushed back inside her apartment.

She knocked on Kay's door again. Footsteps sounded inside, shuffling, then the door opened a crack. A dishwater-blonde woman in a terrycloth robe stood on the other side, her hair disheveled, her eyes glassy with alcohol or drugs.

"I ain't buying nothing," the woman snarled.

Mona offered her a friendly smile. "I'm not selling anything, ma'am. Are you Kay Marlin?"

The woman lifted a coffee mug and took a sip, although it smelled like it held whiskey. "Yeah. Who wants to know?"

Mona introduced herself and explained the reason for her visit. "I'm looking for my birth mother. She left me this." She showed her the baby bootie charm.

Kay's eyes flashed cold. "Well, you come to the wrong place. I don't have a daughter."

"But you gave birth to a little girl, didn't you?" Mona persisted.

Kay's pale face twisted into a grimace. "Yeah, but I got rid of that kid. I don't have any idea what happened to her, and I don't wanna know."

Mona sucked in a breath at the woman's harsh tone. She started to say something, but Kay slammed the door in her face.

Disappointment flared inside her. If Kay was her birth mother, she obviously didn't want to reconcile with her.

She blinked back tears and ran to her car, a well of emotions balling inside her. She'd been foolish to indulge in this fantasy that her mother might have missed her, that she might be looking for her, too.

◆ ◆ ◆

Cal took Gwyneth's computer to the lab to have the IT department analyze it and asked a crime unit to process her apartment.

When he made it to Blues and Brews, he had to wait for the night bartender to arrive, so he listened to a guy sing the blues, and found himself contemplating what he would say to Mona when he saw her.

I'm sorry for the lies Brent told you. I'm sorry I wasn't honest with you.

I wish I'd asked you out before Brent had. But then he did, and I owed him, and . . . Brent always got what he wanted.

A seed of resentment wormed its way to the surface. He hadn't realized until now that Brent was just calculating enough to use Cal's debt to him to his advantage. A little reminder here and there—subtle, but it had worked.

Brent had risked his life and the wrath of their foster father to keep Cal from being beaten and tossed in the place the man called the "thinking hole."

The singer finished his set, and a young woman with white-blonde hair and black eyeliner took the stage. She jumped into a dark tune about death and resurrection that made the hairs on the back of Cal's neck bristle.

Finally the bartender arrived. Cal flashed his badge and explained why he was there, then showed him Gwyneth's and Rosalyn's pictures. "Do you remember either of these women being in here two nights ago?"

"Yeah, that Rosalyn chick is in here a lot. Hooks up with this guy named Eddie."

"How about her friend, Gwyneth?"

"There were a lot of people in here. I'm afraid she doesn't stick out."

"Can I view the security tapes from that night?"

The young man looked sheepish. "There's only one camera that works right now. It's by the back door."

"Let me take a look."

The bartender escorted him to a back room and introduced him to a bouncer, who apparently didn't remember Gwyneth either.

Minutes later, Cal was scrutinizing the tape. Mostly routine stuff. A couple of guys snuck out to make a drug deal, and the bouncer shoved some guy who'd started a fight out the door.

Then . . . back in the corner, he spotted a figure that looked like Gwyneth. Yes, it was her. A man approached her as she left the restroom, took her arm, and ushered her through the back exit.

She was staggering slightly as if she was intoxicated.

Bastard had probably slipped something in her drink.

But all he could see was the back of the man. He wore all black and had pulled a hoodie up over his head, shielding his face.

Dammit. He'd have the lab analyze the tape to see if they could get a better look at the man.

He told the manager he was taking the tape, then left the bouncer and bartender each his card. "If you remember anything or hear anything about the girl, give me a call."

They agreed, and he left, anxious to get the tape to the lab.

Felicity drove around for what seemed like hours.

First she visited the grave.

She plowed through the woods to find the spot she'd dug so many years ago, her heart pounding so hard she thought she was going to pass out. The trees seemed thicker than they had back then, and for a moment, panic hit her that she might not find it. Those first few years she'd visited often, but then she'd stopped coming because seeing the small clump of dirt with weeds growing on it only dredged up the pain.

She veered to the left, stopped, and scanned the clearing, then recognized the cluster of rocks near the creek. Shivering with the cold, she moved forward.

She had to make sure the grave was still there.

That no one had found it and dug up the body.

That no one knew her secret.

Only Sheriff Buckley . . .

She halted at the sight of the grave. She'd nestled her baby's body beneath a tree where the branches curled inward as if they were a mother's arms. She dropped to her knees and laid one hand on top of the mound, the memory of that night flashing back in nightmarish clarity.

Her premature labor. The pain. How alone she'd felt. How terrified.

And then the baby coming . . . all the blood . . . she wasn't breathing . . .

A sob choked her as she remembered, and she allowed herself to mourn as the wind cried out its own soulful sound through the trees. But the cold finally got to her, and her tears were freezing on her cheeks, so she buried her face in her scarf and tried to collect herself.

Leaves and snow whirled around her as she finally pushed herself up and ran back to her car. The grave was intact.

No one knew.

But why had that woman Mona Monroe come knocking on her door asking questions today?

She said she was looking for her birth mother.

Yes, Felicity had been pregnant back then. But she hadn't been the only high schooler who'd gotten knocked up that year.

Only she was the one who'd told Sheriff Buckley that story about Johnny.

Then she'd accepted Sheriff Buckley's help and done everything he'd said.

If she hadn't, she might have gone to jail just like Johnny Pike.

She had to warn Sheriff Buckley about Mona Monroe. Maybe he could stop her from making trouble.

Cal dropped the tape off with the deputy and had him courier it over to the lab.

His phone buzzed as he was leaving. Peyton from the lab. "It's Cal."

"I looked into those two Facebook friends. One was a man named Aaron Brinkley. He lives in Atlanta but was traveling to Knoxville when he posted that invitation. That was three weeks ago. This past week he's been in North Carolina on business."

"So he's not our unsub." He paused. "What about the second?"

"That one is more interesting. Whoever it was posted his name as Bill Williams. Profile says he's thirty, lives in Tennessee, that he's a craftsman and hunter, and that he's not married. His posts indicate he's looking for a serious relationship. That he wants a wife."

"Did he meet up with Gwyneth?"

"She was supposed to meet him at that bar the night she disappeared."

Cal's pulse kicked up. "Send me his address."

"That's the problem. The IP address is a coffee shop not too far from Graveyard Falls. And there are dozens of people named Bill Williams in Tennessee. I'm trying to narrow the list down now."

"OK. Send me the address for the coffee shop, and let me know what else you find."

"I'm on it. I'll also text you the photo the guy posted on his site, although I have a feeling it's a fake."

Cal ended the call, checked the address, and drove through another light snowstorm.

Thirty minutes later, he entered Moose's Coffee, a rustic-looking structure topped with a giant moose head. Inside, plain wooden tables, fireplaces, and support beams made from tree trunks gave the feel of being in the woods.

He glanced around the interior, irrationally hoping to see the man in the Facebook photo, but didn't spot him. A group of women had gathered around one table, chatting and looking at magazines. Another table held students with computers and study guides.

Most everyone had their own laptop, although a bar to the side held three computers, which could be used by guests for a fee. On a shelf above the computers, a stuffed falcon sat, its talons bared, eyes beady as if watching for prey.

A geeky-looking college-aged student with square glasses was using one computer, an Asian girl the second. The third was empty.

Cal crossed the room to the counter, ordered a plain coffee, and asked to speak to the manager. The young kid behind the counter disappeared through a swinging door and returned a second later with a middle-aged, burly man with thick beard stubble. He reminded Cal of a grizzly bear.

"Eric Brothers." The man wiped his hands on a kitchen towel, and Cal noted the scars on his fingers and palms. "What can I do for you?"

Cal introduced himself. "I'm investigating the murder of a young woman from Graveyard Falls. She communicated online with a man who posted from this IP address. She was supposed to meet him the night she disappeared." He flipped his phone around to show him the photo on the Facebook page. "Do you recognize him?"

Eric rubbed at his chin and leaned forward to study the picture. The man in the photo had short-cropped hair, was wearing a suit, and looked like he belonged at a bank. He certainly didn't fit the image of a killer.

"No, I can't say as I do." He gestured around the shop. "We get mostly college students in here. Although a few businessmen traveling through stop in, and of course the hunters in winter."

"His profile said he was a hunter."

Eric frowned. "He doesn't look like any of the hunters I know."

Cal silently agreed. Just as Peyton had suggested, he suspected the picture was a fake.

That the man had posted it to lure Gwyneth to the bar.

He texted the picture of the man to Eric. "Pass this picture around and see if any of the employees recognize him."

As soon as he got in the SUV, he cranked up the defroster to melt the ice particles clinging to the window, then flipped on the radio to the local station. To Mona's show.

"Yes, this is Mona," a familiar voice said. "What's on your mind?"

"You're a fake, Mona."

Cal stiffened. Whoever it was had disguised his or her voice.

"What do you mean?" Mona asked, a note of caution in her tone.

"How can you give people advice on marriage when your own was a lie?"

"What?"

"Why don't you just leave town instead of nosing around? Nobody wants you here."

"Who . . . is this?" Mona asked.

Heavy breathing followed, along with an ominous silence.

Heart pounding, Cal punched the accelerator and raced toward town and Mona.

He was a romantic at heart.

He bought flowers on the way back to the cabin. The thick snow and ice on the mountains forced him to drive slowly, although with his snow chains he bypassed several idiots who'd skidded off the road near town.

By the time he wove down the winding road through the woods, his stomach was growling. He rubbed his belly, dreaming of a big, hot pot of stew and corn bread.

Excited at the possibility, he barreled to a stop in front of the cabin. But one glance at the chimney and he realized the fire had gone out.

Dammit to hell. He had to teach Constance how to keep it going while he was gone. He didn't want the house getting so cold that Mama took a chill.

He held a load of firewood under one arm while carrying the roses in the other hand. But the minute he opened the door, he smelled urine.

Pure rage shot through him. He jerked Constance up by a hank of her hair and shook her.

"What's wrong with you? You haven't done anything all day? You didn't help Mama to the toilet."

Constance stared up at him with wide bloodshot eyes, her cheeks red, her face swollen. "Please let me go."

He looked at the breakfast dishes still piled in the sink, then at his mama, who was slumped in her wheelchair. The poor thing hadn't even had lunch.

"You were supposed to clean up the kitchen. Help Mama get her bath before I got home, and make dinner!"

"How could I? Your mother wouldn't untie me."

"I was scared to. She was going to run," his mother said.

Constance started to sob, and he slapped her once, twice, until she fell silent and simply stared up at him. Respect. A wife had to respect her husband.

He looked over at his mother for advice, then knelt beside her. "Mama?"

"I'm sorry, honey, she said she was too good to do dishes and chores."

"That's not true. She made that up." Constance shook her head wildly back and forth. "Please just give me another chance. I can be everything you want."

He looked into her eyes and wanted to believe her. She was so beautiful, and she would give him perfect children. So he smiled and kissed her cheek where he'd hit her.

"One more chance," he whispered.

But this time she'd better get it right.

CHAPTER NINE

Mona gripped the phone, an uneasy feeling rippling through her at the caller's tone. Locals had called in all evening, upset over the recent murder.

And now this . . . What did the caller mean about her marriage? She glanced at Chance through the glass partition, but a perplexed expression covered his face.

"Tell me your name and why you don't want me here in town."

But the caller didn't reply. Instead the phone clicked into silence.

Mona gritted her teeth. "I'm afraid that's it for tonight," she said. "Take care and have a safe evening." She took off her headphones, then hurried to talk to Chance.

"Did you get that caller's name?"

"No, I'm sorry. And the number showed up as an Unknown."

Mona sighed. The voice had sounded disguised. She couldn't even tell if it was a man or a woman. "What did he say when you screened the call?"

"Just that he needed your advice." Chance pulled at his chin. "Why? Do you think you know who it is?"

"No . . . I mean, I can't be sure."

Earlier, both Felicity and Kay had been upset with her questions. Maybe it was one of them calling. Or one of her clients' spouses. She did have one troubled woman whose husband was abusing her.

Although it could be that man Will.

♦ ♦ ♦

Cal parked in front of Mona's house, his instincts alert.

Why taunt Mona with the fact that her marriage hadn't been as it seemed? Who else knew Brent had been a pathological liar?

Hell, Brent had lied to him so many times that he'd begun to wonder if he'd known his friend at all. If Brent had manipulated situations when they were young to get Cal in trouble, then took the blame in an attempt to make Cal feel indebted to him . . .

He pulled his hand down his chin. He hated that that thought had occurred to him, but once it had taken root, Cal viewed their years with the foster families in a different light. Little things that had seemed inconsequential at the time now took on new meaning.

The sound of an engine rumbling jerked him from his thoughts, and he glanced in his rearview mirror and saw Mona's Honda barreling down the drive. He cut the engine and stepped from his SUV, bracing himself to see her.

She slipped from the car and picked her way through the snow. When she looked up at him, a wariness washed over her face.

Still, his body hardened with the same intense attraction he'd always felt for her.

The first time he'd laid eyes on her he'd been drawn to her. But she'd been upset and vulnerable because her parents had just been murdered.

Brent had declared his interest on the way home that night, and had moved in on her so quickly that Cal's head had spun.

"Cal, I'm glad you came," Mona said as she approached.

He gave a quick nod. "I can't stay long, the case . . ." He let the sentence die, hoping she'd buy the excuse.

But the memory of that cryptic caller made him want to pull her into his arms.

Disappointment flared in her eyes, but the look quickly faded, and she led the way to the door. Her hand shook as she jammed the key in the lock. Was she upset about the caller? Or . . . had she discovered one of Brent's lies?

"Come on in, Cal. I have some lasagna I can heat up for dinner."

"You don't need to do that."

"Don't argue. I know you're working a case, but you have to eat. And I could use the company."

It was so unlike Mona to say she needed anyone that his senses prickled. "What's wrong?"

Mona tugged off her shawl and scarf and hung them on the coat rack. "It's been a long day. I had a really odd call right before I left the station."

"I heard it," Cal said, earning him a surprised look.

"You listened to my show?"

He shrugged off his jacket. "It was on the radio on the way over."

Her movements were agitated, and he followed her to the kitchen, where she put the food in the oven. Then she poured herself a glass of wine and handed him a beer from the refrigerator.

He caught her arm, startled when a frisson of electricity shot through him. "Talk to me. Tell me about the caller."

Her eyes softened, a yearning in them that tempted him to pull her into his arms. But if he did, he might not be able to resist a kiss. So he released her and gripped the beer bottle just to have something to do with his hands.

"Do you know who the caller was?"

She ran her fingers through the tangled strands of her silky hair. "No. Chance, the producer, screens the calls, but some callers want anonymity, and it showed up as an Unknown."

He hesitated. "The voice sounded disguised."

"I know."

"We can put a trace on the phone at the station in case he or she calls again."

Mona sipped her wine. "Let's hold off. Maybe it was just a prank. Some disgruntled client or client's spouse who wants to antagonize me.

Besides, if callers think I'm tracing their calls, they'll stop phoning in to the show."

She sank onto a barstool and faced him. "Cal, you knew Brent better than anyone." Mona's eyes held a hint of vulnerability when she looked up at him. "Why would the caller say my marriage was a lie?"

Cal's pulse pounded. This was the moment he'd been dreading, the reason he'd avoided her. If he told Mona the truth, he'd hurt her.

But if he lied, he was no better than Brent.

Mona hated the questions nagging at her, but she couldn't shake the caller's comment. There were times during her short marriage when she'd felt like Brent had secrets, when she'd sensed he hadn't exactly lied but that he'd embellished the truth to impress her.

At the time she'd been flattered that he wanted to impress her.

But when she'd lost the baby, he'd shut down, and she'd wondered if he might leave her, if he thought she'd failed him by miscarrying their child.

Although when she'd confronted Brent about her feelings, he'd assured her he loved her and that whether or not they had a baby made no difference to him.

"Cal?" Mona asked, disturbed by his silence. "How would anyone here know about my life with Brent? I didn't move here until after his death."

Cal shifted and scratched at the label on his beer bottle.

"What's wrong, Cal? Is there something you're not telling me?"

"No, of course not." His professional mask slid back into place, and he leaned against the breakfast bar. "I think the question is—who made that call? And why do they want to upset you? Is there a client you've pissed off recently?"

Mona pulled out salad fixings and began to chop green peppers and onions to add to the mix. "I'm always pissing off someone," she said with a halfhearted laugh.

"Do you have a name, someone you think might want to hurt you?"

"No. Well, there is one man I suspect of abuse, but I've only seen his wife once."

"His name?"

"I don't feel comfortable sharing that yet, Cal."

"Anything else happen recently, any odd encounters?"

"Well, I have been looking for my birth mother."

Cal raised a brow. "I didn't know you were adopted."

She toyed with the chain around her neck. "I didn't either, not until my parents died. They left me a letter with this charm saying my birth mother gave it to me, and that she was from Graveyard Falls." She tossed the lettuce in the bowl. "Today I searched county records and found the names of three women who gave birth around the time I was born."

"You went to see them?"

"One woman passed away. But the second lady, Felicity Hacker, said her baby died. She seemed upset, and then after I left, she sped by me on the highway."

"That does seem odd. But people who give their babies up for adoption usually want privacy. Sometimes they want to remain anonymous with good reason."

A long hesitation. "It's still hard not to know the truth. Not to know why someone didn't want you."

He sipped his beer, and Mona silently chided herself. "I'm sorry, Cal. That was insensitive. I know you grew up in the system with Brent."

His eyes darkened. "We survived. But I understand your need to know. What else did you learn?"

Mona shrugged. "The other woman, Kay Marlin, has a record for prostitution."

"You met her?"

Mona sipped her wine. "Yes. Let's just say she wasn't happy to see me. And if she is my mother, she doesn't want a reconciliation."

"I'm sorry, Mona. But maybe it's better if you leave it alone."

"That's what everyone keeps telling me." But she didn't know if she could let it go. She felt incomplete, as if a part of her were missing. "I'm sorry for dumping on you, Cal," Mona said softly. "I realize you're working that murder investigation. I had several callers tonight in a panic about it. Do you have a suspect?"

A shuttered look passed over Cal's face, indicating he was troubled.

"Not really. I searched the victim's apartment, which yielded nothing, then questioned the mother and a friend. According to them, Gwyneth Toyton had no boyfriends, lovers, or exes, or any enemies who would want her dead." He heaved a weary breath. "The night she disappeared, she and her friend went to a bar. The friend met up with an old flame and stepped outside, leaving Gwyneth alone. The bartender and bouncer didn't remember her. I spotted her on the surveillance camera but can't see the face of the man she left with."

"What about her phone?"

"We haven't found it yet."

"You searched her computer?"

"Yep. No online dating sites or solicitous emails, although the tech team is looking over the computer and her phone records, and checking into a couple of private Facebook messages."

Mona set the salad on the bar, slathered butter on a loaf of French bread, then popped it in the oven. She liked that he was talking to her about the case. It felt like old times.

"There's another disturbing aspect of the murder," Cal said. "First of all, the killer cut Gwyneth's hair."

Mona frowned. "That *is* odd. Maybe it's a trophy. Or maybe he wanted her to look like someone else. Someone he knew?"

"You mean he's fixated on someone from his past, and he's trying to replace her?"

Mona nodded. "What else?"

Cal straddled the barstool. "The victim was wearing a wedding gown when she was found."

"But you said she didn't have a boyfriend?"

"She didn't. She wasn't engaged."

Mona's pulse clamored as a profile began to take shape in her mind. A profile indicating this wasn't an isolated murder.

That other women in Graveyard Falls were in danger.

♦ ♦ ♦

Her father was having a bad night.

"Why did you come back here?" he shouted at Anna.

Anna battled tears. Why *had* she come? She hated him and he hated her. But . . . she felt this damn obligation because he was ill.

"Daddy, just take your medication and go to bed."

Suddenly his eyes clouded over, and he began to tremble and cry like a baby. "Who are you? Where's Lilith?"

She swallowed hard, took his arm, and ushered him toward his bed. "Mom is gone. I'm your daughter and you're sick. You need to take your pill and go to sleep. You'll feel better in the morning."

Although she had no idea what the morning might bring.

He cursed but washed the pill down with water, then crawled into bed. She pulled the covers over him and turned off the light, although the bitterness inside her couldn't be doused in the dark.

She had lost so much because of him.

Needing distance between them, she shut the door and roamed the house where she'd grown up. The antiques that her mother had loved looked dated and worn, the pale walls faded from age, the blue-and-white dishes she'd collected old-fashioned but still classy on the sideboard in the dining room.

Her mother had had a great eye for detail and had kept an immaculate home.

Too bad she hadn't related to her daughter more.

Too restless to sleep, Anna made a cup of tea, then poured a dollop of whiskey in it, stoked the fire, and flipped on the television. A special news report was airing.

"Police have identified the young woman whose body was found at Graveyard Falls as Gwyneth Toyton, a student at TCAT. FBI agent Cal Coulter has been brought in to assist Deputy Ian Kimball with the investigation, but police have not revealed any details at this time or if they have any suspects. Women are urged to be cautious and to travel in pairs until the killer is apprehended."

Anna's hands trembled as time swept her back thirty years. The faces of the young women who'd died at Graveyard Falls her senior year of high school haunted her just as they had crowded her nightmares for years.

Skeletal faces, girls with wide, white, empty eye sockets, their shrill cries for help boomeranging through her mind. The vile accusations of the families, the accusatory looks from the residents of Graveyard Falls, her father's condescending, damning tone, her mother . . . leaving to escape it all.

It was your fault, Anna. Your fault . . . your fault . . . your fault . . . You should have known . . . but you loved him. You were blind to what he did. To the monster he was.

To the beast within who stole young girls' lives.

Nausea flooded her.

Had she known? Or had she loved Johnny so much she couldn't see past his sexy smile?

She punched her daughter Josie's number into her phone, anxious to make sure she was safe. Where was she now? She'd said she was going to the library to work on a research paper, but Anna had a feeling Josie had simply wanted to get out of the house.

How could she blame her? Her father barely acknowledged Josie.

Finally Josie picked up. "Hey, Mom."

"Where are you, honey?"

"Still working on my research. I'll be there soon. Don't wait up."

Anna cautioned her that a murderer was on the loose, then closed her eyes as she ended the call, anxiety riddling every bone in her body.

It was almost like the past was repeating itself. Like the murders were starting all over again . . .

CHAPTER TEN

Sheriff Buckley beat at the side of his head with his fist and spit the sleeping pill into the plant in the corner.

Fucking brain tumor was robbing his mind. And that girl Felicity . . . she had come to see him, reminding him of what they'd done years ago.

Worse, now Anna was home, messing with his head by being in the house. He never should have let her leave Graveyard Falls.

But he'd had to send her away to protect her.

Just like he'd had to send that damned Johnny Pike to jail. By God, he'd had the pictures and evidence to prove what a sick son of a bitch that kid was.

And that other girl who'd come forward—she'd cried in his arms and told him all the things Johnny had done to her.

He had to save his precious Anna from that horrible fate.

He switched on the radio and heard a newscaster talking. "With Johnny Pike's parole hearing less than a week away, letters are pouring in from both sides, some advocating that he be denied parole while others believe that with so much time passed, the police should review the evidence presented at the trial.

"The fact that a woman was killed on the day of the memorial honoring the Thorn Ripper victims has also raised suspicions that the two cases might be related. Police have not released details of the MO, although some speculate that Pike may have garnered a copycat. Others have even suggested that Pike was innocent, and that the killer may have moved to another area after his arrests to avoid being caught. And now they fear he's back.

"An investigation is under way, but the town of Graveyard Falls will not sleep soundly again until the killer is apprehended. One body has been found at Graveyard Falls this week. Will there be another?"

Buckley flipped off the radio and grabbed his winter coat. He'd damn well go watch those falls himself and make sure no psycho took another girl up there and left her to die.

And if this was someone with an itch to help set Pike free by casting doubt on his guilt, he'd find the asshole and lock him up just like he had Pike.

He'd done what he had to do back then, and he'd do it again if he had to. He didn't care if he'd crossed the line.

♦ ♦ ♦

The killer had dressed her in a wedding gown?

Mona massaged her temple with two fingers, contemplating what Cal had said. "What was the cause of death?"

"She was strangled," Cal said. "And left with a garter around her neck. The blue kind like women wear at their weddings."

Mona envisioned the garter she'd worn at her own ceremony and remembered Brent cracking a joke about what else he was going to take off as he'd slipped it from her leg. When he'd tossed it toward the single men, Cal had caught it.

Her gaze met his, and she realized he was remembering that moment as well.

But he quickly moved past it. "According to the girl's mother and friend, Gwyneth didn't have any enemies or old boyfriends," Cal said. "That suggests the killer chose her at random."

"Or that someone was stalking her," Mona interjected. "Someone she might not have even known was interested in her."

"That's possible. He could have been in one of her classes, a professor, hell, the guy at the grocery store or online . . ."

"That makes it more difficult to catch him, doesn't it?" Mona asked.

"Yes, but that doesn't mean we won't." Cal raked a hand through his hair. "We're looking into the dress angle—maybe if we find out where it came from, we can figure out who bought it."

"That makes sense," Mona said. "Was there anything unusual about the crime scene? Did he pose the victim?"

Cal nodded. "He painted her lips with red lipstick, although it was smeared in a grotesque way as if he was mocking her. We're also testing the lipstick for the color, where he might have gotten it." He paced the kitchen, glanced at the photo of Brent and him on the sideboard, then jerked his head back toward her. Some emotion she couldn't quite define darkened his eyes.

"He also left her at the edge of Graveyard Falls like the Thorn Ripper did. I'm thinking he could be a sicko who's fascinated with the story, even a fan of Pike's. He wants to be legendary like him."

Mona worried her bottom lip. "That would imply a certain pathology."

"I know." Cal's voice dropped a decibel. "And if he copies Pike's crimes, then there will be two more murders."

A chill chased up Mona's spine. "You're suggesting a copycat. But the MO is somewhat different this time, isn't it?"

Cal nodded. "There are similarities and differences. The location and the roses are part of both MOs, as is the hair. But the wedding dress and garter are new."

Mona tried to put herself in the mind of the killer. "That could imply motive. This killer is older. High schoolers, prom dates—he's past that stage. He wants a wife or he lost one recently."

"Maybe we should look into widowers?"

"That's not a bad idea."

Cal nodded. "So the unsub fixates on Gwyneth, and when she doesn't go along with his plan, he strangles her." Cal paced as he spoke. "Then he has to get rid of the body, so he carries her to the falls and leaves her, hoping no one will find her body for a while. That way he'll have time to cover his tracks. Create an alibi. Bury evidence at his house or wherever he killed her before he dumped her."

"And he makes it look like the Thorn Ripper so he'll get attention. Maybe he does it to glorify Pike in some way."

Mona took a sip of wine, her pulse pounding as she envisioned the man dragging the poor woman's body through the snow and leaving her out in the elements. "Or he could be mimicking the Thorn Ripper to remind the town of those murders and that Pike shouldn't be paroled."

A heartbeat of silence passed while Cal considered her suggestion. "What else can you tell me about this man?" Cal asked. "Who should we be looking for?"

Mona traced her finger around the stem of her glass. "I would say he's a loner, that he suffers from low self-esteem. He may have been abused as a child. And he desperately wants love." Worry made her chest clench. "He wants it so badly that he'll kill if he doesn't get it."

♦ ♦ ♦

Cal rolled Mona's observations over and over in his mind as they ate and cleaned up the dishes.

He needed to say good-night, he thought, as Mona sank onto the sofa and offered him a tentative smile. But with a murderer on the loose, he couldn't bring himself to leave her alone. Hell, he wanted to pull her up against him and hold her until his need for her dissipated.

Although holding her would be too tempting. It would make him want more, make it impossible to leave without touching her. Kissing her. Confessing that he wanted her.

"Did the killer take anything from the woman?" Mona asked, dragging his mind back to the case. "Like a photo from her house, a piece of jewelry, or . . . again, could that be the reason he cut her hair? So he'd have something to remember her by."

And relive the kill. "I don't know. I'll ask her mother if anything was missing." He scraped a hand over his chin. "If this man is so desperate to be loved and this woman didn't work out, do you think he'll keep looking?"

Mona sighed. "I hope I'm wrong, but yes."

Cal muttered a sound of frustration. "And if she doesn't work out, he's gotten a taste of killing and he'll kill again."

"That's usually the way a serial killer is born," Mona said. "But there has to be a trigger for him to start killing now. Something in his life changed recently. Some big event that set him off."

"Like he was recently rebuked by a girlfriend?"

"Yes. Maybe his fiancée broke off an engagement or his wife left him or he lost a family member . . ."

Her gaze met Cal's. He wondered if she was thinking of Brent then. The thought brought reality crashing back.

Mona had loved his friend, not him.

He drained his beer and set the bottle on the table. "I should go and let you get some sleep."

A wary look flashed in her eyes, and he remembered the earlier phone call. "Unless you think that caller might try something and you want me to stay." God help him, he *wanted* to stay. The thought of a madman hurting Mona made fear streak through him.

"I have a gun, Cal. I'm not afraid," Mona said, her voice strong. "But if you need a place to sleep while you're in town, you're welcome to sleep here." She hesitated. "Brent would have wanted that."

Hearing her say his friend's name made him fist his hands.

He was a fool to torment himself by being close to her.

"Thanks." Needing some distance between them, he stood and squared his shoulders. "But I rented a cabin on the river."

"Oh."

Was that disappointment in her voice, or had he imagined it because he wanted her to want him?

"Thanks for your opinion on the case, Mona." He grabbed his coat and headed toward the foyer.

"Cal, wait."

Cal paused by the door, one hand on the doorknob.

Mona hurried to him. "I almost forgot. I wanted you to have Brent's medal," she said softly.

The memory of that day was like a punch in Cal's gut, a reminder of the wrongs Brent had done.

He didn't want that medal anywhere near him.

But how could he refuse without explaining to Mona that her husband hadn't been the hero she'd thought him to be?

◆ ◆ ◆

"Cal, I know you miss Brent, and I don't mean to upset you," Mona said, struck by the pain in Cal's eyes. "But I know Brent would want you to have that medal."

"I'm not so sure about that."

Mona took his hand in hers and squeezed it. "Why would you say that? You were his best friend."

"I . . . a young man died that day, Mona. It's not something I feel like celebrating."

"I'm sorry. Brent didn't tell me that part."

"Yeah, he was a kid."

She took a deep breath. "That was a tragedy, but his death wasn't your fault," Mona said.

Cal released a heavy breath as if he wanted to say more, but he took the medal and jammed it in his pocket.

Mona squeezed his hand. God, she wanted to hug him. "I'm sorry, Cal. Is there anything I can do to help?"

His dark gaze skated over her, despair and anger and a dozen other emotions flickering in the depths. Brent always claimed Cal needed him, that Cal might have gotten lost years ago if he hadn't taken him under his wing.

When they were young, Cal had been smaller than Brent, had borne the brunt of their last foster father's abuse. Brent admitted he'd stepped in a half dozen times and taken beatings for Cal. He'd been afraid Cal wouldn't survive.

Of course, in their late teens, Cal had had a growth spurt and shot up four inches taller than Brent. He'd also developed broader shoulders, muscles that flexed when he moved, and a fierce look that stopped most perps in their tracks.

"I just need to focus on this case." Cal opened the door and the blustery wind swirled dead leaves inside. "If you're right about this unsub, I have to stop him before he kills again."

CHAPTER ELEVEN

Cal battled the fierce winter wind as he climbed into his SUV. The dark clouds above mirrored his mood.

He hated to leave Mona on a night like this, especially knowing someone had called making insinuations about her marriage. Someone who might reveal the truth about Brent and destroy her world.

Worse, a killer was in Graveyard Falls and might be hunting another victim.

His nerves on edge, he studied Mona's house and property as he phoned the lab.

Peyton answered.

"Did you get anything on that surveillance video?" Cal asked.

"I'm afraid not."

"How about biological evidence or DNA on the victim?"

"Actually, Dr. Wheeland sent over a loose brown hair that he collected from the body. It was short, not the victim's," Peyton said. "We'll run DNA, but that'll take time. And if it's not in the system, we'll need someone to compare it to."

"Anything else you can tell me?"

"The particles beneath her nails were wool fibers from an old blanket or coat. The garter is a dime a dozen. The brand is sold at all discount stores, bridal shops, party stores, the Internet."

A needle in a haystack. "What about the dress?"

"That's more interesting," Peyton said.

Mona's silhouette appeared through the sheer curtains, and Cal watched her walk into the kitchen. He needed to tell her to get blackout curtains, or shutters.

"The dress wasn't purchased in a store or online."

Cal started the engine to warm the car. "Where was it purchased, then?"

"It wasn't. The dress was homemade."

"Homemade?" The lights in the house flicked off, and he realized Mona was headed to bed. The urge to go back inside and guard her tonight ripped through him.

"Yes. I'll try to find out where the fabric came from. The beads on the dress are unusual, old, so that might help."

Cal's mind raced. "So whoever this killer is either sews or knows someone who does."

"That's a possibility. Or the dress could have been passed down in the family," Peyton pointed out. "The lace was yellowed as if it had been kept in a closet for a while."

A family heirloom would complicate matters. There was no way to track where the materials might have been bought. "All right. But just to cover our bases, run a search on seamstresses in the area, bridal shops, and businesses that specialize in alterations."

"I'm on it."

"Also look at Craigslist, garage and estate sales, antiques houses, and personal ads. Maybe someone in Graveyard Falls recently bought this dress or sold it, and we'll get a name."

Then they might be able to nail this bastard.

♦ ♦ ♦

Unable to sleep, Mona combed through the yearbook again. She found the pictures of the girls who'd died—Tiffany, Candy, and Brittany.

Judging from the number of candids of them together, they had been inseparable. All cheerleaders. All on the homecoming court. All served on the prom planning committee.

A fourth girl caught her eye, and Mona tried to distinguish her face. She looked familiar.

She flipped back to the individual shots and found her.

Felicity Hacker.

Her breath caught. Felicity was in several shots with the other three girls. She had volunteered on the prom committee and had helped decorate one of the homecoming floats.

She'd also been an alternate on the cheerleading squad but had to give that spot up.

Hmm. Had she been close to the girls, or had she been ostracized because she'd been pregnant? Had she resented being rejected from the group? And if she was pregnant, who'd fathered her baby?

Felicity had been upset when she was talking to the sheriff at the memorial. Had she known something about the Thorn Ripper?

Mona had no access to the original case files, but she'd ask Cal.

Because Felicity was definitely hiding something.

♦ ♦ ♦

The house smelled like rotten eggs. And bleach.

Constance shivered at the sight of the skulls and dead animals in the house. Will preserved them. Talked to them. Called each one by name as if he knew them.

He moved up behind her to watch her clean the dishes, and she fought nausea.

She had already failed and been punished twice. Now she had to scrub the frying pan again. No dishwasher in this house. She needed to dry the glasses and polish the silver until it shined.

He liked egg salad and deviled eggs. She had to get it right. Boil the eggs by the timer. Peel them without tearing apart the egg. He liked them smooth and shaped to look pretty like his mama made.

He was crazy.

Tears blurred her eyes as she carefully chopped the pickles into tiny bits as his mother instructed. The ropes around her wrists had been loosened just enough for her to work in the kitchen.

She considered cutting them with the knife she was using to chop the ingredients for the salad, but it wasn't sharp enough.

Even if she did free her hands, he'd bound her ankle to the floor with a thick chain so it clanked against the wood as she walked, and it wasn't long enough for her to reach the door to escape.

Hopelessness welled inside her, threatening to bring her to her knees. All day she'd tried to get free, but she'd only managed to rub her skin raw and wear herself out.

He moved over to the fire with his mother and sipped his whiskey.

Then he leaned toward his mother and whispered something in her ear.

Constance's hand was shaking so badly she dropped the knife and knocked the platter onto the floor. The glass shattered, and eggs, mayonnaise, and sweet pickles splattered the kitchen rug, an old braided monstrosity that should have been thrown out years ago.

Will shot up from his perch on the hearth. "Yes, Mama, she made a big mess." He stomped over to her, and she instinctively cowered.

"I'll clean it up. I can do better."

"Mama says you're just like the other little liars, pretending to be something you're not."

She screamed as he closed his hands around her neck.

She was young, had her whole life in front of her. She wanted to finish her degree, get a job. Have a family.

"Please don't," she begged.

But a cold rage flashed in his eyes, and he threw her down and forced her lips apart, then jammed a thorny rose stem in her mouth.

"Shh, bite down now, sweetheart. We don't want to disturb Mama."

She gagged as thorns stabbed her tongue and blood filled her throat.

♦ ♦ ♦

He carefully buttoned the wedding gown his mother had stitched for Constance, her beautiful scream still echoing in his ears.

He slipped the garter around her neck, then removed her locket.

It would look so pretty on Mama.

The photo she'd taken of him and Constance lay on the table waiting for the frame. Although it wouldn't go in the frame.

He'd put it in his Bride's Book, the scrapbook Mama had made for him to show off pictures of the ceremony. She'd glued lace to the front in the shape of a heart so he could place his wedding photo in the center.

Tears leaked from his eyes. "Mama, I'm sorry, she wasn't right."

"I'm sorry, too, son. Come here." She motioned for him to sit with her, and he dropped to his knees and laid his head in her lap. She stroked his hair gently, her voice a soothing murmur.

"I have to take her to the falls," he said, choking on the words. "But tell me the story about the little liars first."

He'd been infatuated with the story ever since his mother had first told him she'd known the Thorn Ripper and the girls he'd lured to the falls.

Pretty girls who'd acted like Goody Two-shoes but were whores instead. They'd all expected to get the rose from their lover as an invitation to prom.

But none of them were worthy. That was the reason they had to die.

CHAPTER TWELVE

Carol Little hated this podunk town. Outside the Falls Inn, wind battered the window and icicles dangled like sharp knives along the awning.

She scrolled through all the articles on the area with a grimace.

The name Graveyard Falls gave her the heebie-jeebies and reminded her of growing up in New Orleans, where floods had once uprooted graves. Where gators swarmed the bayous, the sound of their gnashing teeth echoing in the eerie silence as they floated, hidden predators in the murky water.

She'd been in the city when Katrina hit and seen such horrors that she'd never be able to erase them from her mind.

Later, she'd had a bad breakup with her boyfriend, so she'd driven to Knoxville, landed a job at the paper, and although she'd started out writing light human-interest pieces, her propensity toward the morbid had eventually driven her to ask for a chance to work on crime stories.

Maybe it was because her own daddy had been chewed up by a gator when she was little. The day it happened, he'd taken her out on a pirogue to go fishing, but he'd known she was terrified of the water, especially the gators. He was pure evil, though.

He liked to see how close he could get to the gators and taunt them, then laugh when she cried. But that day, he hadn't won. He'd taken his bottle with him and guzzled it while he fished, but when he got up, he'd lost his footing and he'd fallen in and . . . She shuddered, the memory of blood so vivid her stomach clenched as if it were yesterday.

Now, here she was in another town that had known its own share of death.

She'd done her homework, had photographed the falls and mountain, although she hadn't yet seen the crimson color the water turned in the sunlight. The color of blood.

The water had probably always looked that way, caused by some kind of particle or plant indigenous to this part of the country, but she understood the way small-town legends took root and became embellished over time.

The height of the falls had astounded her. When she visited, she'd imagined standing at the top of the mountain and being thrown over the ridge into the jagged rocks and rapids.

She clicked on the old story about the murders and skimmed the details. A man named Johnny Pike had been arrested for the gruesome crimes and was serving a life sentence. She'd requested an interview with him, but he had rejected her request.

She had to figure out just what he would want in order to talk to her. Cigarettes? Cash? Some kind of special privilege?

She jotted down the names of his victims, and decided that, while she was here, she'd interview their family members. Many of whom had avoided her at the memorial. She punched Deputy Kimball's phone number but got his voice mail.

Frustrated that he'd only given her the bare minimum about Gwyneth Toyton's murder when they'd spoken before, and that Agent Coulter had refused to talk to her, she grabbed her coat, gloves, and purse and hurried outside.

Blues and Brews was just across the street. Bars were great places to mingle with the locals.

It was open-mic night, so she ducked inside, eased onto a barstool, and ordered a beer, hoping to fit in. Inebriated locals often had loose lips.

Loose lips were just what she needed now. Someone who knew more about Gwyneth and how she'd ended up dead.

◆ ◆ ◆

Cal ran his finger over the edges of the medal, his memory of the day Brent had received it still fresh, his anger still pulsing.

"Do you really think you should accept that?" he asked Brent.

Brent shrugged. "Why not? We made a big bust tonight. Just think about all the drugs we got off the streets. All the kids we saved."

"What about the one we didn't save?" Cal asked, the pain raw. He could still see Milo's young face. Eager to escape being trapped in a gang, he'd agreed to help Brent get info on the Ten-nines. But the leader of the gang caught on to Milo's undercover ruse and shot him in the head.

The fourteen-year-old boy's life had been snuffed out in seconds, his brain matter splattering Cal's shirt.

"He knew what he was getting into," Brent said. "Besides, the gang already considered him in. They never would have let him leave."

"We were supposed to protect him," Cal argued. "He trusted us."

Brent's eyes flared with impatience. "Look, Cal, I've spent half my life wiping up other people's messes, taking care of kids like Milo. Kids like you. We can't save them all."

The phone jarred Cal from the memory and Brent's callous words. They should have saved Milo.

He hadn't deserved to die so young.

◆ ◆ ◆

Mona booted up her computer and skimmed the stories online about some lawyer trying to get Pike paroled.

Sheriff Buckley had made the arrest, but a couple of teenagers claimed that Buckley's daughter, Anna, was dating Johnny, and May Willis said she thought Buckley had it in for Pike.

Others dubbed Sheriff Buckley a hero for locking away a serial killer. If he'd railroaded Johnny Pike, he wouldn't want that conviction overturned. But if Pike hadn't killed the girls, who had? Once he was arrested, the murders had stopped.

May Willis was not around any longer to question, though. She had passed away.

Mona searched for the original story about Pike's arrest, and like a rubbernecker, she couldn't turn away. The sheriff had found a box of photos of the dead girls under Pike's bed.

Another teen had come forward and claimed Pike had attacked her, but she'd escaped. The sheriff stated that the young girl did not want her identity revealed, and had kept her name confidential.

The reporter who'd covered the story had also tried to interview the sheriff's daughter, but the sheriff had sent her away to avoid the ugly press and rumors.

Was Anna the girl who'd claimed Pike had attacked her?

She skimmed another article, but didn't find the answer anywhere.

Although there was a small story about Pike's parents. Apparently they'd left town after the conviction. Eventually the mother had committed suicide and there was speculation that the father had changed his last name.

She leaned back in her chair and considered the recent murder. If Gwyneth's killer wanted a bride, it suggested his age was probably midtwenties to forties.

The typical age for a serial killer.

♦ ♦ ♦

Carol knew she shouldn't climb into bed with a stranger, especially for a story, but Deputy Kimball was sexy and mysterious, and he was working on the recent murder case in Graveyard Falls.

So far, none of the other patrons at Blues and Brews had offered any information. And she was sick and tired of being the grunt person at the paper. Her daddy had once told her she'd never amount to anything, and she was determined to prove him wrong. Even if he was dead and would never know.

Various scenarios regarding the murder had surfaced. A disgruntled boyfriend probably killed her. Or a jealous girlfriend? Both reasonable if you didn't know the details of the case. Carol did, but she hoped Deputy Kimball would be able to offer more. An angle she could run with.

"You look tired," she said as she slid a beer onto the table in front of him.

He cocked a sexy blond brow at her, his gaze raking her from her sinful stilettos to the short skirt showcasing her legs to the dip of her silk blouse, which exposed just enough cleavage to pique a man's interest without making her look like a slut.

Then recognition dawned. "You're that reporter I talked to on the phone."

Carol pasted on her sexiest, most seductive smile. "Yes. Anything new to tell me?"

He shook his head. "I'm off duty."

She didn't think cops were ever off duty, especially when a killer was on the loose, but she bit back her opinion.

A cowboy in a black Stetson strode on stage and strummed his guitar. "I'd like to sing a new song I wrote called 'Backyard Blues.'"

He launched into the ballad, and Carol made small talk as the music flowed around them.

"How long have you been the deputy?"

He rolled his shoulders and sipped his beer. "A couple of months."

She noticed he didn't mention that a Fed was in town heading up the murder investigation.

They ordered a pitcher, then chatted for an hour while the last set played, the drinks and soft music weaving a seductive spell around them. By the time the show ended, she could feel the heat simmering between them.

"Come back to my place," the deputy said.

Carol hesitated just long enough to seem appropriately moral, then smiled. "All right, Deputy."

He pushed his big body up, tossed some cash on the table to pay the bill, and placed his hand at the small of her back. "Call me Ian."

"All right, Ian."

"Let's go to my place. I live just down the street. We can walk."

"All right," Carol agreed

He threw his arm around her and they left, then walked down the street and veered onto a long drive that led to a small log cabin set back in the woods on the river.

For a brief second when they entered and he shut the door behind her, Ian's gaze penetrated her with such an intensity that fear racked her body.

Just because he was a deputy didn't necessarily mean he was safe.

But she liked living on the edge. So she reached for the buttons on his shirt and began to loosen them. Seconds later, he walked her backward toward his bedroom, tearing at her clothes and shucking his as he fused his mouth over hers and pushed her onto the bed.

The sex was hot, wild, physical, passionate. And bordered on being rough.

His big hands skated over her, positioning her the way he wanted, shoving her legs apart with his knee, holding her hands above her head to keep her still for his torture.

His kisses became urgent, driven, his moans of need triggering her own until she begged him to come inside her.

He shook his head, grabbed a condom and rolled it on, then flipped her to her stomach and gripped her hips. She cried out as he pushed her legs apart and drove his sex between her thighs. A moan tore from her throat as he entered her, then he lifted her hips and angled her so he could thrust deeper. She felt as if she were coming apart inside, he was so big.

But she loved it.

She braced herself on her hands, reveling in his hungry words as he thrust inside her, pumping in and out until she cried out as an orgasm claimed her.

His grunt of pleasure followed, his movements faster and more intense, his hands stroking her breasts as he groaned and his release spilled from him.

Carol sighed, ready to roll over into his arms and rest, but Ian was too virile to stop. They made love over and over in the night until exhaustion claimed them both in the wee hours of the morning.

Just as he was about to drift off, she curled up next to him. "You have more stamina than any man I've ever been with."

He scrubbed a hand over his face. "It's been a stressful couple of days."

He was half-asleep and inebriated, so she took advantage of the moment. "Do you know who killed that girl?"

He gave her a heavy-lidded, confused stare before shaking his head and closing his eyes. "No, but she had a rose stem in her throat."

Carol perked up. "A rose stem, hmm." Images of crime photos from the Thorn Ripper case flashed through her head. "That's exactly what Johnny Pike did to his victims."

"Yeah, but this was different." He yawned. "This woman was dressed in a wedding gown."

Despite her racing thoughts, Carol tried to keep her voice even. "That's strange."

"Actually that's not the weird part."

"What do you mean?"

"She wasn't engaged."

Carol's heart hammered. This was the angle she needed.

The details that would make it a front-page story.

♦ ♦ ♦

He surveyed the area around the falls where he'd left Gwyneth.

That federal agent was probing around, asking questions. He'd even been to Moose's Coffee looking for him.

He'd almost bumped into him at the door, but managed to duck into a booth without being noticed. Then he'd heard the Fed talking about the body.

He had to be more careful.

Worried they might post someone in these woods to watch for him, he searched the shadows of the thornbush. The sound of birds fluttering toward it echoed in the silence.

But he didn't see anyone now, so he gently laid Constance at the base of the falls, then carefully placed a stone beneath her head as a pillow. He smoothed the lacy wedding dress, then straightened the garter so the bow was centered on her pale, thin neck.

The white gown fanned out around her like angel wings in the snow.

If only she'd been the one . . .

Tears had dried on her cheeks, and the crisp air swirled around her face and caught a strand of her newly chopped hair across her forehead. He brushed it back gently.

She had been a fighter. And a crier. All those tears as she'd begged him to let her go.

But what was she worth to any man if she couldn't make a decent wife?

Her porcelain skin looked a bluish color now. Her eyes frozen in death.

He crossed her hands on her chest, then painted her lips a beautiful red like the roses she would have carried if they had married.

The one she'd bitten down on protruded from her mouth now, macabre and ugly, in stark contrast to her beauty.

"Rest in peace," he whispered as he leaned over and kissed her cheek. "No more crying or pain now, Constance. Dead girls don't cry."

CHAPTER THIRTEEN

Cal stared at the morning newspaper, furious.

A BRIDE KILLER IN GRAVEYARD FALLS

By Carol Little

Local police in the small town of Graveyard Falls and FBI agent Cal Coulter have not yet solved the recent murder of twenty-five-year-old Gwyneth Toyton, whose body was found at the base of the falls.

Sources have revealed that in addition to the location where the body was discovered, there is another significant similarity to the infamous Thorn Ripper case from thirty years ago—the victim was found with a rose stem in her throat.

Although the victim was not engaged, she was wearing a bridal gown. So far, the police have not determined the Bride Killer's motive, but women are urged to be cautious until the homicide is solved.

Anyone with information regarding the case should call the Graveyard Falls police department or the FBI.

Cal shot up from his chair with a curse. Dammit to hell, how had that reporter found out about the rose stem and wedding gown? Worse, if they were dealing with a serial killer, Carol Little had just fed his ego by giving him a name.

Cal had specifically withheld details from the public for interrogation purposes and to weed out false confessions.

He snatched the paper and strode outside to his SUV, started the engine, and drove around the mountain to the town square, then parked at the sheriff's office. Early-morning traffic was minimal, although Cocoa's Café was packed with the breakfast crowd and a school bus chugged by.

He clutched the paper in his hands and rushed into the office. Deputy Kimball was pouring himself a cup of coffee from the side counter, where a box of doughnuts sat. He looked up at Cal with blurry eyes.

Cal slammed the door and the deputy winced.

"Hey, man, not so loud." The deputy rubbed his forehead and sank into the desk chair.

"What's wrong?" Cal's anger mounted at the sight of the bleary-eyed cop. "Are you hungover?"

"Yeah, if you must know, I am," Deputy Kimball muttered. "What's it to you?"

Cal shoved the paper on the desk in front of Kimball. "Do you know anything about this?"

Kimball slurped his coffee, blinked several times, then seemed to focus on the article. His eyes widened in distress. "Shit."

"You leaked that information?" Cal asked, not bothering to disguise his fury.

Panic streaked Deputy Kimball's face. "I . . . don't know. I mean . . . maybe."

Cal tapped the paper, indicating the woman's name. "Do you know this woman Carol Little?"

Kimball's face went ashen. "Fuck. She . . . set me up."

Cal silently counted to ten to keep from jerking the idiot by the collar. "What do you mean, she set you up?"

"I went to Blues and Brews last night to unwind and had a couple of drinks."

"Let me guess," Cal said when Kimball hesitated. "She joined you for some drinks, then you slept with her."

"I told her I didn't do interviews," Kimball argued. "But then I guess . . . maybe I said something when I was half-asleep."

"Do you realize you could have just blown the case?" Cal said. "The rose stem and the bridal gown were details I wanted withheld to weed out false confessions. Now that it's public knowledge, we may get a string of calls claiming to be the killer. And there's the chance of copycats."

The deputy scrubbed his hands over his face. "I'm sorry. I—I screwed up."

"Yeah, you did. Did you tell her about the victim's hair being cut, too?"

"No," the deputy said, although his voice lacked conviction.

Cal's phone buzzed, and he checked the caller ID. Linnea Toyton. Now the shitstorm would begin.

He pressed Connect. "Agent Coulter."

"Did you have to tell everyone about that wedding dress?" Linnea cried. "My phone has been ringing off the hook. And that blasted reporter is at the door demanding an interview!"

Cal gritted his teeth. "Don't open the door. I'll be right there. I need to talk to you anyway. I want you to go with me to your daughter's apartment to see if anything is missing."

"Fine, just get over here and stop this craziness. I don't want my daughter's death used to get publicity for some psycho lunatic."

Cal jogged toward the door. "I'm on my way."

As long as Anna had lived away from Graveyard Falls, she'd felt safe.

But two nights back in the town, back in the house where she'd grown up, back under her father's thumb, and the nightmares had returned.

That story about the murdered girl hadn't helped. In fact, she had déjà vu.

Remembering that she'd tucked her high school diary under the mattress of her bed, she dug it out, surprised but relieved it was still there. She'd worried her father had found it and destroyed it.

She ran her hand over the pale-pink cover and carried it to the kitchen to look at while she had coffee. These pages were filled with her innermost thoughts and dreams and pain. No matter how far she'd run, she'd carried the shame and fear and disgust with her.

Disgust for the boy she'd loved who'd turned out to be a killer.

Disgust with herself for loving him anyway.

How had she not seen what he was doing? What he was really like? The sheriff and press had asked her that a million times. She'd asked herself the same question for the past few years.

Aching for her lost innocence, she skimmed the diary entries.

Today I watched Johnny at football practice. Everyone on the team looks up to him. He's the star quarterback. So good-looking with his bronzed skin and dark-brown hair. And his muscles. Lord, Daddy says it's a sin to notice such things, but I can't help it. That boy is built in a way that I can't help but lust after him.

Daddy says that's wrong. That good girls don't have carnal thoughts.

But I'm weak, and at night when I go to bed, I look at the ceiling and dream about him. I imagine him smiling at me. Kissing me. Wanting me to be his girlfriend.

Sometimes I close my eyes and I feel him touching me. Only, Johnny is so popular he doesn't even know who I am.

She flipped to another entry, four months later.

This is the best day. I can't believe it! Johnny failed his geometry test, so Ms. Grover asked me to tutor him. I'm actually going to get to talk to Johnny!

A loud knock at the front door punctuated the silence, startling Anna. Who in the world could that be?

No one knew she was home. She'd intentionally planned it that way. And her father's friends had dwindled after she'd become the center of the town's gossip.

Her father's footsteps echoed as he shuffled from his room. What little of his gray hair was left stood up in tufts, his robe was undone, his pajama bottoms sagged on his bony frame. He'd lost so much weight he was just a skeleton of the big, brawny man who'd raised her.

"Who the hell's at the door?" he growled.

Anna shoved the diary into her purse on the floor, jumping as the knock sounded again. "I don't know."

"If it's that nasty Johnny boy, you tell him he ain't welcome here."

Pain wrenched her heart as anger surged inside her. Her father's dementia grew worse every day. Sometimes he could remember things that happened forty years ago but not her name or how to get to the grocery store.

"Dad," she said calmly. "It's not Johnny. You put him in prison, remember?" *And you ruined my life.*

"Then get the damn door."

Anna frowned, then picked a piece of lint off her sweatshirt, anxious to get rid of whoever it was. She'd had to come here to try to convince her father to go into an assisted-living home. God knows they couldn't live together.

The knock came again, and she yanked the door open with a scowl. A thin, attractive woman about her age dressed in a suit stood at the door, the wind whipping her bob around her face.

"Hi, my name is Carol Little. I'm looking for Sheriff Buckley. Are you his daughter?"

Panic shot through Anna, resurrecting memories of the newspapers that had plastered her name across the South.

"I'm a reporter—"

"I know who you are, but my father isn't well. He can't help you."

Carol pushed at the door, trying to shoulder her way in. "Then I'll talk to you. You were involved with Johnny Pike years ago, weren't you?"

Sweat broke out on Anna's neck. "Go away and leave us alone. I don't want to talk to you."

Fighting tears and paranoia, she slammed the door in the woman's face.

A knock came a second later. "I said go away," Anna shouted. "If you don't, I'll have you arrested!"

She leaned against the door, trembling as she waited until the woman's car disappeared out of sight.

She couldn't go through this again. She didn't know the girl who'd just been murdered, and Johnny wasn't involved. He was in prison.

This time they had to leave her alone. She had her own secrets to protect.

◆ ◆ ◆

Sheriff Buckley's head throbbed as if the devil had lit it on fire. He paced his bedroom like it was an eight-by-eight cell.

Ever since Anna had come back, shoving pills down his throat and watching him like he was some sick, old demented man, he'd felt like he was losing his mind.

He'd mixed up names and places. Hell, he'd thought that Johnny Pike was at the door knocking.

A minute later, he'd remembered that he'd taken care of that boy a long time ago.

But something else nagged at his mind . . .

He walked into the bathroom and washed his face, but when he looked in the mirror, he didn't even recognize himself. He needed a shave, his eyes looked bloodshot and red, and he had scratches on his cheek.

What the hell? How had he gotten those?

He dried his face with the towel, then tossed it down, but saw his clothes on the floor in a pile. His heart banged with fear.

He stooped down and examined his jeans and shirt. They were damp, covered in leaves, and thorns were stuck in his jeans.

Then he saw blood on the handkerchief he always carried.

His vision blurred, the room faded, and he was suddenly staring at woods.

Thick trees stood side by side like sentinels, the branches winding together like arms guarding the secrets inside.

Between the branches he saw the falls. The thornbush.

Twigs snapped as he stepped forward and inched his way to the falls. Someone was there.

A body.

Shit. The woman was lying on the ground in a wedding dress, the stem of a blood-red rose jammed down her throat, the rosebud on the ground beside her.

He staggered back against the wall as he remembered going to the falls the night before. He had stayed all night.

But he'd lost time somewhere in there.

Then he'd seen the dead girl's body, and it had sent him back thirty years to when it had all started . . .

The roses the boys at high school used as an invitation to prom . . . just as he'd done with his wife, Lilith.

Just as the Thorn Ripper had . . .

Nausea choked him, but he grabbed his jacket and boots, then snuck out the door. He had to go back there now.

See if what he'd remembered was real.

♦ ♦ ♦

Cal braced himself for Mrs. Toyton's wrath as he approached him outside her daughter's apartment. She had a right to be angry.

"That reporter left, but she's called me twice since," she said. "She knew about the dress. Please tell me you didn't mention that that maniac cut Gwyneth's hair."

"I'm sorry, the information about the wedding gown wasn't supposed to be leaked. But no, she doesn't know about the hair." He gestured for her to lead the way into her daughter's apartment. "And I promise you whatever you tell me will remain confidential."

She opened the door, her face paling as she glanced around the interior. A picture of Gwyneth and her mother hung on the wall in the foyer, and the woman broke down.

Cal patted her back. "I'm sorry, ma'am. I really am."

She swiped angrily at her tears and straightened her spine. "Just find out who hurt my little girl."

"Yes, ma'am, I will." Cal stepped into the entryway. "I need you to see if anything of your daughter's is missing."

"Like what?" Mrs. Toyton asked. "You think her death was about a robbery?"

No, he didn't think that at all. But he didn't want to share his theory yet.

Or that this unsub might kill again.

"It's just routine. Was she wearing something personal like a favorite scarf or a piece of jewelry?"

Mrs. Toyton's eyes widened as if she'd just thought of something, then she hurried to her daughter's bedroom. Cal watched as she rummaged through Gwyneth's jewelry box. She looked frantic for a minute, then searched the top dresser drawer.

"She had this charm bracelet she always wore." Anguish darkened her eyes. "Was it with her when you found her?"

Cal mentally ticked through the personal items recovered with the body—nothing but the bridal dress. She hadn't been wearing any jewelry.

"No," he said. "I'm afraid not."

Mrs. Toyton dropped onto the bed, her chin quivering. "Her father gave her the bracelet on her birthday right before he died. She never took it off."

"Was it valuable?"

"No." Her voice cracked. "The charms were inexpensive, but it was special to her."

Cal gritted his teeth.

Serial killers took souvenirs . . .

So it obviously meant something to the killer.

Cal drove straight to the state prison. It was time to talk to Johnny Pike.

He met with Warden Brisbin as soon as he cleared security, and explained the circumstances. "I want you to analyze his mail one letter at a time. See if anyone is enamored with him and his MO, if someone wants to emulate or impress him, if he's been in contact with someone and mentored them."

"We're behind on the mail, but I'll personally see that his is pulled going back the last year."

"Send anything suspicious to my lab." He handed the warden his card. The warden escorted him to an interrogation room, where a guard had already brought Pike.

Pike had been eighteen when he'd been locked up. The years incarcerated had hardened him from a young boy to a tough, angry man who bore the scars of prison life.

Cal crossed his arms. "My name is Agent Cal Coulter. I'm here because of the recent murder in Graveyard Falls."

Pike muttered something beneath his breath.

"What was that?" Cal asked, his voice hard.

"I said I knew you'd show up here."

Cal raised a brow. "Because you knew the murder was going to happen."

"No," Pike said, his tone controlled but lethal. "Because I was rail-roaded by that sheriff once. It stands to figure with my parole coming up that he'd do anything he could to keep me locked up, even point fingers at me for some random crime."

"It's not a random crime." Cal dropped the folder of pictures on the table, opened it, and spread them in a row.

Crime photos of Gwyneth lying in the snow in the wedding dress, the rose stem jammed down her throat, blood dotting her mouth and tongue, her hair hacked off.

"Good God," Pike whispered.

His shocked expression appeared to be genuine. But Sheriff Buckley had painted him as a psychopath.

"Have you had contact with anyone from that area?"

Pike shook his head, but his eyes were glued to the picture.

"How about a visitor? Someone who wanted to pick your brain about the Thorn Ripper case?"

"The only people who contacted the warden to see me are the report-ers, and I refused to talk to them."

"If you tell me what you know, it might work in your favor when the parole hearing comes up."

"Right. If Sheriff Buckley has anything to do with it, that will never happen."

Cal cleared his throat. "Then do it to prevent another girl from suffering. Because if this guy is copying you, he's going to kill again."

Pike clenched his jaw. "I can't help you because I don't know any-thing," he said in a low voice. "Now this interview is over."

He looked to the guard. "Take me back to my cell."

Cal watched him disappear out the door, the man's anger lingering like a dark force.

Hopefully Pike's mail would offer them a lead. And if he learned the man was hiding something, he'd make sure parole never happened.

CHAPTER FOURTEEN

Mona tried to shake off the disturbing idea of a serial killer in town as she met with her clients.

Her first patient of the morning was a repeat. A woman named Leslie Combs, whose husband had been abusing her. The fresh bruises on the woman's face triggered Mona's protective instincts. This time Leslie had called the deputy, who'd arrested Whit Combs.

But this was a cycle, and when he was released, which he probably would be, he would come back after her.

Mona gave Leslie the name of a friend who would help her take refuge in a women's shelter until she could relocate.

A knock sounded, and her assistant, Aimee, cracked the door. "You have a new patient. She just called this morning, and I told her we'd fit her in."

"Background?"

"Her name is Sylvia Wales. She needs grief counseling."

Mona's heart clenched with sympathy. "Send her in." She walked around her desk to greet the woman, and was surprised to recognize her.

It was the same woman with the baby she'd seen at the housing development where Kay Marlin lived.

Sylvia was about her age, late twenties, with dark-blonde hair and expressive green eyes full of pain. "Thanks for fitting me in."

Mona clasped her hand. "Of course. My assistant said you came for grief counseling. May I ask who you lost?"

"My husband." A wariness flared in her expression that suggested the loss was recent. Her gaze landed on the photo of Mona and Brent on the bookshelf, and Sylvia started to back out the door as if the sight of any happy couple made her sad.

"I know this is hard," Mona said. "But stay and talk to me."

Sylvia hesitated, but finally gave a short nod, then chose the love seat. Mona's heart immediately went out to the young woman as she seated herself across from her. "I'm sorry for your loss," Mona said. "I know people say they understand and that they know what you're going through, but I really do. I recently lost my husband as well."

Sylvia seemed surprised at her admission. Mona was surprised herself. Normally she didn't discuss her personal relationships with a patient. But Sylvia had noticed the photograph and she'd thought sharing might help, that they were kindred spirits.

Mona reached for Sylvia's hand and squeezed it. "Tell me about your husband. What was his name?"

For a moment, Sylvia looked as if she was going to bolt, but she took a deep breath and began. "Ted. He was a wonderful man." Sylvia's eyes glittered with unshed tears. "He was tall, handsome, a hard worker. He liked to renovate houses."

"I saw your baby. Was he Ted's son?"

Sylvia studied her hands.

"Sylvia?"

"Yes." When she looked at Mona, she lifted her chin. "We were so excited to have a little boy."

The pang of her own loss hit Mona, but she swallowed back a comment about her miscarriage. "What happened to Ted?"

"He was killed in an accident," Sylvia said. "A month after our son was born."

Mona's heart broke for the woman and for the child.

Sylvia stood, hands fisted by her sides as if she might punch someone. "But he'll never know his father, and Ted wasn't supposed to die.
We were a family, he was going to build us a house with a fenced yard
and a walk-in closet—"

Mona started to respond, but the door swung open, and suddenly
Leslie's husband, Whit Combs, burst in, waving his arms around. Aimee
was on his tail trying to stop him. "You can't go in there!"

"You bitch, where is my wife?" Whit shouted.

Sylvia ducked behind the chair, and Mona raised a hand to calm the
man. "Please, Mr. Combs, settle down. If you want to talk—"

He lunged forward and grabbed her. Mona's legs buckled as she
reached for the panic button on the side of her desk.

Cal parked, battling the fierce winds rolling off the mountain as he
hurried to the morgue.

Peyton and Dr. Wheeland met him in the lab.

"What did you find?"

"The lipstick is called Ravaging Red," Peyton began. "It's an inexpensive brand that I thought was probably found in most drugstores, which
would make it more difficult to trace. But the interesting part is that the
cosmetic company who made that brand no longer manufactures it."

"So it's old?"

She nodded. "The killer may have had it for a long time. It might
have belonged to a sister, girlfriend, or mother."

Cal cleared his throat. "I consulted the counselor in town, Mona
Monroe, who studied criminology. She suggested he cut the victim's
hair to make her resemble someone he knows."

"That makes sense," Peyton said.

"Anything on the bridal gown?"

"As I mentioned before, it was homemade." Peyton indicated a sample of thread on a slide. "That thread is so old it's rotting."

"So the unsub got the dress from a family member or a vintage store?"

Peyton nodded. "That's possible. I ran a search for vintage gowns on Craigslist, eBay, and other stores and sites but haven't come up with anything so far. I also posted a picture of the dress and asked anyone recognizing the seamstress's work, the stitching or beadwork, to contact me."

"Good work," Cal told Peyton.

Dr. Wheeland raised a finger. "I have something else, too. We found DNA on the victim's cheek that doesn't belong to the victim."

Cal's pulse hammered. "You think it belongs to the killer?"

Dr. Wheeland nodded. "I believe he kissed her on the cheek before he left her at the falls."

"Sick bastard."

"I've already run the DNA through the databases, but nothing popped," Peyton said. "If you bring us a suspect, we can run a comparison."

Cal's phone beeped, and he checked the ID. Deputy Kimball. "I need to take this. Anything else?"

Peyton handed him a slip of paper with a number and name on it. "This is for a tailor shop in Graveyard Falls. The owner might be able to look at the dress and stitchwork and help."

"Good." He'd get one of the deputies to check it out. "Peyton, I asked the warden at the state pen to send any suspicious mail Pike received to you for analysis."

"I'll put my assistant on it right away," Peyton said. "If there's a lead there, we'll find it."

Cal's phone buzzed again, and he pushed Connect. "Yeah?"

"I just got a call from Mona Monroe's assistant," Deputy Kimball said. "There's trouble. A man I brought in earlier for spousal abuse made bail and went to see her."

"I'm on my way." Cal rushed outside, the gray clouds painting a gloomy darkness across the sky as he jumped in his SUV and headed toward Mona's office.

If that man had hurt her, he'd tear him apart with his bare hands.

♦ ♦ ♦

Mona yelled for the security guard. Whit shoved her against the desk and her hip hit the corner hard. He raised his fist, but the security guard snatched his arm back and dragged him away from her.

Whit swung his fist back and connected with the guard's jaw. He landed another punch, and they tangled for a few minutes, trading blows.

Mona reached inside her purse and grabbed her gun, then raised it. "Let him go, Whit. I don't want to use this, but I will."

Whit ignored her and again punched the guard, who dropped to the floor in pain. Aimee was at the door, her eyes panicked. She waved Sylvia past, and Sylvia rushed out the door.

"Whit, let him go!" Mona shouted as Whit raised his fist again.

"Do what she says." Cal's deep voice echoed from the doorway, his big body tense.

Whit jerked his head toward Cal, then raised his hands in surrender at the sight of Cal's gun.

Damn man. He wasn't afraid of her, but he respected Cal. Typical abuser. Picked on someone smaller and weaker than himself.

Cal's boots pounded as he crossed the floor, then he yanked Whit's arms behind him and handcuffed him. Cal's eyes narrowed as he looked at her gun, and she instinctively lowered the weapon.

"You got no right to arrest me," Whit bellowed. "That bitch kidnapped my wife and pulled a gun on me!"

"I did not kidnap her," Mona said, grateful to see the security guard getting up. Aimee helped him sit in a chair to collect himself. "You need psychiatric help, Whit," Mona said.

"Where did you take her?" Whit snarled.

"I didn't take her anywhere," Mona said. "She left to protect herself from you. If you really love her, you'll let her go and get some counseling."

Cal jerked the man's arms behind him and handcuffed him. "I don't know how you made bail, but this time you're going to sit in a cell for a while."

Ignoring the man's litany of curse words, Cal hauled him toward the door.

♦ ♦ ♦

Cal made sure the jerk was locked up, then returned to the front of the sheriff's office. He'd driven Mona here to file a statement, and she was waiting, arms crossed.

He reminded himself to be calm, that Mona meant nothing more to him than anyone else, but that was a lie, and his tone reflected the surge of fear that had shot through him when he'd thought Combs might hurt her. "What the hell were you thinking pulling a gun?"

Mona glanced at him with a calmness that only infuriated him more. "I told you about it. I carry it for protection," Mona said. "And before you ask, yes, I know how to shoot. Brent taught me."

Of course he had.

"If your job is this dangerous, maybe you need to rethink your line of work."

Mona released a bitter laugh. "You're worried about my job? Cal, you put your life on the line every day."

"But I can handle it. I'm trained."

"I'm not going to debate this," Mona said. "It's the same argument Brent and I used to have."

Cal gritted his teeth. One thing he and Brent had agreed on was keeping Mona safe.

In spite of her bravado, her adrenaline must have been waning, because a shudder coursed through her. He couldn't help himself. He pulled her to him and closed his arms around her.

She laid her head against his chest, and he stroked her back. He didn't know what the hell he would have done if the bastard had killed her.

Still terrified inside, he lifted her chin and looked into her eyes. For a brief second, he thought desire flickered in the depths. His own hunger spiraled.

Her sweet scent teased his senses, and the soft whisper of her breath made his pulse pound. She felt so fragile, yet Mona had always been strong, and that strength stirred his desires even more.

Unable to resist, he leaned toward her and touched her lips with his. A soft sigh escaped her as her lips met his in invitation.

Their mouths fused, need seeping between them, unspent hunger making his body harden.

Cal wanted more. He might never have enough.

He deepened the kiss, tasting her sweetness, yet a fiery heat ignited inside him. She clutched his back, her chest rising and falling against his own, driving him crazy with the ache to have her.

But a second later, his phone buzzed, jolting him back to reality. He cursed the phone. He cursed himself for kissing her. But the haze of passion glittering in her eyes made him want to drag her back into his arms.

His phone buzzed again, though, and he gave her a look of regret, then reluctantly pulled away and connected the call. "Agent Coulter."

"This is Sheriff Buckley. There's another dead girl at Graveyard Falls."

He knelt at a pew in the church he'd attended since he was a kid. Granted, his mama didn't take him regularly 'cause she'd been sick so much. But when he was little, they'd come every time the doors were open.

He'd been so scared when he was little he'd nearly peed himself when that big preacher had stalked up and down the aisles, hunting for someone to save.

Preacher would shout and pound the pulpit, sweat streaming down his ruddy cheeks, then he'd comb the aisles, stopping to glare at the children, at the men and women, at anyone he thought might have strayed from God that week.

Sometimes the preacher lingered on his face as if he thought Will was evil just because he didn't have a daddy.

But Mama was dying, and Will didn't know where else to turn. Maybe if he prayed hard enough, the good Lord wouldn't take her from him.

Tears choked his throat, and he gulped them back, snot bubbling in his nose. Sometimes at night when he lay there in that big metal bed by himself, he cried like a baby. He didn't know how he'd go on without her.

You have to find a wife.

Then he wouldn't be alone.

He wiped his nose with his sleeve and glanced up to see that girl Josie DuKane kneeling at the pew across from him. He'd heard the preacher talking to her and asking her name. Her head was bowed, her lips moving as she prayed.

There was something about her that seemed so familiar. Her cheekbones? They were high . . . Her eyes an odd shade of green. And she had pretty hair. The wavy brown strands fell down her back, making him itch to run his hands through it.

She looked up at him then, and her gaze met his. Her cheeks looked flushed from the cold, and she lifted her scarf and tied it around her head.

"You look sad," she said softly.

He didn't like to talk about his mama, but she sounded so kind that he decided to open up. "My mama's ill."

"I'm so sorry." She knelt beside him and covered his hand with hers. "I was praying for my grandfather. My mother and I came back to Graveyard Falls to take care of him because he's sick, too. But he doesn't seem to like me."

How could he not like her? She was beautiful and sweet, and she cared about family.

Would she be a good wife? "Can you cook?" he asked.

She looked startled by the question. "Yes, why?"

A slow smile curved his mouth. "Just wondering."

CHAPTER FIFTEEN

Cal didn't have time to drive Mona home, so he let her ride with him to the falls. But he tried to convince her to stay in the car.

"Maybe I can help," Mona said as she climbed out to follow him.

He couldn't argue with her reasoning. This was the second murder within three days. If they were dealing with a serial killer, he needed all the help he could get.

Because the killer could already be hunting for another victim.

But hell, part of him didn't want her anywhere near this mess. Whoever the unsub was, he was dangerous, and Mona already had enough trouble on her tail.

That man Whit was a loose cannon, and Mona had pissed him off.

Cal didn't intend to leave her unguarded again.

Mona stumbled on a vine, and Cal caught her arm, helping her down the slope. Again, he was struck by the fact that the unsub must be strong to carry his victims to the base of the falls, where the water pooled before continuing downstream over the jagged ridges and rocks.

Icy wind bit at his cheeks, and Mona tugged the ski cap she'd retrieved from her office over her ears. It was so damn cold he felt like the hairs on the back of his neck were literally freezing.

Mona gasped when they made it to the clearing. Sheriff Buckley was standing beside the body, his hat tilted askew on his head, his face chapped from the cold. Deputy Kimball was already assessing the scene.

What the hell? He thought Buckley had retired.

The white wedding gown caught his eye, although it nearly blended with the snowy ground. God, the woman looked angelic with her blonde hair and that satin dress.

Except that the whites of her eyes showed reddish spots of blood called petechial hemorrhaging, her irises shockingly wide, her mouth frozen in a scream.

Mona's breathing rattled in the silence as they crossed the remaining distance to the victim, and he realized she was taking deep breaths. Had she ever seen a dead body?

"I'm sorry, Mona, I told you it wouldn't be pretty."

"I can't imagine doing that to another human. And she's so . . . young."

Yeah. She'd had her entire life ahead of her. But this maniac had stolen it from her before she'd had a chance to live out her dreams.

Cal hadn't officially met the former sheriff, so he introduced himself. "And this is Mona Monroe."

"Yes, I saw her at the memorial service," Sheriff Buckley said with a scowl.

"Who found this woman?" Cal asked.

"I did," Sheriff Buckley replied.

Cal's pulse quickened. What had the sheriff been doing in these woods? "How did that happen? Did you get a tip?"

"No, but I started thinking that if this killer was copying the Thorn Ripper, there would be another victim, so I decided to revisit the area."

He didn't know whether to be irritated that the sheriff had decided to check the falls or to question his involvement. They'd need to get officers out here to monitor the area. "I thought you retired."

Sheriff Buckley shot him a condescending look. "Once a cop, always a cop. Graveyard Falls is still my home."

"And you were here during the original murders," Cal said.

"Exactly. I don't aim to let another serial killer destroy this town."

◆ ◆ ◆

Mona felt uncomfortable around the former sheriff, although she didn't know why.

The medical examiner arrived, and the men gathered around the body.

"Cause of death appears to be asphyxiation due to strangulation just like Gwyneth Toyton, but I'll verify it with the autopsy." Dr. Wheeland opened the victim's mouth and examined her tongue and throat. "Thorns are embedded in her tongue and throat same as the first victim. Her teeth are bloodstained, so she bled from biting the thorns while he strangled her."

Revulsion filled Mona. Why would a man force a woman to bite on a thorny rose as he killed her? Was it his way of keeping her quiet? Of making her suffer because she'd rejected him?

"Did anyone ever ask Johnny Pike why he used the rose?" Mona asked.

Sheriff Buckley cleared his throat. "According to town tradition, the high school boys gave a girl a rose when they asked her to prom."

Was killing the girls his way of saying he didn't want to go with them? Definitely excessive behavior.

"Did they ever do a psychological exam on Pike?" Mona asked.

Sheriff Buckley shrugged. "Lawyer talked about pleading insanity, but it was clear that Pike was lucid, not insane."

She still didn't understand Johnny's motive. "Did he have problems with his mother? Had he ever been abused?"

"Listen, Ms. Monroe," the sheriff said in a tone laced with disdain. "We're not here to probe Pike's mind. We've got a killer to find."

Dr. Wheeland checked the victim's wrists and ankles, and Mona cringed at the sight of the bruises and raw skin. "It also appears that her foot was bound with a heavy chain."

"How about time of death?"

"TOD was sometime last night." He gestured toward marks on the back of her neck. "Looks like he used a stun gun on her as well."

Cal knelt. "The dress, the garter, the cut hair, the red lipstick smeared on her lips . . . it's the same MO." Even though the reporter had revealed the information about the rose and wedding gown, no one but the killer, the investigators, and the people who'd found the bodies would know all the other details.

Dr. Wheeland lifted the woman's head and searched inside the back of her dress. "No tag. This gown looks homemade as well."

A shiver rippled through Mona. "Are they family heirlooms?"

"We don't know yet. They could be, or he could have purchased them. We're looking into that angle." Cal stood and glanced at the medical examiner. "You said you found DNA where the unsub kissed Gwyneth. Make sure you check for saliva on this girl's cheek as well."

He gestured toward her hands. "How about her fingernails? Do you think you can get any forensics there?"

Dr. Wheeland scraped beneath her nails, and his brow puckered as he sniffed her fingers. "Her fingernails have pieces of eggshells beneath them." He indicated a particle he'd extracted.

"Eggshells?" Cal frowned. "They were cooking or eating before he killed her?"

Dr. Wheeland arched a brow. "That's possible."

But not much of a lead. "We need an ID." He turned back to the sheriff. "Do you recognize her?"

"No," Buckley said.

Cal approached the crime team and instructed them to search the area for the victim's purse, ID, and any evidence they could find.

A growing horror rose inside Mona. The killer had obviously gotten away with murder the first time, likely had even enjoyed the kill.

"What are you thinking?" Cal asked.

She rubbed her hands together to warm them. "I think he may be suffering from delusions. He's a loner and keeps to himself, probably lives off the grid. If he's trying to satisfy some fantasy in his mind, he won't stop until he finds the woman who can fulfill that delusion. He wants her to look like a woman in his past, maybe a former girlfriend or someone who rejected him. In some cases of abuse, he may be fixated on his mother."

"You mean he wants someone like her, but he also hates her?"

"I would only be guessing, but yes."

"It may be too early to tell if he has a type," Cal said.

Mona stared at the body. "So none of the females in Graveyard Falls are safe."

♦ ♦ ♦

"I'm afraid not." Cal held back a torrent of curses. It was his job to protect them. "Do you think this man could convince a woman to go with him willingly?" he asked.

Mona scrunched her face as she considered it. "It's possible he's handsome, maybe even charming. Or he's the opposite, the quiet, mysterious type who draws women. But he doesn't stand out in any way, not overtly."

"So no one notices him?" Cal said.

"Exactly. He's probably quiet and unassuming. He blends in, and no one suspects what he's capable of."

"You think he's another teenager like Johnny Pike was?" Sheriff Buckley asked.

Mona shook her head. "If he was, he would probably choose younger victims like high schoolers. Looking at the profile of the victims, he chooses young, single women in their twenties. The fact that he puts them in wedding dresses suggests he's around their age, maybe a little older. Early thirties. He's looking for a wife, so he may have never been married, or like we talked about earlier, he could have recently lost his wife. Something triggered his need to marry now, though."

"Hopefully the homemade wedding dresses will lead to something," Cal said, frustrated. "But we need more."

Mona winced as the medical examiner studied the girl's bare feet. "I wonder what he does with the clothes the women were wearing before he changed them."

Cal shrugged. "We didn't find anything at the first scene. Maybe he disposes of them or keeps them as part of his trophies. We think he took a charm bracelet from Gwyneth Toyton. Once we ID this victim, we can ask her family if she's missing anything."

"Pike took a piece of jewelry from his victims, too," Sheriff Buckley said. "That's one thing we never recovered."

One of the CSIs shouted that he'd found a partial boot print by a damp muddy spot, but the water from the falls had washed most of it away. Another found a small piece of tattered lace from the dress that must have caught on a branch when the unsub carried her through the woods.

Cal pinched the bridge of his nose. "You know we've been thinking that the killer is trying to mimic Pike's MO to get attention. What if Pike being up for parole is the trigger, and he started killing to remind everyone how much horror Pike caused, by making the town relive that fear?"

Mona contemplated that theory. "That would make sense."

"You want me to check out the family members of the original victims?" Deputy Kimball asked.

"Yeah, get a list together and start talking to them," Cal said.

Sheriff Buckley cleared his throat. "I know the families, and none of them would do this."

Cal frowned. "How can you be so sure?"

"These are my people," Sheriff Buckley said. "I've known them for years."

The sheriff was obviously defensive of the locals. And he probably didn't want anyone questioning the original case—the case that had made him a hero.

"One thing to keep in mind is that this killer may have had psychotic tendencies growing up," Mona said. "Oftentimes, serial killers start out killing animals when they're young."

"Maybe he hunted with a father or uncle?" Deputy Kimball suggested.

"He could have grown up hunting," Mona agreed. "But even if he didn't, he may have enjoyed cold-bloodedly killing just to watch an animal suffer." Mona paused. "You might contact the schools for kids who acted out, maybe ones with juvenile records. If he's in his early thirties now, I'd go back fifteen to twenty years."

"I'll have the lab look at that," Cal said.

Mona glanced at her watch, and he realized she needed to get back to town for her radio show.

"I'll check prisons and mental hospitals for recent releases." He punched Peyton's number, anxious to get started.

The killer might already have abducted his next victim.

Josie DuKane had a strange feeling about the young man praying in the pew near her. He seemed so humble, nice . . . a little unsure of himself. But he obviously cared about his mother or he wouldn't be in church praying for her.

"Maybe we could have dinner sometime," he offered.

She considered his offer but remembered why she was here. She had things to do while in town. Answers to find.

So she declined his invitation.

Disappointment flickered in his dark-brown eyes for a moment. He looked so dejected that she scribbled her phone number on a pad she pulled from her purse and handed it to him. "Give me a call."

His disappointment faded. "Maybe tomorrow?"

"Maybe."

She gave him a little wave, then headed outside into the chilly evening.

She and her mother hadn't been in town long. In fact, her mother had resisted coming to visit her father, Josie's grandfather, for years.

Something bad had happened between them when she was young. She wished she knew what it was.

Her mother hated the town and the people here.

She'd already told Josie they wouldn't stay long.

But Josie was tired of all the secrets and lies.

Her mother said Josie's father had died before she was born. But she suspected that wasn't true.

Maybe her grandfather knew his name. If she could catch him on a good day, he might be able to tell her where he was.

Then she could finally meet him and find out why her mother claimed he was dead.

◆ ◆ ◆

He jabbed the pin against his palm as Josie left. He wanted her so bad he almost chased after her.

He could see her dressed in white, the lace curling around her delicate wrists and ankles, the hint of that garter beneath her skirt.

Adrenaline surged through him as he imagined lifting the folds of the wedding gown, sliding that garter off, then planting kisses up her thigh.

But first they had to walk down the aisle. The roses would look so beautiful against the white lace.

Yes, Josie looked like the one. She seemed sweet and . . . inexperienced. And she was a churchgoer like him.

But something didn't feel quite right about her. Something about those eyes . . . who was it she reminded him of? A picture of a girl his mama had shown him . . .

Torn over what to do as he headed toward his truck, he remembered that Mona woman who gave advice on the radio. He crawled into the front seat, cranked up the heater to ward off the chill from the blustery wind, and punched her number.

That damned man answered first. "This is the *Ask Mona* show. Can I tell her who's calling?"

"She'll know me. It's really important."

A heavy sigh. "One moment, sir."

He thumped his fingers up and down while he waited. While her sweet voice spoke to him.

"This is Mona. How can I help you?"

"I think I may have found the one."

A second of silence passed. "Who am I speaking to?"

"You don't remember me?" he asked sharply.

How could she not remember him? He thought he'd made an impression on her the last time, but women seemed to look right through him. Forget him. Act like he was nothing.

His temper reared its head, and he gripped the steering wheel, following Josie in her car. She stopped at a nail place and hurried inside, and he watched as she slid into a seat across from a pretty redhead. Two other women were seated at the nail stations, hands extended as the workers gave them manicures.

"Oh, yes, we talked before. I thought you might call back." Mona's voice sounded a little too light. Fake. Like she was trying hard to be nice to him.

Was she one of the little liars Mama had told him about? Was she only pretending to care when she really didn't?

"Tell me about her. Why do you think she's the one?"

Because she was nice to him. But that made him sound pathetic. "Forget it," he snarled. "You don't care."

"Yes, I do," she said quickly. "Please, talk to me."

"I just want someone to love me," he said, hating the quiver in his voice. Fuck. He didn't want to sound pitiful.

"I'm sure your family loves you," Mona said. "Do they live close by?"

His eyes blurred, images of his mama confined to that wheelchair haunting him. He wanted to go back and crawl in bed beside her and have her hold him and tell him everything would be all right just like she had when he was little.

But everything wasn't all right. She was dying and soon he'd be all alone. And he hated to be alone.

He breathed out deeply, ended the call, and drove to the Boar's Head. He wouldn't be alone for long.

CHAPTER SIXTEEN

Mona's instincts warned her that the man who'd just hung up on her was either dangerous or teetering on the edge of violent behavior.

And that he might break any second.

She glanced at Cal, who was watching her through the glass. He'd insisted on escorting her to the radio station and left the police covering the crime scene, saying he didn't intend to leave her alone until he knew Whit was no longer a threat and the Bride Killer had been caught.

Chance cut to a commercial, and Cal rushed to her. "That was the same man who called before. Do you think he could be the Bride Killer?"

Mona chewed her lip, hesitant to point fingers. "I need more information. If he calls back, I'll try to keep him on the line talking."

"His phone number didn't show up again," Chance said. "My guess is he's calling from a throwaway cell."

"I just requested a trace on the phone here anyway," Cal said. "He might slip up and call from a landline somewhere and we can get a location. Why don't you invite him to call back?" Cal suggested.

Mona agreed and returned to her microphone, then waited for Chance to give her the cue.

"This is *Ask Mona*. I want to implore that last caller to phone me again. I don't like the way we left things. I can tell you're lonely and that you need to talk. I'm here when you're ready."

Hopefully he'd take the bait, and she could find out more about him.

Still, the possibility that she might have been talking to the Bride Killer chilled her to the bone.

She'd seen the violence and anger in the bruises on the woman's throat, arms, and wrists. She'd felt his regret in the fact that he'd kissed Gwyneth good-bye before leaving her.

But that wouldn't stop him from doing it again.

Carol Little stopped by the deputy's office, hoping he'd have more information on the murder. But the deputy met her at the door and jerked her inside.

She ran a finger along his jaw. "What? Do you want a quickie on the desk?"

She rubbed her foot up his calf, playing. He was a passionate man, virile, and she wouldn't mind doing him again. He seemed to loosen up after sex.

He clenched her wrists, his jaw rigid. "Stop it," he hissed. "You got me in a shitload of trouble by printing that article."

She pulled back, a scowl on her face. "You knew I was a reporter, and murder is news. Don't you think the people in town have a right to know if they're in danger?"

"Yes," he said, a dangerous glint to his eyes. "But you weren't supposed to reveal the part about the wedding dress. The Feds are up my ass. They wanted to hold that back in case we have grandstanders coming in with false confessions."

"If you didn't want it printed, you should have said so," Carol shot back.

His eyes widened. "We were in bed, I was half-asleep and drunk." Anger hardened his tone. "Or was that your plan all along? Fuck me so you could pick my brain when you had me off guard? Is that why you're here now, because you heard there was another victim and you think I'll talk?"

Carol went still, her heart pounding. "There's another victim?"

The deputy exhaled on a curse. "You didn't know?"

She shook her head. "Who is it?"

"We haven't IDed her yet," he said between gritted teeth. "But even if we had, I wouldn't tell you."

Carol flinched. "I'm not the enemy here. I just want to report the news and warn people if they need to be on guard." She turned and mimicked surveying his office, nodding her approval, before casually wandering to his desk and glancing at the open notepad. Apparently he'd been researching the families of the Thorn Ripper's victims.

"See, we're on the same page. I was going to look into these folks. Thought one of them might have motive to replicate the Thorn Ripper's work."

Deputy Kimball walked over and snapped the notepad closed. "You want to share? Tell me what you found out."

Carol smiled, playing along. "Tiffany Levinson's mother still lives in town. Father is deceased. Brittany Burgess's parents divorced after her death, and the mother moved away. The father remarried and lives in Knoxville. He comes back once a year for the memorial."

"And the Yonkers?"

"They're more interesting. They had troubles and separated. The mother lives in a cabin in the mountains. Husband was a vet and started a pet crematorium but died. Candy's brother, Doyle, runs it now."

But that was all she was ready to divulge. "Your turn."

"You got more than I did."

She doubted that. "Come on, Deputy." She ran her hand up his arm. "Play nice."

"No, you tricked me before, but I won't fall for it again. You want to sensationalize these girls' murders to make a name for yourself."

He dragged her toward the front door, then pushed her outside. "I have no comment. Now get out."

"Ian," Carol said, ignoring the curious locals on the street. "The town deserves to know what's going on."

"I told you I have no comment." He slammed the door.

Carol muttered something ugly beneath her breath. She wanted to go back inside and shake the truth out of him, demand he give her the story.

But he was too angry at the moment. She needed to let him cool down. Meanwhile, she'd dig around some more on her own.

She hadn't yet talked to Tiffany Levinson's mother, Sara. She would pay her a visit and hope she wasn't viewed as a pariah like she had been at the memorial.

♦ ♦ ♦

Cal watched Mona through the glass, anxious for the caller to phone again.

If he was the Bride Killer, he might be stalking another victim now.

Dammit. He needed a lead. He phoned Peyton, hoping she had some information.

"There are two men in Graveyard Falls who lost wives in the last few months," Peyton said. "First, Darby Holland. His wife died of an aneurism three months ago. He has three children and works at the post office."

"Anything in his background to indicate he might be violent?"

"No. He's a deacon at his church and teaches Bible study on Wednesday nights. No police reports, not even a traffic ticket. I talked to his boss at the post office and he said he's hardworking, kindhearted, and never misses a day of work."

He didn't sound like their man. "Who else?"

"Virgil William Mulhaney," Peyton said.

William—it might be Mona's caller Will. "Tell me more about him."

"He owns several chicken houses outside town. He provides eggs to local stores and chickens to several parts of Tennessee."

This latest victim's fingernails had had eggshells beneath them. And Mona had said the killer might have killed animals as a child. If this man relished slaughtering chickens, it wouldn't be a stretch for him to choke a woman to death.

"What happened to his wife?"

"That's a little murky. The death certificate said she died when her car ran off the road. But she told someone at her sewing circle that she planned to leave Virgil."

A sewing circle . . .

"He denied knowing about it?"

"Yes. And the sheriff couldn't find any proof he'd caused his wife's death." Peyton paused. "But this is interesting. When the husband was young, neighbors reported instances where their animals had died. The sheriff suspected Virgil killed them, but they found no proof."

So far he fit the profile. "Text me his address."

"On it." A second passed. "There's another name you might want to check out, too. Doyle William Yonkers."

"Yonkers? He related to Candy Yonkers?"

"Her brother. He's forty and was released about three weeks ago from a psychiatric ward at Peninsula. You know medical records are hard to access, but I spoke to one of the psych nurses and she said he suffered from depression and bipolar disorder. They medicated him, and he was released under his mother's custody. I'll send you that contact info as well."

His adrenaline surged. He had two possible persons of interest now. And one was connected to the Thorn Ripper case.

He hurried to tell Mona that he needed to leave.

♦ ♦ ♦

"I'll go with you to question them," Mona offered.

"What about the show?"

"We're done for the evening. I'm sorry that man didn't call back. Maybe he'll call tomorrow." She just hoped that if he was the Bride Killer, he didn't take another life tonight. The last few callers had been panic-stricken about the recent crime. Already word was spreading that there had been a second victim.

Cal walked her to the car. "No, I think it's best I question this man alone."

They climbed into his SUV and he pulled from the parking lot. Thankfully the snow had ceased, but the roads were still icy. Night was setting in, the stars minimal, the moon barely a sliver through the dark winter clouds, making the forests look eerie and thick with hidden dangers.

A patch of black ice could send them skidding off the mountain in seconds. And according to Cal, the man he needed to question lived in the hills.

"I might be able to help," Mona said.

"You have been helpful, Mona, but it's too dangerous. If this is our unsub, he may be armed. I don't want you anywhere near him." Cal's beard stubble made a coarse sound as he ran his hand over it.

A tingle of awareness seeped through Mona, tempting her to lean into him.

"What about you?" she said, unable to hide the anxiety in her voice. "If he is armed, you could be hurt." Or worse.

She could lose him just as she'd lost Brent.

"I can take care of myself," Cal said, his voice deep.

"Brent thought that, too." The words came out more harshly than Mona intended. But she couldn't retract them.

"Brent died in an accident."

"I know, ironic, isn't it?" Fresh pain clawed at her chest. "We argued about the dangers of police work, but he died in his car."

"I'm sorry, Mona, I know you miss him."

Cal's voice was flat, but his expression said so much more. He was in turmoil and missed his best friend, too. They should be bonding over their shared grief.

But that kiss between them teased her mind.

Instead of making the turn toward the hills, he veered onto the street leading to her house. "I don't want to leave you alone, but Whit is in jail for the night and I have to go, Mona."

She nodded, resigned, as he parked in her drive. In spite of her determination to be strong, and the fact that Cal was a seasoned, trained agent, she knew anything could happen on that mountain.

"Mona?"

A tear fought past her resolve and lingered on her eyelash, and she averted her eyes. "Be careful, Cal."

Tension vibrated between them, thick with questions and the threat of him facing down a killer. He reached across her to open the door, and she braced herself to put on a brave face, but he touched her cheek with his thumb and tilted her face toward him.

His dark gaze met hers, and his jaw hardened. "Ah, God, Mona . . ."

"I'm sorry, Cal," she whispered. "I lost Brent. I don't think I could bear to lose you, too."

A low moan that sounded like a mixture of pain and hunger rumbled from him. His gaze locked with hers, and emotions flooded his face. She told herself to get out of the car, to run to the house, that she couldn't show Cal how much she cared for him.

But the thought of him leaving tonight and not coming back terrified her.

"Nothing is going to happen to me," he said.

She squeezed her eyes shut, his husky assurance only making her ache to hold him.

Another sigh escaped him, then he pulled her into his arms and held her against him.

Cal silently cursed himself for giving in to his need to hold Mona, but he'd wanted her too damn long to walk away when she looked terrified and heartbroken.

She was missing Brent.

But she said she couldn't stand to lose *him*.

He didn't want to be second to Brent, but Brent was gone and he was here, and for the life of him, at the moment, he couldn't think of one damn reason he shouldn't touch her.

Kiss her.

Have her.

His lips closed over hers, hungrily, greedily, and she wrapped her arms around him and rubbed his back, parting her lips for his entry. He drove his tongue inside her, aching to be naked and hot in bed with her.

She slid one hand into his hair, tangling her fingers through it, her need just as evident.

Mona had wanted Cal for so long that she shoved thoughts of all else from her mind as he teased her mouth with his tongue. She threaded her hands deep in his hair, urging him closer, hoping the kiss would last forever.

Need and desire collided. Heaven help her, she wanted more.

She reached for the top button of his shirt, desperate to feel his bare skin, and twisted the top two buttons free. His breathy moan echoed between them as he gripped her hands to stop her from undressing him.

"Please," she whispered.

His dark gaze met hers, hungry and passionate. "Not here in the car."

She smiled, her body rippling with sensual sensations as she opened the car door. He was right behind her, his hand at the small of her back.

By the time she unlocked the front door, their lips were locked again and he was tugging at her coat.

Her scarf hit the foyer floor, along with both their jackets, his body moving against hers as he claimed her mouth again. They kissed fervently, tongues dancing, bodies humming to life with need.

He carefully removed his gun and laid it on the side table. She tugged at his shirt, popping buttons in her haste to feel his chest, and he walked her backward toward the den. She kicked off her boots, frantically raking her hands over his muscled torso, and he trailed his fingers over her back, then slid fingers beneath the bottom of her sweater to slide it off.

But her hip bumped the back of the sofa, and suddenly she stumbled. Cal caught her before she fell, and she glanced down to see what she'd tripped over.

Shock made her go very still.

"What the hell?" Cal muttered.

He gripped her arms, both of them looking around the room in shock.

Someone had been inside her house and trashed it. The frames holding photographs of her and Brent were shattered, the pictures torn to shreds and scattered across the floor and sofa.

Even more disturbing, the words *LEAVE TOWN* had been spray-painted on the wall.

◆ ◆ ◆

Carol slipped into the Boar's Head, anxious to talk to Sara Levinson, mother to one of the Thorn Ripper's victims.

The vacant eyes of a bobcat stared at her from the counter that ran along the wall. In fact, dead animals were everywhere she looked in the bar/restaurant.

Even though her father had been a hunter and had the same fascination with preserving the animals he'd caught, they gave her the creeps.

She'd had nightmares about the gators attacking her during the night and ripping her apart. Sometimes when she'd tried to sleep, she could hear their teeth gnashing as their hunger for human flesh intensified with the smell of blood.

Shaking off her sudden nerves, she chose a corner booth. The place was half-full with men chowing down on burgers and steaks. Country music boomed from an old-fashioned jukebox while three men played pool in the back corner.

She'd talked to the nail tech earlier, and she'd been a wealth of information about the town's history and told her that Tiffany Levinson's mother waitressed here.

She recognized Sara from the memorial, her frizzy reddish-brown hair piled on top of her head, a pencil stuck in the teased, lacquered strands. "What can I do you for?" she asked in a smoker's voice.

Carol ordered a draft beer and the venison stew. She waited until the woman placed the order, then when she returned to bring her drink, Carol introduced herself.

"I heard you might be willing to talk with me about your daughter's murder."

"I don't know who told you that." The waitress's eyes glazed over with anger. "Why are you dragging the families through the past?"

"I'm a reporter covering the recent murder in town."

"I know who you are," Sara hissed.

"People are wondering if there is a connection between the Thorn Ripper and the Bride Killer," Carol continued, ignoring Sara's obvious disdain for her.

Sara's face paled. "How should I know? The man who killed my baby is in prison. Has been for nearly thirty years."

Carol had done her research. "But his parole hearing is in less than a week. Don't you think it's odd that a similar murder has occurred?"

"I don't want to think about it," Sara said, her lips stretching thin. "Sheriff Buckley locked up the man responsible for my daughter's death. I owe him for that."

Carol didn't quite know where to go with this, but she wanted emotion in her story. Emotion sold copies.

"Are you sure Pike was guilty?"

Anger slashed the woman's face. "What are you saying?"

"I looked at the files for the original investigation, and he never confessed. In fact, over all these years, Johnny Pike has maintained his innocence. He said he was framed."

"He wouldn't have taken a plea bargain if he was innocent."

"I'm not so sure of that. He was young and scared, and was facing the death penalty."

Sara leaned over, her nostrils flaring. "Listen here, you nosy bitch, those of us who lost kids back then have suffered enough. Leave it alone and let Johnny Pike rot in jail."

She stomped away, leaving Carol irritated and with nothing to report. But a man with short brown hair seated across from her was watching her with interest. He looked to be in his late twenties and was slightly nervous.

If he was a local and had grown up in Graveyard Falls, he might be useful. He raised a brow, a shy smile curving his mouth, and she smiled back, then motioned for him to join her.

♦ ♦ ♦

His blood heated with excitement. The blonde woman had just invited him to join her.

When he'd heard her order venison stew, he'd decided she might be his soul mate. Venison stew was his favorite. Well, next to rabbit stew.

He wondered if she knew how to make them.

Fancy meeting her here at his favorite spot, surrounded by the animals he'd preserved with his own hands. A hobby he'd turned into a side business.

Beer in hand to give him a little liquid courage, he walked over and claimed the chair beside her.

Her hazel eyes were almost a muddy color, but as she looked up at him, he envisioned her in the wedding gown his mama had made.

"Tell me about yourself," he said, remembering what Mama had told him. *Don't talk about yourself all the time. Ask about her.*

"My name is Carol Little," the woman began. "I'm a reporter. You might have seen the front-page story I wrote about the Bride Killer in Graveyard Falls. And you are?"

"Will." He slipped the pin from his pocket and stabbed his palm with it in an effort to stifle a reaction.

He didn't know whether to be thrilled that she thought writing about him was newsworthy.

Or nervous she might know who he was.

Either way, she wasn't wife material.

She would have to die.

CHAPTER SEVENTEEN

Mona trembled at the sight of the message.

LEAVE TOWN.

The torn pictures and shattered glass strewn across her living room made her feel violated. "Why would someone do this?"

Cal retrieved his gun. "Stay here. Let me check the house."

She nodded, fear clogging her throat as she strained to listen for signs the intruder might still be inside.

Cal held his gun at the ready, glanced in the kitchen, and murmured that it was clear, then eased his way to the bedrooms.

For a moment, she couldn't move. The fact that someone had been inside her house made her feel sick inside. What else had the intruder touched?

She stooped down to pick up the photograph she and Brent had taken on their honeymoon in the mountains, but Cal's voice stopped her.

"The house is clear. Don't touch anything, Mona."

She curled her fingers into her palms and straightened. God . . . now her house was a crime scene.

Cal held his phone to his ear and was already calling for a crime team. When he hung up, his expression was grim. "The bedroom is a mess, too, Mona."

She exhaled a shaky breath and rushed toward her room. Cal caught her at the door, and she gasped at the sight. Her underwear and nightgowns had been shredded and scattered across the bed like confetti, the mirror above her dresser marked with another message—*LIARS MUST DIE.*

Cal fisted his hands to keep from pulling Mona back up against him. Dammit, he hated the fear in her eyes. He moved closer and examined the message.

"It's lipstick." Maybe the same kind the Bride Killer had used. He'd have the lab check.

"Who hates me enough to do this?" Mona whispered.

"That's a good question," Cal said. "And one only you can answer." Unless the intrusion had something to do with her dead husband and his secret.

"The only person I can think of is Whit Combs, and he's still locked up."

"Let me make a call and verify that," Cal said. "Meanwhile, think about your other clients. Is there someone else you're seeing who recently split? Maybe a couple who divorced after undergoing therapy with you?"

Mona's face paled. "Even if they did, I can't name names, Cal."

"You can't protect someone if they're dangerous."

"But—"

"Just make the list, Mona," Cal said. "We can keep it quiet until we know more."

She still looked hesitant, but walked back to the kitchen, grabbed a notepad from a drawer, and sat down at the table. She was still sitting there lost in thought fifteen minutes later when the CSI team arrived.

"I want this place processed," Cal said. "And be sure and compare the lipstick on the mirror to the one the Bride Killer used."

Mona wrapped her arms around her waist, her face stricken at the thought. "You think he did this?"

Cal squeezed her hand. "I don't know, but we'll find out."

Unable to sleep or leave Mona alone tonight, he finally agreed to let her ride with him to check out the names Peyton had given him while the crime team processed her house.

They talked about her patients as they drove. "A couple of my clients are filing for divorce," Mona said. "But I don't think their spouses are dangerous or angry enough to break into my house."

"How about a stalker? Maybe a man you've dated since Brent died?"

"It's only been three months, Cal. I haven't seen anyone else," she said in a strained tone. She fiddled with her purse strap. "Although I've been asking questions about my birth mother. But I haven't gotten very far. No one seems to want to talk to me about it."

"Jesus, Mona, you may have opened up a can of worms."

"I realize that, but I have to know the truth."

He laid his hand over hers. "Listen, drop the search for now, and when this case is over, I'll help you. Right now, I have to focus on finding the Bride Killer. Another woman's life might be in danger." *And that woman might be you.*

His phone buzzed. The medical examiner. "Yeah?"

"Coulter, we have an ID on the second victim. Her name is Constance Gilroy. Twenty-three years old. Cause of death is the same as the first victim, asphyxiation due to strangulation. The lipstick on her lips is not only the same brand, but it's from the same tube."

"You're certain?"

"Yes. Traces of Gwyneth's DNA were found in the lipstick on this girl's mouth."

Jesus. "What else?"

"We found traces of saliva on her cheek as well."

"So he kissed her good-bye just as he did the first victim."

"It looks that way. There was also a burn mark from a stun gun, just like with Gwyneth."

"How about the dress?"

"Peyton said she sent photos of it to local tailors, but they didn't recognize it. She's still searching the Internet, but so far no hits."

If the person who'd made the dresses had sold them online, they would probably find one similar. But the seamstress could have sold them in some little mom-and-pop boutique across the country, which would be more difficult to track down.

Unless the dresses were hand-made for the victims . . .

"Anything more on forensics?"

"Yes. We found a strand of hair in the lace of the dress. Must have caught it when he leaned over to kiss her."

"Then if we find the guy we can nail him."

"Yes. I just wish I could tell you *how* to find him."

"I'm working on it," Cal said, determination kicking in. "Right now I'm on my way to check out a possible lead."

He maneuvered the switchbacks, slowing as they passed a white van going too fast. The damn thing suddenly sped up and careened toward them.

Mona gasped as he cut the wheel to the right to avoid hitting it, and they slammed into the mountain wall. His front end crunched, air bags exploded, and rocks tumbled down.

Cal looked up, saw the car spin around and head toward them. He braced himself as the front end of the van rammed his side.

Fuck. The driver had intentionally hit them.

Dr. Wheeland was yelling his name over the phone, asking what was happening, but Cal had dropped his phone. He ripped the air bag with his pocketknife, determined to get a look at the driver or get the license plate.

But his eyes were blurry from the impact.

The van backed up, then accelerated and slammed into his side once more. Metal crunched and glass shattered.

"Cal!" Mona cried.

"Hang on!" He grabbed his gun from inside his jacket, aimed, and fired at the maniac. One, two, three shots.

Tires screeched, the van revved its engine and backed away, then it swung around and flew down the mountain.

Cal fired at him again, hoping to at least hit a tire, but the van was too fast.

◆ ◆ ◆

Mona was shaking all over as the van roared away. She pushed at the air bag, her chest sore from the impact, and Cal took his pocketknife and sliced through it. "Who was that?"

"I don't know, the windows were tinted," Cal said. "Are you okay?"

She nodded, although she was trembling so badly her teeth were chattering. Wind swirled through the shattered glass, and shards had pelted Cal's face and arms.

"You're bleeding." She reached up to pluck a small glass fragment, wincing at the drops of blood splattered across his cheek.

"I'm fine." He brushed off her concern, then leaned down to retrieve his phone.

Wheeland was still on the line.

"We got ambushed by a van," Cal said. "Have Peyton search for anyone who owns a white cargo van around Graveyard Falls." A pause. "No, I didn't get the license. It was an older model, tinted windows. Also have her issue an alert to all body shops and garages in the area. Look for a dented front fender. If anyone tries to get a van repaired, I want to know about it." He angled his head toward Mona. "Call the deputy and tell him to send a tow truck up here, and to bring an extra car."

Mona touched his cheek with a tissue to dab at the blood. "You need to go to an ER, Cal."

He shook his head. "No way. For all we know, the unsub has another girl right now and her life is in jeopardy."

◆ ◆ ◆

Fifteen minutes later when the tow truck and Deputy Kimball pulled up, Cal was royally pissed. While the mechanics loaded the SUV onto the tow truck, Cal coaxed Mona to sit inside the Jeep the mechanic had brought for him to drive, then he talked to the deputy. Kimball filled him in on what he'd learned about the families of the Thorn Ripper's victims.

"Do you think the driver of the van was the unsub?" Deputy Kimball asked.

Cal swiped his hair back from his forehead. "No. It doesn't fit his MO. But earlier Mona had a break-in, so whoever did this may be after her."

The deputy blew on his hands to warm them. "I checked. Whit Combs is still locked up."

So that ruled him out. "Then we'll concentrate on finding the van. First I need you to notify the second victim's sister of her death." Cal skimmed the text Peyton had sent. "The victim's name is Constance Gilroy. She was twenty-three. Studied early-childhood development and worked part-time babysitting her sister's two kids. The sister's name is Tanya Gilroy, she's a—"

"Nail tech," Deputy Kimball muttered.

"You know her?"

Deputy Kimball's eyes darkened. "Yeah. Tanya and I had a couple of dates. She's going to be devastated. She raised her little sister after their folks died." He pinched the bridge of his nose. "She was a good girl, Coulter."

"I'm sorry." Cal didn't know her, but no young woman deserved to have her life snuffed out before she'd had a chance to live it. "I would offer to break the news myself, but I have two possible suspects I intend to question."

Deputy Kimball wiped a hand over his eyes. "Then get to it. I'll talk to Tanya and find out everything I can about Constance, if she was seeing anyone, had any male friends, if she met someone online."

"Also find out if she knew Gwyneth," Cal said. "If we find a connection between the two victims, it might tell us where or how the unsub is choosing them."

The deputy nodded and jogged to his car. Cal gave the mechanic his card and told him to call with an estimate for the repairs, then slid into the driver's seat of the Jeep.

"You okay?" he asked Mona.

She nodded but she looked pale, and he squeezed her hand. How could she be okay when someone had just tried to kill them?

Carol knew she'd messed up big-time. The look in this man's eyes was eerie. Like a gator appearing to snooze lazily in the swamp, his body buried just beneath the surface while he lurked for prey.

"What do you know about that dead girl?" Will asked.

"The police aren't talking," she said. "I'm not sure they have a clue. Did you know her?"

He folded his hand on the table, an odd look on his face. "No, never met her."

His fingers closed around a pin in his hand. A drop of blood dripped from his palm.

Her eyes were glued to the blood. Like a cutter, he needed to punish himself. To rid himself of the pain.

Then his eyes became sinister, darting across her face. "What are you looking at?"

"Nothing." She jerked her gaze back to the wall of animal heads and shivered again at the eyes staring back at her. "Are you a hunter, Will?"

The wary look turned to one of . . . pride?

"Yeah. Matter of fact, I am."

"You shot some of these?"

"A couple. But I preserved all of them."

"You're a taxidermist?"

A smile twitched at his mouth, drawing her gaze to the small jagged scar at the corner of his lip. "Yeah. You want to see my studio?"

He made it sound like a joke, but a bad premonition took root in her gut.

"Maybe some other time. I . . . have to go now." Hands trembling for reasons she didn't even know, except that her instincts warned her this guy was dangerous, she removed her wallet, tossed some cash on the table, then grabbed her keys. "It was nice meeting you."

"You too," he murmured, although his voice sounded odd, and he closed his hand around the pin again. Another drop of blood fell to the table, making her stomach churn.

She gave him a fake smile and headed to the door. Her keys were braced between her fingers the way she'd learned in self-defense classes, and she hit the Unlock button for her car a few feet away, jogging toward it as the wind whistled shrilly through the night.

The parking lot was nearly vacant, but gravel and snow crunched behind her, and she whirled around, her keys ready.

But he pounced, shoved something over her face, then pressed a stun gun to her neck.

She tried to scream but felt herself jerking and spinning, then sinking as if the murky water of the bayou was sucking her underneath.

CHAPTER EIGHTEEN

Virgil William Mulhaney's chicken farm was nothing more than two chicken houses situated on a hill on several acres in the mountains.

His house, a small, older wooden structure, tilted sideways as if the land below it was sinking. A mangy-looking, three-legged dog loped toward the Jeep as Cal parked.

Could Virgil be the man who'd posed as Bill Williams on Facebook and lured Gwyneth to that bar? The one who called himself Will on the phone with Mona?

Cal held a hand up to warn Mona not to get out yet. "Let me see if that dog is dangerous."

Mona still looked shaken from the accident, but a smile softened her face. "He looks too old and feeble to be dangerous."

"You never know." If Mulhaney was their killer, he might have beaten or abused the animal. Hell, the animal could have lost that leg because of his owner.

Cal laid his hand on his gun just in case he needed it as he slid from the Jeep. "Hey, boy," he murmured in a low voice. "You gonna be friendly or bite my head off?"

The dog looked up at him with the saddest pair of eyes Cal had ever seen. He also reminded him of a stray he and Brent had taken in at their foster parents' house.

He'd cried like a baby when his foster father used to hit the animal. The night the old man had shot it, Cal had lost it and attacked the man.

He was only seven and still had the scars from the beating.

Slowly he extended his hand, and the dog limped toward him, sniffed his fingers, then wagged his tail. Mona must have seen it; she climbed from the Jeep, tugging her coat tighter around her. The wind was rolling off the mountains, beating the trees into a frenzy and sending snow swirling like a fresh storm.

Just as they approached the house, a man wearing bloodstained overalls loped down the hill, carrying two chickens in his right hand, both with their heads cut off.

A prosthetic served as his left hand.

Cal motioned for Mona to stay behind him. When the man noticed them, he threw his shoulders back, but Cal couldn't see his eyes for the hat pulled low over his forehead.

He estimated his age to be mid- to late twenties—the right age for their unsub.

Mulhaney spit chewing tobacco on the ground, the black spittle streaking the white snow at their feet. "What you doing on my property?"

Cal identified the two of them, although Mulhaney made no indication that he recognized Mona's name. Then he angled his phone to show the man Gwyneth's photo. "Do you know this woman?"

Mulhaney shook his head. "Never seen her."

"How about this one?" Peyton had just sent him a photo of Constance Gilroy.

Mulhaney spit again, then wiped his mouth with the back of a sleeve. Blood trickled from his hand, dripping onto the snow. "Don't know her either. What's this about?"

"Both women were murdered," Cal said. "I'm sure you heard about it on the news."

Mulhaney veered into a shed and laid the chickens on a steel table. "Yeah. What's that got to do with me?"

"We thought you might tell us that," Cal said. "Where's your wife?"

Mulhaney gestured toward his prosthesis. "She ran off and left me. What does that have to do with those murders?"

"The police report said she lost control and ran off the road," Cal pressed.

"That's what they told me."

"You think something else happened?" Cal asked.

"No. She was drinking before she left, then she was driving too fast 'cause she was in a hurry to get away from me. Said she couldn't stand me touching her with this."

"You must have felt rejected," Mona said. "Bitter."

"Maybe you wanted to replace her," Cal suggested.

Mulhaney made a sound of disbelief. "Listen, I ain't got a girlfriend or wife and don't want one. I seen what women can do to a man. My daddy killed himself when my mama run out. And then when I lost my hand, my wife left me. I'm done with the sorry lot."

Cal gestured toward the chicken houses. "How do you kill your chickens?"

"Is that what this is really about?" The man squinted, looking confused. "I follow American Veterinary Medical Association standards. Use cervical dislocation," Mulhaney said. "Then I asphyxiate them with carbon dioxide."

The pieces didn't fit. The killer had used his hands and a garter. Mulhaney's handicap would make it difficult for him to attack and strangle a woman.

And he didn't appear strong enough to carry a body through the woods to the falls.

He could have used a sled or something similar to transport her, but they hadn't found evidence of tracks in the snow.

"Mind if we look around?" Cal asked.

Mulhaney frowned. "You got a warrant?"

"You got something to hide?"

"I didn't kill those women," Mulhaney said.

"Then let us look around," Cal said with a challenging look. "And if you really want to prove it, let me take a DNA sample."

Mulhaney hissed. "All right. Look your fill, then take your damn sample and get off my property."

♦ ♦ ♦

Mona didn't like the way Virgil Mulhaney looked at her, as if she were to blame for all the wrongs women had inflicted on men in the past.

Which didn't fit the profile of the killer. The guy they were looking for was lonely and desperately wanted a companion.

Only his delusions held certain expectations, and when the woman didn't meet those expectations, something inside him snapped.

That *did* fit Virgil. He obviously was disillusioned by the opposite sex.

Cal took a DNA swab from the man's mouth, bagged it, and stowed it in the crime kit he'd transferred from his SUV to the Jeep.

Mulhaney laid the bloody rag he'd used to wipe his hands on the worktable beside the dead chickens. "All right, now look around. You won't find any dead women here."

He gave Mona a lecherous grin that revealed a missing front tooth.

She forced herself not to feed his sinister side by reacting—he seemed to enjoy taunting her. Scaring her.

Although he definitely wasn't charming enough to lure a woman into going with him. But the stun gun she saw on the workbench would do the trick.

She leaned close to Cal and whispered, "Cal, were there stun gun marks on the victims?"

"Yes."

Mona considered this as Cal gestured for the man to lead the way, and she and Cal followed Mulhaney into his house.

The furnishings were old and faded, dust mounting on the tables and books scattered around. Mona quickly scanned his collection—books on the poultry business, hunting and fishing, and best hiking trails in the Smokies.

The refrigerator held milk, packaged meat in butcher paper, several whole chickens, eggs, condiments, and bread.

She followed them to the bedroom, which was dusty, the metal bed covered in an ancient quilt that needed mending. The closets revealed work boots and overalls.

No signs of a wedding dress. No garters in the drawers or closets. No sewing supplies.

Mona huddled inside her coat but opted to stay in the car while Cal went to search the chicken houses. If he found a dead body in there, she didn't want to see it tonight.

Constance's face was already going to torment her in her sleep.

◆ ◆ ◆

Cal drove down the mountain, his expression grim. Mulhaney was a jerk, but he hadn't found any evidence suggesting he was the unsub.

Apparently his wife's desertion wasn't Mulhaney's only problem. His business had virtually died. He had a few chickens in one house but not enough to support himself and was drawing disability.

There had been no evidence he'd had a woman to the house, much less one he'd murdered. And no rosebushes, although with winter lingering, the killer had to have picked up a rose from a florist, grocery store, or road stand.

He cranked up the defroster and heater, hoping to warm Mona, who'd been shivering ever since he'd returned to the Jeep. "What do you think?"

"He's strange. A loner. Was probably bullied as a kid. But I don't think he's the killer."

"Neither do I," Cal admitted. "I think we would have found something. A sewing machine, a wedding gown, the jewelry he took from the victims, something." He paused. "That is unless he has another place where he holds the victims."

"That's a possibility."

"Although it would be extremely difficult to strangle the victims with one hand. That prosthetic would have also left definitive marks, which we didn't find on the victims."

She nodded. "Where to now?"

"There's one more name on the list. Doyle William Yonkers. He runs a pet cemetery."

Mona hugged her arms around herself, then lapsed into silence, the sky painting a gloomy atmosphere across the sharp ridges as they drove.

"Yonkers? I saw him at the memorial service," Mona said when they finally pulled down a winding drive in the midst of a forest of hemlocks and snow-covered pines.

"Yes, he's Candy Yonkers's brother. Deputy Kimball said Doyle's parents separated after his sister's murder."

"How old is he?"

"Forty. He was younger than Candy. He also recently spent time in a mental hospital and was released into his mother's custody."

"Pike's upcoming parole hearing could have been a trigger for him." Mona shivered. "Why was he hospitalized?"

"According to his medical report, he suffered from depression and bipolar disorder."

"He fits the profile," Mona agreed. "And he has a motive."

Cal scanned the property as he parked. A log cabin sat by a nicer brick building and a graveyard named Pet Heaven. The stone markers shimmered with new-fallen snow, and instead of vases of flowers, concrete food bowls held ceramic bones and chew toys along with statues and figurines of cats and dogs.

But through the window, he saw roses in vases, blood-red just like the ones the killer left with his victims.

◆ ◆ ◆

Mona spotted a battered van parked in the drive. Not white, though, like the one that had hit them.

Another small outbuilding sat beside the cabin, probably a storage building.

Stone bird feeders flanked the entrance to Pet Heaven, with a walkway that wove through the graveyard. Concrete benches were scattered throughout for those who might want to sit and visit.

The wind whistled off the mountain, stirring snow and dead leaves around Mona's feet, and sending an uneasy feeling through her as Cal led the way to the cabin. He knocked and she waited, but no one answered.

Cal gestured that he was going to check out the brick building. Mona followed, noting a gold-embossed nameplate on the side of the building—CREMATORIUM.

Cal rapped his knuckles on the door and footsteps shuffled inside, then a young man greeted them. His round face was slightly covered in beard stubble, his hair clipped short, his hands scarred with what Mona assumed to be animal bites.

"Hello," the man said with his thick eyebrows raised. "Welcome to Pet Heaven."

"You're Doyle Yonkers?" Cal asked.

"Yes. I'm with a customer now. You can hang out in the waiting room."

He gestured toward a small room to the left with a love seat and chairs. One wall held photos of animals he'd laid to rest, while another bank of shelves displayed a selection of urns.

Mona heard a woman crying in the back room, and Cal flashed his badge. "I'm Agent Coulter. What's going on?"

"A lady's having a hard time saying good-bye to her basset hound."

"Your cremation chamber is in the back?" Cal asked.

"Yes."

"Let me see."

Yonkers suddenly looked worried. "Are you here because you have a pet?"

"No, I'm investigating two homicides. Gwyneth Toyton and Constance Gilroy. Did you know either of them?"

Yonkers's eyes darted between Cal and Mona. "I didn't do anything to them."

"I didn't say you did," Cal said.

Yonkers glanced at Mona. "Jesus. I should have seen this coming. You think it was me 'cause I was in that mental hospital?"

"Your sister was one of the Thorn Ripper's victims, and Johnny Pike's up for parole," Cal pointed out.

Mona lowered her voice. "You wanna talk about that?"

Yonkers crossed his arms. "I did have some problems, but you would have too if you'd grown up with your parents depressed and obsessed over your sister's murder. Hell, sometimes I wished I *had* died. I would have finally gotten their attention."

"That must have been difficult," Mona said softly.

He shrugged. "It was. But I'm on meds now. You can ask Mama. She's sick, has been for a while, and laid up in bed. But she can tell you I'm not crazy. I take care of her."

Mona frowned. "I saw you at the memorial service. If you're so bitter, why did you go?"

"Because I did love my sister." His eyes widened nervously. "Besides, a couple of the family members are clients."

Cal cleared his throat. "Show me the back room."

The scars on the man's hands looked more prominent as he rubbed his chin.

As soon as Mona stepped through the door, the strong scent of cleaning chemicals assaulted her.

This man was certainly big enough and strong enough to overcome a woman. He could easily have killed Gwyneth and Constance.

Maybe he wanted the attention his sister and Johnny Pike had gotten badly enough to kill for it.

"Some folks can't stand the thought of cremation." Yonkers showed them the cremation chamber. "We only cremate one animal at a time," he explained. "We do our best to be humane and honor the family's wishes."

Through a glass partition, Mona saw a middle-aged woman rocking herself back and forth as she dabbed at her tears with a tissue.

Cal's scowl grew more intense as he strode through the rooms, as if he was searching for a hidden chamber where Yonkers might be hiding another victim.

The temperature chilled Mona again as they left the brick building and trudged through the snow to the man's home. When he opened the door, the scent of soap assaulted her again, yet it was the stuffed creatures, animals that had once been alive but now had been preserved, that made her go cold inside.

A stuffed coyote sat on a table, two bobcats on a shelf by the wall, raccoons and squirrels and a . . . beagle, which looked so real it made Mona's stomach roil.

CHAPTER NINETEEN

Cal had searched for a secret room or chamber in the crematorium building, someplace where Yonkers could hold a woman, but he didn't find one.

Logic nagged at him. If Yonkers had murdered those women, why not get rid of their bodies in his cremation chamber instead of carrying them to the falls?

Moving the bodies and leaving them so they could be discovered increased his chances of getting caught.

Maybe he wanted to get caught . . .

Or he was arrogant and enjoyed watching the town's reaction and the police scurry to find the truth.

"You like preserved animals?" Mona asked.

"I couldn't save my sister or keep her alive for my folks," Yonkers said in a disturbingly calm voice. "But I do what I can to help honor the animals when they die."

The inside of the cabin was just as disturbing as the crematorium. All those dead animals preserved, their eyes watching him.

Nothing in the tiny den or the man's bedroom. Just jeans and flannel shirts and a book on taxidermy. Although it was possible that he'd hidden the jewelry he'd stolen from the victims somewhere in the house.

Hell, he could have sewn the jewelry inside the animals.

Dammit, if Cal found probable cause, he could obtain a warrant, then he could tear the place inside out.

"Mama isn't well," Yonkers said when they reached the door to the second bedroom.

Cal shrugged. The sound of Christian music echoed from inside the room. Yonkers knocked gently. "Mama?"

Mona looked warily at Cal as the man opened the door. A mixture of smells assaulted Cal—some kind of cleaner mixed with sickness.

A dim light glowed from a lamp in the corner and allowed him to see inside the room. A frail woman lay in the bed, her thin gray hair matted. An oxygen tube was attached to her nose, but her eyes popped open as they stepped in the doorway.

"I'm sorry, Mr. Yonkers. What's wrong with her?" Mona asked softly.

"Liver cancer," Yonkers said. "After my sister died, she drowned herself in the bottle. She can't get around very well now, and her organs are failing."

The entire family had been torn apart by Candy's murder. "Shouldn't she be in a hospital?"

"No, she wants to die at home." He walked over, patted her shoulder, and offered her a drink of water.

The woman tried to speak, but her words were slurred. "Not today, Mama. Just rest."

"What did she say?" Mona asked.

Yonkers cut her a dark look. "She asked if I'd brought a nice girl home for her to meet. Mama always wanted to see me marry and have a family. I think she was hoping a daughter-in-law would replace Candy. But no one ever measured up to her."

Cal silently cursed. So much for questioning her about her son's whereabouts.

As they stepped back into the hall, Yonkers turned to Cal.

"And before you ask where I was the night the Toyton woman was murdered, I was here. I'm afraid to leave my mother for too long. I don't want her to die alone."

If Cal didn't suspect him of murder, he would feel sorry for the guy. But Yonkers fit the profile of the unsub.

♦ ♦ ♦

Josie knew her mother was keeping secrets.

She'd promised to stay with her grandfather while her mother ran to the drugstore to pick up his medication.

Desperate for answers, she sneaked into her mother's room, searched the dresser drawer, and pulled the diary from beneath some lace doilies. She had to hurry if she wanted to skim through it. Her mother might be back any minute.

She sank into the chair in the corner, opened the diary, and began to read.

Daddy doesn't understand how much I love Johnny. He forbid me to see him today. But I won't stop seeing him. I'm going to meet him at our special place at the falls. Johnny is the love of my life. He noticed me when no one else did.

And the other girls, the plastics—Brittany, Tiffany, and Candy—they're all furious that Johnny likes me.

They want Johnny to give them the rose for prom. But I'm hoping he'll give it to me.

Josie skimmed a couple more entries, until another caught her eye.

I told Johnny he was my first. I want him to be my only.

But tonight Tiffany was murdered. They say someone pushed her over the falls.

The police are questioning everyone at school.

> I wish I hadn't argued with her yesterday. They might think I did it.

Josie's heart pounded. Her mother had been questioned in a homicide investigation?

> Brittany died last night, just like Tiffany, at the falls. Everyone at school is in a panic. Candy accused me of being jealous and asked if I killed them.
> But Johnny knows I would never hurt anyone.
> He loves me. I think we're going to run away together and get married.
> Although if Daddy finds out, he'll kill me . . .

Josie was so engrossed in the diary that she didn't hear the door open. But her mother's sharp voice startled her. "What are you doing?"

Josie jerked her head up as her mother ripped the diary from her hands.

◆ ◆ ◆

Mona studied Yonkers as they walked through the pet cemetery. He was handsome in a dark, macabre kind of way. Intense dark eyes. Short-cropped brown hair. Olive skin.

Of course, some psychopaths were charming. "How did you get into this business?"

"I took over from my father. He was a vet and started the cemetery years ago when he saw the need for it."

Cal crossed his arms. "Did your parents ever talk about Johnny Pike?"

"Everyone talked about him," Yonkers said. "Have for years. The town is in a panic now just thinking he might be granted parole and be released."

"Did your folks believe he was guilty?"

He shrugged. "Yes. Why? You aren't trying to get him out, are you?"

"No, I just want to find the truth," Cal said. "If you had nothing to do with the recent murders, give us a DNA sample and we can eliminate you from our suspect list."

Yonkers glared at them. "Don't you need a warrant for that?"

Cal shifted, his expression challenging. "Like I said, if you're innocent, you won't mind helping us."

"I am innocent," Yonkers said. "But Johnny Pike said he was, too, and they sent him to jail anyway."

"I thought you believed he was guilty."

"That's not the point," Yonkers said.

"Tell us about yourself," Mona said, changing tactics. "Do you have a girlfriend?"

Yonkers swung around, every muscle in his body tense with rage. "I have a feeling you already know the answer to that. My girlfriend left me the day I went in for treatment."

Mona sucked in a sharp breath. Yonkers obviously felt betrayed. If he was off his meds, that betrayal could have triggered enough rage to make him kill.

◆ ◆ ◆

Cal called Director Vance to request a warrant for Yonkers's DNA as he drove away from Pet Heaven. Vance also agreed to send another agent, one of Cal's buddies, Dane Hamrick, to run surveillance on Yonkers. If he made a move tonight, they'd know about it.

His phone buzzed and he told Vance to keep him posted, then punched Connect.

"It's Deputy Kimball."

Cal shifted into low gear to wind down the mountain. The damn roads were slick with ice. "Yeah?"

"I just talked to Constance Gilroy's sister, Tanya."

"And?"

"Her sister broke up with her boyfriend a few months ago because he'd become obsessive and pressured her to marry him. She wanted to finish her degree and turned him down. When he persisted, she filed a restraining order against him."

Cal slowed as he maneuvered a switchback, the memory of their earlier crash still fresh. "Who is this guy and where is he?"

"His name is Steve Fulton. He runs a fishing camp in the mountains."

"He grew up around here?"

"Yeah," Deputy Kimball said. "And that camp is not too far from Graveyard Falls."

"Give me the coordinates. I'll check it out."

"I'm texting them to you now," Deputy Kimball said. "Also I looked into the sewing circles like you asked. There's one at the Presbyterian church, but they didn't recognize the wedding gown. I'll check with a couple of others and get back to you."

Cal started to hang up, but remembered the jewelry. "Kimball, did Tanya Gilroy say her sister was missing any jewelry?"

"As a matter of fact, she did. Constance always wore a silver locket that had a picture of their parents inside."

"It looks like taking the jewelry is part of his signature," Cal said. "But don't tell that reporter."

A hesitation. "Don't worry. She won't be a problem anymore."

Cal thought he detected an odd note to Kimball's voice, but the deputy was probably embarrassed he'd screwed up.

Hopefully he'd learned his lesson.

Cal checked his GPS, then turned down a side road that led to Steve Fulton's fishing camp.

CHAPTER TWENTY

Cal didn't like the location of the fishing camp.

"This would be a good place to hide out," Mona said.

"And so off the grid that if you wanted to murder someone here, no one would ever hear the victim scream." Cal surveyed the property. "I have a bad feeling about this guy. Deputy Kimball said he was obsessed with Constance and pressured her to marry him."

"That sounds like our guy," Mona commented.

He nodded. "Wait in the car."

Mona didn't argue. Instead she huddled next to the door.

Cal removed his gun and hiked up the path to the camp. An old, weathered building that served as a lodge sat among the pines, the mountains rising behind it.

Cal knocked on the door as the wind screamed off the mountain. He tapped his boot while he waited and scanned the property. To the left of the lodge sat a carport, which housed a broken-down lawn mower, a three-wheeler, and assorted tools.

A faded, rusted-out black pickup was parked underneath. Not a white van, though.

He listened for sounds that someone was inside, and thought he heard footsteps so he knocked again. "Fulton, this is Agent Coulter from the FBI. I need to talk to you."

Inside something rattled. Then a thump as if someone had knocked something over.

Cal gripped his gun at the ready and pushed at the door. It squeaked as it opened, and he peered inside. Battered wood floors, old fishing caps piled on a side table, a stuffed fish on the wall.

A noise echoed from the back, and he inched inside, scanning the open area to the living room, which was furnished with an old plaid couch and a coffee table.

A lamp burned from the back, giving him enough light to see as he combed through the living room. He veered to the left to the kitchen and stopped cold when he spotted photos of Constance covering one wall like a shrine.

Candids of the woman in various places—at school, her apartment, catching a bus, undressing . . . photos he had a feeling she hadn't posed for.

An article Carol Little had written about Gwyneth Toyton's murder was tacked on a bulletin board, then another one about the Thorn Ripper murders and the yearly memorial.

Cal frowned. Had Fulton gotten the idea for killing Constance from the articles about the original murders? He could have murdered Gwyneth first to cover for his real target and make it appear both were murdered by a serial killer.

The floor creaked again, and he jerked his head up, then thought he detected a movement outside. Instincts alert, he pushed open the screen door and stepped onto the landing.

There was another movement to the right and he crept in that direction, wood bowing beneath his weight as he descended the rickety stairs and headed around toward the shed.

He couldn't let this guy get away.

A scream suddenly rent the night.

Mona.

Dammit.

He took off running, his heart hammering when he circled to the front yard and saw the man dragging Mona from the car.

The bastard grabbed her around the neck, pushed her in front of him as a shield, then raised a knife to her throat.

Terror shot through Cal. One wrong move and Fulton would kill her.

♦ ♦ ♦

The knife at Mona's neck cut off her scream. She went still, terrified that one movement would set the man off and he'd slit her throat.

Cal came to a halt, his hand frozen in midair, his weapon trained on Fulton.

"You don't want to hurt her," Cal said. "Just put down the knife, Fulton."

Mona could feel the tension in his big body. His hand shook at her throat. "No, if I do, you'll take me in."

"Please, Steve," Mona said softly. "Put the knife down and talk to me."

"When Tanya called and told me Constance was dead, I knew you'd come up here and try to pin her murder on me!" Fulton shouted.

Cal lowered his gun. "Listen, man, put the weapon down and let's talk."

Fulton's voice cracked. "Talking won't bring back my girlfriend."

"I know you loved her," Mona said, keeping her voice calm. "But hurting me isn't the way to honor her."

"She was everything to me," he muttered bitterly. "But she wouldn't marry me."

"She was ambitious," Mona said. "But I'm sure she didn't mean to hurt you."

His breathing became raspy. "If she'd cared about me, she wouldn't have told me to leave her alone."

"Is that why you killed her?" Cal asked.

"I didn't kill her, I loved her!" The man's gaze shot to Cal. His hand was shaking so badly the knife pricked Mona's neck. She felt the sting of the point, a blood drop pooling . . .

She didn't want to die.

◆　◆　◆

Cal kept his gun by his side, but his fingers were clenching it, ready to fire at any moment. He just had to take the guy off guard.

Get him away from Mona.

"I saw your photographs of Constance," he said.

"She was beautiful," Fulton murmured, his tone far away as if he was remembering a specific day. Maybe one of the pictures from that damn shrine.

"What happened the last time you saw her?" Cal asked. "Did you try to convince her to marry you again?"

"Of course I did," Fulton shouted. "But she refused just like before."

Cal eased forward. "Is that why you strangled her?"

The man's eyes widened, his nostrils flaring. "No, I told you I didn't hurt her. I would never hurt her."

Cal inched closer. "If you aren't dangerous, then drop the knife."

"But you're going to put me in jail," Fulton yelled. "I can't be locked up."

The man staggered backward, dragging Mona with him. Cal didn't hesitate. He fired a shot into the man's right shoulder. Fulton dropped the knife and bellowed in pain.

Mona ran toward him, and Cal rushed forward and kicked the knife aside.

"What the fuck?" Fulton snarled. "You shot me."

"You held a knife to a woman's throat. What did you think would happen, asshole?"

Fulton started to fight, but Cal pressed the gun to the back of his head. "Move and I'll kill you this time."

The fight went out of the man, and he went limp. Cal snapped the cuffs around his wrists, then tossed Mona his phone.

"Call an ambulance." He glared at Fulton. "You ready to confess now?"

"I didn't kill anyone," Fulton insisted.

Cal ignored him. "Here's what I think happened. You decide to kill Constance but figure everyone will look at you so you come up with a plan. You kill Gwyneth Toyton first, then kill Constance and make it look like some kind of nutcase serial killer is in town."

"That's not true," Fulton shouted. "I wanted to win Constance back."

"So much that you stalked her," Cal said. "So much that you decided if you couldn't have her, no one would. So you dressed her in a wedding gown and then left her at the falls."

"What?" Fulton's voice broke. "Why was she wearing a wedding gown?"

Cal ground his teeth. "Because you dressed her that way. Because you wanted her as your bride."

The man shook his head. "I didn't kill her. You have to believe me. I loved her, I didn't do it, you have to find out who did . . ."

Cal looked up at Mona, his pulse still pounding as he remembered the man holding that knife to her throat. Even if he hadn't killed Constance—and Cal wasn't sure yet either way—he had almost slit Mona's throat.

For that, he had to be punished.

The next two hours passed in a blur for Mona. She watched the paramedics load a handcuffed Fulton into the ambulance. Deputy Kimball sent an assistant to ride with them and guard Fulton while he was treated at the hospital.

She tried to gather her composure while Cal met with the crime team, and they searched the house and fishing camp for evidence that would tie Constance's ex-boyfriend to her murder and to Gwyneth Toyton's.

"The photographs are damning," Cal told her. "But I'm hoping for more. If they find garters or sewing supplies and fabric, or the jewelry he took from the victims, it would make the case."

And if his DNA matched the sample from the crime scene, it would confirm that they had the unsub in custody.

The lead CSI approached them. "Except for those photographs and the articles, we haven't found anything damning in the house," CSI Ward said. "It looks like the guy's been hitting the booze a lot and is behind on his bills. There are a couple of items of women's clothing in the closet, a pair of underwear and a sports bra, but no wedding attire or jewelry."

"Nothing in the truck," another investigator said. "No blood, signs of a body, or anyone being held against their will on the property either."

"How about underground storage units, maybe a cellar?" Cal asked. "Or a key to a storage unit or gym locker."

"We haven't found one." CSI Ward pointed to the truck. "The battery on that truck is dead, the engine rusted. If he did kill those women, he didn't use it to transport their bodies."

Mona dug her hands in her pockets to ward off the chill from the relentless wind, and the realization that Fulton might not be the man they were looking for.

Which meant the killer was still out there. That women were still in danger.

And they were no closer to finding him.

♦ ♦ ♦

Frustration knotted Cal's shoulders as he listened to the CSI's findings. Or the lack thereof.

Dammit, he wanted this to be over. To pin both murders on Fulton.

But he had to listen to the facts. While the man was unstable, had stalked his ex-girlfriend, and had taken Mona hostage out of panic, he wasn't sure he was their man.

"See if you find a computer or his cell phone," Cal said. "I'll have the tech team analyze his calls. If he made any contact with Gwyneth Toyton, it might be enough to solicit a confession and nail his ass. And we have DNA from the first victim for comparison."

The investigator nodded. "I'll keep you posted. Meanwhile, is someone watching the falls?"

"Yes, Deputy Kimball's assistants are supposed to be rotating." Although if the unsub spotted them, he might just pick another spot on the trail by the falls as a dump site.

Cal placed his hand at the curve of Mona's back. "Come on, I'll drive you home."

Mona didn't argue. She looked exhausted and shaken, and she still had to face the vandalism in her home.

She wrapped her scarf around her neck as she climbed in the Jeep, and he cranked up the heater, the night wearing on him as well.

Fresh snow flurries blurred his vision, forcing him to drive slowly as he maneuvered the switchbacks, the tires grinding ice and slush.

"Do you think he did it?" Mona finally asked.

Cal wanted to say yes. To have this case tied up. To be able to leave Graveyard Falls with the town—and Mona—safe. To get away from the temptation to touch her and confess that he loved her.

He scrubbed his hand through his hair. Dammit, this case was getting to him. He had an ache all through his body and the only thing that could make it better was to hold Mona tonight.

"I don't know yet. The evidence will tell."

By the time they reached Cal's cabin, he thought he had his libido and emotions under control.

"You're not taking me home?" Mona asked softly as he parked by the cabin.

He shook his head and turned to her, terrified his heart was in his eyes. But she looked so vulnerable and fragile, and an image of Fulton piercing her neck with that knife flashed behind his eyes, and he shook his head.

"Not after what happened tonight." He meant her near-death experience, the accident on the road, the vandalism at her house—hell, he meant it all.

She shocked him by reaching for the door and sliding out. He inhaled sharply, grateful she hadn't argued. He wouldn't leave her alone tonight. He wanted her with him where he knew she'd be safe.

◆ ◆ ◆

Carol stirred, the darkness consuming her. She tried to move, but her hands and feet were bound, her body felt weighted, and her head ached.

Her memory rushed back, causing panic to blind her.

God . . . she'd been in the Boar's Head, asking questions about the Thorn Ripper. She'd been onto something, had met that man with the strange eyes and wicked smile, had sensed something was off about him.

Then the world faded . . .

She struggled to sit up, but her head bumped the top of something, and she realized she was in a covered truck bed. A truck that was moving. Knowing her chances for survival plummeted if she arrived at the second location, she banged her feet on the door, kicking as hard as she could. But it didn't budge.

She frantically searched for a tire iron or a lever, but it was so dark she couldn't see, and her finger caught on something sharp and jagged. Metal. Blood dripped down her hand from the cut, but she ignored the pain and continued to search.

Seconds later, the vehicle stopped, slamming her against the side. Then the truck bed cover popped and a hulking shadow appeared, hovering over her. She tried to scream but the sound died in the wind.

"No one's gonna hear you up here," he growled.

Her heart pounded in terror as he dragged her from the truck.

He had a ritual—he dressed his victims like brides.

She had to get him to talk. To stall. Maybe someone in the restaurant would have noticed them leaving. Maybe Deputy Kimball would call looking for her.

Except he was furious with her . . .

The man trudged up an incline of snow, carrying her like a bag of garbage over his shoulder, tree branches slapping her in the face as he wove through the woods.

Dear God. She knew where he was going. Graveyard Falls.

"Why are you doing this?" she cried.

"You asked too many questions," he snarled. "You're going to ruin it all."

"No, I won't," Carol said in a raw whisper. "Don't you see? I'm here to help you."

He threw her to the ground by the edge of the falls. "Help me?"

"Yes," Carol said, desperate. "Let me tell your side of the story. Tell everyone who hurt you how they wronged you. I'll make you famous."

He suddenly lunged at her, his hands sliding around her throat in a punishing grip. "I don't want to be famous! I just want a wife, someone to love and cherish me."

Carol tried to nod her understanding, tried to make the words come out, but he stuck a rose stem between her teeth and forced her to bite down on it, then his fingers dug mercilessly into her throat, and she couldn't breathe.

Couldn't swallow.

The sound of the water raging down the falls filled the air, and the screams of the girls who'd died here before echoed in terror as she joined them.

♦ ♦ ♦

"Amazing Grace" drifted through the cold house as he let himself inside. He knocked off snow from his boots and stuck them in the shoe bin, but the floor felt like ice, and he hurried over to rebuild the fire.

Mama had let it go out during the day. In fact, she hadn't come into the den at all today.

Panic zinged through him. What if . . . no, she couldn't be gone. It wasn't time yet.

She had to stay around, had to live long enough to see him take his bride.

He threw another log on the grate, lit a match and tossed it in, then stoked the embers beneath it to stir up the flame. Throat raw with fear, he washed his hands in the sink.

He still smelled like that vile woman Carol.

All her talk about fame and glory and making a name for himself—all blasphemy.

All he wanted was love, just like anyone else.

He dried his hands, then shuffled toward his mama's room, pausing to listen to the end of the song, before he eased open the door.

Mama was lying on her side in the bed, so still that, for a moment, he nearly shouted in horror.

But the whisper of her breathing rattled a second later. Still shaky at the thought of losing her, he lifted the quilt and crawled in bed beside her.

Her body felt cold, frail, and her bones poked through the thin fabric of her flannel gown.

Tomorrow he'd find a way to get some food in her. Make her some chicken soup just like she had for him when he was five and sick with the chicken pox.

Tonight, though, he'd warm her up.

He wrapped his big hairy arms around her and buried his head against her neck. She smelled like talcum powder and flannel, the sweet scents that had calmed him as a kid.

"You can't leave me, Mama," he whispered. "Not yet."

He closed his eyes and curled against her, holding on for dear life.

CHAPTER
TWENTY-ONE

Cal ushered Mona inside, the remnants of fear from seeing her in danger still thrumming through him.

"You rented this place?" Mona asked, a hint of nervousness in her voice.

"For as long as I'm in town." Something akin to disappointment flickered in her eyes, giving him hope that she'd missed him.

"You didn't come back after the funeral," she said, her eyes searching his. "I thought you were upset with me."

Regret swelled inside him. "No, Mona, it was just . . . too hard." *Because I wanted you for myself.*

"I know you miss Brent." Mona gently touched his cheek. Her hand was so soft that he wanted to curl her fingers beneath his lips and kiss each one of them. "I understand that he was your best friend, Cal. And I was afraid . . . you blamed me for his accident."

Cal's heart thumped crazily. "God, no, Mona, why would I blame you?"

"Because Brent and I argued the night of the crash."

"It wasn't your fault, Mona. You were good to Brent." *Too good.*

He didn't want to talk about Brent tonight.

"I thought we were friends, and then you disappeared, too."

The loneliness in her voice ate at Cal. He'd been selfishly thinking of how angry he was at Brent for not loving her the way he should have, at himself for not stepping up in the beginning and claiming her.

Because he'd owed Brent.

But he'd repaid Brent long ago.

How much was a man supposed to sacrifice for a friend, even one like Brent who'd thrown himself into the line of fire to save Cal's ass?

"Mona, it's complicated. But I'm sorry I wasn't here for you."

Mona's breath rushed out in a soft whisper. "You're here now."

The yearning in her eyes made his body harden with desire.

"I thought I'd go crazy when Fulton put that knife to your throat," he admitted.

Mona shivered. "I was terrified, but I trusted you."

There was that word—trust. He wanted her trust. Hell, he wanted her love. But could she love him if she knew he'd kept secrets? "I'm always here for you."

Mona leaned toward him, her lips parted on a sigh. "I'm here for you, too, Cal."

Her sweet voice washed over him with tenderness, causing his hunger to spike. Mona had almost died tonight.

He had almost lost her . . . for good.

"Mona . . ." He cradled her face between his hands. "I . . . tell me to stop." He leaned toward her, his mouth an inch from hers.

"Don't stop," she whispered.

His heart tripped overtime, and the irrational voice inside his head urged him to kiss her anyway. To finally go after what he wanted.

And he'd wanted her for too long to walk away now.

◆ ◆ ◆

Mona sighed with pleasure as Cal closed his lips over hers. His touch was so titillating that her knees almost buckled, and pinpricks of desire rippled through her.

Cal cradled her face so gently that she threaded her fingers in his hair and drew him closer. He moaned low in his throat, fueling her need, and she deepened the kiss, teasing his mouth with her tongue, until he gave her what she wanted.

He plunged his tongue into her mouth, greedily kissing her, his movements becoming more urgent, hands sliding down her shoulders, over her arms to her waist, then her hips.

With one hand, he pulled her up against him, and she felt his sex harden against her belly. Long-dormant needs stirred, and she rubbed her foot against his calf.

"God, Mona, it feels so good to touch you, to hold you."

His husky admission intensified her need and erased any hesitation she had. "You feel good, too, Cal."

He froze for a moment, his eyes searching hers, and she tried to show him with her eyes how much she wanted him.

A second later, he swept her into his arms and carried her to the bedroom. He didn't bother with a light. She didn't ask.

She wanted him naked and loving her all through the night.

◆ ◆ ◆

Cal forgot everything as he slowly undressed Mona. The bedroom was dark, but a dim light from the adjoining bathroom filtered through the room, painting Mona with an angelic glow.

She was so beautiful he could barely breathe.

He kissed her again, deepening his tongue and tasting her sweetness and passion as she gave herself into the kiss.

Pleasure rocked through him as she teased him with her tongue and her hands urged him closer. He brushed her hair back from her neck, trailed kisses along her throat, then slowly slid his fingers to her waist and lifted her sweater over her head.

She wore a black lace bra that barely contained her breasts, lace that made him want to rip off her clothes instead of taking his time.

But he didn't intend to rush. He wanted to savor every moment.

Mona pushed at his jacket and he yanked it off, carefully setting his gun on the nightstand. For a second, fear flickered in Mona's eyes.

"Mona?" He rubbed her arms, watching. Waiting. If she said to stop, he'd walk away.

A soft sigh escaped her, and she looked into his eyes. No regret or hesitation there now, though. Only need and desire.

Fueled by her silent invitation, he kissed her again. Their movements became frenzied, heated, desperate, and he pulled off her jeans, then shucked his own. Mona took his hand and led him to the antique sleigh bed.

He pushed the covers back, his body aching to have her as he lowered her onto the bed. Her hands raked over his bare chest, her look of appreciation for his physique making his erection swell, and he kissed her neck and throat again, then trailed his tongue down her cleavage. He kissed her through the lacy bra, emboldened by the way her nipples turned to stiff peaks at his touch.

She moaned and ran her hands through his hair as he peeled away the lacy barrier and closed his lips over one nipple. He traced his tongue around the areola, then sucked the tip into his mouth and laved her with his tongue.

She groaned, then wrapped her legs around his body, urging him between her thighs. His hard sex pulsed between her thighs, and she opened to him, welcoming him.

But he made her wait while he laved her other breast, sucking her until she shoved at his boxers. He peeled her panties down at the same time, and finally they were naked and touching, bare skin to bare skin.

Passion burned hot through him. His cock throbbed, aching to be inside her. But he wanted to pleasure her first, wanted her to remember what it was like to be loved by him.

She stroked his calf with her foot again, and he hissed between his teeth, forcing himself to hold back as he slid down her body. He kissed her belly and her inner thighs, then gently parted her legs so he could reach her innermost secrets.

He trailed his tongue up and down her delicate skin, teasing her feminine folds until she moaned again and undulated her hips. Raw need shot through him, and he worked her clit with his tongue, then plunged it inside her.

She clawed at his hair, whispered his name on a throaty sigh of pleasure, and her body quivered as the first strains of her orgasm claimed her. The throbbing in his body intensified, and he grabbed his jeans from the floor, yanked a condom from the pocket, ripped it open with his teeth, and quickly rolled it over his length.

He lowered his head and suckled her sweetness again, and she cried out and urged him to come inside her.

Hot with hunger, he rose above her and replaced his tongue with his cock. One thrust and he closed his eyes and moaned. He'd never felt such intense passion before.

Because this was Mona.

The woman he'd denied himself from having. The woman he loved.

♦ ♦ ♦

Mona whispered Cal's name on a breathy sigh of passion. Pure erotic sensations splintered through her body, a million butterflies fluttering in her belly as Cal thrust inside her. Brent had always held something back during their lovemaking, acted as if he was performing.

But Cal felt real. Hungry for her. And so masculine that his hard muscles stoked her curves in all the right places. Her skin tingled, her mind blurred, and all she could think about were his fingers on her skin.

His lips touching her intimately.

Her soul finally connecting with his.

He groaned her name, slowly pulled out, then thrust inside her again, intensifying the pleasure rippling through her.

She undulated her hips, meeting him thrust for thrust, and they rocked back and forth, thrusting and stroking and loving each other, until she knew Cal had become part of her.

◆ ◆ ◆

Cal held Mona against him, torn between happiness and regret. They had made love over and over.

He didn't want to let her go.

But she had belonged to Brent.

Brent's gone.

Was he still in Mona's heart? Would she ever love Cal the way she'd loved his friend?

His phone buzzed, and he silently cursed. He didn't want to spoil the mood. But he was working a case.

The phone buzzed again, and he grabbed it before it woke Mona. She looked so peaceful now that he hated to disturb her rest.

"Agent Coulter."

"It's Peyton, Cal. Listen, there are two things. First, we didn't find any calls or connection between Gwyneth Toyton and Constance Gilroy. No phone calls from Fulton to Gwyneth either."

Any shred of hope he may have been holding on to disintegrated. The man was looking less and less guilty.

"Check out Doyle William Yonkers's phone records and see if you find a connection. Also research his financials and see if he bought any wedding dresses."

"I'm on it." Peyton tapped a few keys. "FYI, that Facebook page for Bill Williams has been taken down. And I ran the prints the team found at Mona Monroe's house, and a name popped."

Cal sat up in bed. "Go on?"

"They belong to a female. Her name is Sylvia Wales."

Damn. He'd assumed it was someone like Whit Combs. Or perhaps the Bride Killer.

"She lives outside Graveyard Falls with her baby."

Why would a woman break into Mona's?

"Text me her address."

He hung up, then slipped from bed and dressed. Mona stirred, rolled over, and looked up at him. Her hair was tousled, her eyes hazy with sleep, her lips red and swollen from his kisses. She looked radiant and so damn gorgeous his body hardened with renewed hunger.

But the text came through, reminding him he had a job to do. Protecting Mona meant tracking down the killer.

♦ ♦ ♦

Anna hadn't slept all night.

Nightmares of living in Graveyard Falls and the painful day Johnny had been arrested flashed back as Anna rose and dressed.

She had defended Johnny to her father. And Johnny had claimed his innocence. Until that last day when he'd told her to leave . . .

And now her father had been to the falls and found the second woman dead this week.

A chill slithered up her spine. Something didn't feel right. She'd checked on him during the night and he hadn't been in his bed. Then later, he'd acted confused.

Thirty years ago he'd been obsessed with crucifying Johnny because she'd slept with him. He'd called her ugly names when he'd found out.

Questions nagged at her as she remembered the timing. Right after he'd discovered Johnny and her together, the girls had started dying.

And her father had quickly stacked the evidence against Johnny.

Johnny had begged her to believe that he was innocent, that he loved her and only her.

But her father had shown her those pictures of the dead girls that he'd found under Johnny's bed, and . . . her faith had waned.

Could her father have planted that evidence?

He had been obsessed with the murders . . . he still kept a copy of the case file in his home desk drawer.

His mind was warped now, the past and present a fragmented jumble . . .

She hated the dark road her thoughts were traveling down. If Johnny hadn't killed those girls, someone else had.

Someone her father had let go free . . .

Unless he . . . no, she couldn't possibly think her father was capable of murder . . .

Anxious and needing answers, she finally decided to go to the falls herself. She poured a cup of coffee into her to-go mug, then grabbed her father's shotgun just in case she ran into trouble.

A few minutes later, she parked and found herself hiking to the falls. Foolish, considering there was a killer in town, but she was armed.

Besides, maybe she'd remember something that could help Johnny's parole. Or something to reassure her that her father hadn't done the inexcusable things she suspected.

And maybe one day she could finally let go of the guilt she'd harbored for years over abandoning Johnny.

Or for not seeing the truth and saving those girls.

But she didn't want to believe that Johnny was anything but the loving, sweet guy she'd fallen in love with.

Because if Johnny was guilty, that meant her father had been right about him. And that her daughter's father was a psychopath.

Worse, she and Josie had had a big blowup about Josie reading her high school diary. Josie knew her grandfather and Anna had been estranged for years, but Anna had never explained the reason.

If Josie nosed around too much, she'd discover the truth.

Dark storm clouds made the sky look as if it were nighttime. The trees shook violently in the wind, their shrill echo boomeranging off the mountain walls.

In spite of the freezing temperature, sweat beaded on her skin. Anna should have thrown the blasted diary away. She didn't know why she'd held onto it.

Yes, she did. The days and evenings she'd spent with Johnny had been the best of her life. The most romantic. The time when she'd been young and full of dreams and hopes for her future.

Then everything had gone to hell.

Her boots dug through the snow and brambles, but she pushed the branches aside and followed the trail. She knew the exact spot where Tiffany, Candy, and Brittany had been pushed from, and the spot where they'd fallen to their deaths below.

Yet she had happy memories of that place. She and Johnny had snuck to the falls so many times in the afternoon for a secret getaway. She'd lost her virginity at the base of the falls in a grassy area shrouded by pines and hemlocks.

She'd conceived her baby—their child—by those falls.

Icy snow stung her cheeks, her breath puffing out in a white cloud as she hiked through the thicket to the clearing.

Horror seized her when she spotted something on the ground. For a moment, she thought she must have imagined it.

It looked like . . . a body.

Her lungs begged for air as she inched forward. Snow swirled around the woman's face.

God . . . It was Carol Little, the reporter. The one who'd come knocking on her door wanting to question her about the past.

Tree limbs crackled and popped, twigs snapping off in the wind, and Anna jerked her head around, searching the shadows of the forest as she dragged her phone from her jacket.

The hair at the nape of her neck bristled. Was the killer still here watching her?

A falcon soared above, and two vultures circled the trees. The sound of brush and sticks breaking made her jerk her head to the right. Somewhere a mountain lion growled, then leaves parted as something darted through the trees.

She shivered and glanced at her phone to call for help, but there was no service. Another sound. More footsteps. Leaves rustling. One of the vultures swooped down.

Then a man appeared in the shadows. Deputy Kimball.

She'd seen him arguing with Carol Little the other day on the street when he'd pushed her outside the sheriff's office. And now Carol was dead . . .

CHAPTER TWENTY-TWO

Cal dropped Mona by her house so he could pay a visit to Sylvia Wales. He'd considered asking Mona if she knew the woman, but in light of the fact that Mona's personal photos had been destroyed, he'd been worried that she might be someone from Brent's past.

He wanted to check her out first.

Deputy Kimball called just as he was leaving Mona's. "Yeah?"

"Coulter, I'm at the falls. You won't believe it, but there's another body."

Shit. "Same place?"

"A few feet down."

Made sense. They'd had a rotation of officers monitoring at night, in sync with the Bride Killer's MO. They'd all mentioned difficulties with the darkness and density of the trees, animal sounds, and bitter-cold wind.

"Sheriff Buckley's daughter, Anna—she's here, Coulter. She found the dead woman."

Cal's mind raced. Why the hell would Anna Buckley go to the falls?

Kimball made a sound in his throat. "The victim is Carol Little."

Shock slammed into him, and he turned the Jeep in the direction of the falls. Carol had written about the murders. She'd been asking questions.

She had used Kimball to get the scoop.

Had she been murdered because of the story? And if so, had she discovered something about the unsub that had gotten her killed?

Gray clouds soaked up the early-morning light, making the woods look dark and ominous. He hiked to the bottom of the falls to view the body, shining a flashlight to guide his way. He kept his eyes trained for evidence of the killer—a piece of torn clothing, a hat, a button, anything the killer could have dropped or that had caught in the bushes along the way.

He spotted Anna hovering by a cluster of rocks near the falls. She was shivering in her coat, her hood dotted with snowflakes, her face pale as she stared at the scene.

Deputy Kimball stood by the body on the ground, his shoulders hunched. When he heard Cal approach, he swung his gaze up. His jaw was set hard, a dark expression on his face.

"The MO is different," Deputy Kimball said. "The rose stem is here, but she's not wearing a wedding dress, there's no garter, and the lipstick is missing."

"Her hair hasn't been chopped off either." Cal narrowed his eyes as he approached, his pulse pounding. The deputy was right. Carol Little lay at the base of the falls, her black slacks soaked, her coat half-unbuttoned, her hair tangled around her ghostly white face.

He glanced at the woman who'd found the body and introduced himself. She looked to be mid- to late forties. Dark hair. Green eyes. Attractive but her expression was haunted.

This was the sheriff's daughter. Odd that he'd found a body just yesterday and now she'd come to the falls and found another dead woman.

"My name is Anna DuKane," she said in a shaky voice.

"I know, you're the sheriff's daughter."

"Yes," she said tightly.

"What were you doing up here alone?" Cal asked.

She leaned against a tree. "I . . . it's a long story. I just had to come here and see this place."

"You knew two murdered women were left here and you came by yourself?"

She nodded, looking chastised. "I know it was stupid, but I had my father's shotgun."

"The killer could have turned it around and used it on you," Cal pointed out. He gestured at Carol. "Did you know this woman?"

A wariness crept into Anna's face. "No. Although . . . she stopped by my house wanting an interview. I told her to leave." Anna raised her chin. "That was a bad time, Agent Coulter. I didn't want to revisit the past."

Because she'd been involved with Johnny Pike. He remembered the details now. "Did you know Gwyneth Toyton or Constance Gilroy?"

"No," she said. "I haven't lived here for years. I just came back to Graveyard Falls to see my father. He's . . . ill."

Although he had insinuated himself in the case yesterday.

That was something an unsub might do.

"I still don't understand. You had to know it was dangerous. That the killer might come back."

"Actually, I was thinking about Johnny's parole. I thought maybe if I revisited this place I'd remember something from back then that might help him."

"You think he was innocent?"

She studied her jagged fingernails. "I did. But my father didn't agree." She looked back up at him. "But I'm sure you know all of this."

"Do you think the recent murders are related to those teenagers' deaths?"

She picked at one of her nails. "No . . . I mean, how they could be?"

She was right. Unless they had the wrong man . . . or someone wanted to glorify Johnny or help by killing Gwyneth and Constance to bring Pike's guilt into question.

Although if the sheriff had made a mistake and the killer had gone free, he'd be in his midforties now.

Most serial killers were twenty-five to forty-five. And if it was the same killer, where had he been for the last three decades?

Again, the sheriff's timing at the falls struck him. What if the Thorn Ripper had been living here in Graveyard Falls all along? What if Buckley had some kind of obsession with young girls and had killed them, then framed Johnny to get him out of his daughter's life?

Buckley might not be the Bride Killer, but he could have committed the Thorn Ripper murders. And what if someone knew the truth and they were killing women now to stir it all up?

"Did Ms. Little question your father?" Cal asked.

Anna shrugged. "I don't know. He doesn't share much with me. But I doubt he would have let her. He doesn't like the press. And his illness has affected his memory, so he avoids people. He doesn't want everyone to know."

What if this brain tumor had affected his behavior? Maybe triggered him to relive the past and kill again?

More voices sounded, then the crime team and medical examiner arrived.

Cal motioned to Anna. "Stay here. I'll need you to come to the station and make a statement."

She nodded and huddled in her coat while the other investigators approached.

Cal walked over to study Carol's body. "She was strangled?"

"Looks like it," Deputy Kimball said.

"Her death looks more violent." He had a feeling they wouldn't find DNA from a kiss on her cheek either. "Could be another killer. Someone who had a beef against Carol Little because of her job."

And that could be a boatload of suspects. Someone who'd made it look like she died at the hand of the Bride Killer by placing her at the base of the falls.

He gave the deputy a pointed look, the silent accusation settling between them.

"Don't look at me like that," Deputy Kimball snapped. "I was angry with her but not enough to kill her. Hell, I figured when the case was over, we might hook up again."

"Then maybe she stumbled onto something that could help us find the unsub."

If she had, he would find it. And if the Thorn Ripper was Buckley, he'd find that out, too.

Mona missed Cal already. But it was time she faced the mess in her house. Vandalism was one thing, but she didn't understand why anyone would want to tear her photographs into pieces.

That act seemed personal.

Was it a disgruntled patient or a patient's spouse or significant other? Someone angry because she'd helped give her patient enough strength and courage to leave a toxic relationship?

If so, why not just destroy the house? Why the pictures of her and Brent . . . ?

It almost seemed as if the person was angry with her for having a good marriage. Or was trying to tell her she was a hypocrite, that she shouldn't be dispensing advice when her marriage wasn't perfect.

Although another memory tickled her consciousness as she began to clean up, one so faint that it had seemed insignificant at the time, and she hadn't thought anything of it.

Brent had worked undercover at times, worked odd hours, been gone overnight. One night when he was on a case, the phone had rung and when she'd answered, someone was breathing on the other side.

Then silence and a click.

She'd told Brent, and he'd seemed upset about it, but she'd shaken it off.

She removed the photographs from the broken frames and placed them in a drawer, then swept up the glass and debris.

Brent's face faded in her mind, and Cal's replaced it, giving her a warm feeling. Cal had been so passionate and loving, had made her feel warm and safe and sexy and . . . loved.

Things she'd never completely felt with Brent.

Her phone trilled. Hoping it was Cal, she hurried to answer it. But it was Aimee, her assistant.

"Mona, Anna DuKane just called and wants an appointment. She said something happened, but she wouldn't tell me what."

"Anna DuKane—why does that name sound familiar?"

"She's the sheriff's daughter," Aimee said. "I heard some ladies talking about her at the memorial. She left town after Johnny Pike was convicted, and someone said she got married right after and hasn't been back since."

"But she's back now?" That seemed coincidental, too.

"Yeah, word is her daddy's real sick. Got a tumor that's affecting his brain."

"Oh, that's too bad. Well, call her and tell her I'll meet her at the office. You can text me the time when you talk to her."

She hung up, then rushed to shower and dress. Anna had lived here thirty years ago, so she might have known Mona's birth mother.

◆　◆　◆

Cal knelt by the medical examiner as he studied Carol Little's body.

"She was definitely strangled," Dr. Wheeland said. "The killer used his bare hands this time."

Cal frowned. "If it was the same unsub, he didn't have time for his ritual. He was angry and wanted to get rid of her quickly."

Dr. Wheeland examined Carol's wrists and ankles. "I agree. Although there are stun gun markings, I don't see rope burns or chain marks like on the other two."

Cal imagined a scenario. "Let's say the unsub is out looking for his next victim. He runs into Carol and realizes she's the one writing about him."

Dr. Wheeland nodded. "He may have realized she knew something that could expose him and he had to get rid of her. But she wrote about the killer dressing his victims in a wedding gown," Dr. Wheeland added. "So why didn't he dress her in a bridal dress?"

"He didn't have time." Cal's adrenaline pumped. "That means he's flustered, thrown off his game. So maybe he made a mistake, and we can use it to catch him."

CHAPTER
TWENTY-THREE

Cal made a mental note to look into Sheriff Buckley and probe Anna about their relationship. If there were secrets behind closed doors, he would find out. Carol Little's family needed to be notified of her death, but his contacts told him Carol had no family. Both her parents had passed.

Hoping to find more information on her computer or in her notes, Cal drove to the inn where she'd been staying and walked up the azalea-lined sidewalk to the front. It was a two-hundred-year-old gray-blue Victorian home with turrets, windows that looked as if shadowy ghosts might be looking out, and swings and rocking chairs on the wraparound porch.

A sign pointed to gardens out back and a walking trail to the river. A statue of the man who'd originally owned and built the inn stood in the center of a garden, the story of the man etched on a marker. According to rumors, his ghost could be seen at dusk and dawn, wandering the property.

Cal stepped inside, impressed by the detailed molding and antique wood flooring, yet the painting of the falls and the prison that had once stood by the grounds looked eerie. That prison had flooded years ago and dozens had died.

The town didn't commemorate that loss with a memorial, though.

A short, robust woman wearing an apron and a friendly smile swept in and introduced herself as the owner, Cynthia Humphries. "Are you looking for a room?"

He introduced himself. "I'm here about the recent murders."

The woman shook her head. "It's awful to have that happening in our town. Do you have a suspect?" she asked.

"We have some theories but aren't ready to make an arrest." Dammit, he hated to tell her they were no closer to finding the unsub than they had been after Gwyneth's death. "Unfortunately, there's been another murder. We found Carol Little's body at the falls."

Cynthia's eyes widened. "Oh, my God, Carol is dead?"

"I'm afraid so," Cal said.

Cynthia grabbed the edge of the antique sideboard for support. "This is horrible. She was such a nice lady. A little troubled, but she meant well."

"What do you mean, 'troubled'?"

Cynthia shrugged. "She didn't share much, but one morning over coffee, I asked her about her family, and she said she and her father hadn't gotten along."

He wasn't as interested in her family drama as what was on her computer. "Did she talk about the story she was working on?"

Cynthia smoothed down her apron. "Not really. I mean, she asked about Johnny Pike and the people in town. If everyone thought he was guilty."

"Did you live here back then?" Cal asked.

"Actually, I did. My husband and I had just moved to town. He was a developer and built those cabins up on the river."

"How did you think Sheriff Buckley handled the case?"

She looked at him as if that was an odd question. "I thought he did his job," she said. "All the parents were in a panic. After the first murder, the counselors had their work cut out. Hysterical grieving teenagers and parents didn't make a very happy town."

But Buckley had been the hero. Had he set it up that way?

"Did you believe Johnny Pike was guilty?"

She chewed her bottom lip. "I don't know. His mother was nice and insisted her son wouldn't hurt a fly. But there was so much evidence. I thought they were going to lynch that boy."

Had Carol discovered something that might suggest Pike was innocent? Was that the reason she was killed? It might account for the difference in the MO.

It also meant that anyone in town who didn't want Pike to get that parole could have killed Carol.

Sheriff Buckley especially wouldn't want the case to be overturned.

Cal considered Mona's profile of the unsub, that he was looking for a wife. That detail didn't fit with Buckley.

Yonkers was the one person of interest who did fit.

"I need to see Carol's room."

"Of course." She snatched a ring of room keys, then led him up the stairs to the second floor. When she opened the door, the scent of a woman's perfume swirled around him.

He half expected to see that the room had been ransacked. That the killer had been here covering his tracks before Cal could search Carol's belongings.

But the room was neat and orderly, the bed made, a stack of notepads on the desk. He scanned the room for her computer but didn't see it. Dammit, she must have had it with her.

Maybe it was in her car.

Cynthia hovered in the doorway, looking pale and clutching the doorknob.

"What kind of car did Carol drive?"

"A little red Toyota."

Which was not outside. So if he found the car, he might find her laptop.

"Did Carol have any visitors while she stayed here?"

"Not that I saw. She left early every day to talk to people in town."

"Thanks, Cynthia. I'll lock the room when I leave."

She pulled herself from her stupor and left him alone. He walked over to look at the notepads, hoping to find something, as he called the deputy. "See if you can find Carol Little's car. A red Toyota. Her computer might be inside it."

The deputy agreed, and Cal skimmed Carol's notes. She'd written the names of the Thorn Ripper's victims—Tiffany Levinson, Candy Yonkers, and Brittany Burgess.

Johnny Pike's name was at the top of one column, then she'd listed the evidence the sheriff had gathered against him. Fingerprints, photos of the victims, and a witness, Charlene Linder, who claimed that Pike had attacked her but she'd escaped. Though she'd left town before the trial, her written statement had clinched the case.

He skimmed more notes:

I tried to interview Sheriff Buckley, but he refused. So
did his daughter, Anna. She was dating Pike at the time
of his arrest and insisted that Pike wasn't dangerous.

On another page, she'd created a chart with three columns, listing each of the three original victims and their parents' names.

She'd uncovered the same information Deputy Kimball had about the families of the victims. She'd even circled Doyle Yonkers and written a question mark below his name as if she had her suspicions about him.

Cal texted Agent Hamrick and asked Dane to let him know if he saw Yonkers leave his property.

Beside Sara Levinson's name, Carol had jotted *THE BOAR'S HEAD* in capital letters.

Cal quickly searched the rest of the room in case she'd hidden notes or a flash drive, but he came up empty.

Frustrated but determined, he headed outside to his Jeep to drive to the Boar's Head. He punched the number he'd found in Carol's room for her editor, Wally Gann, and asked to speak to him.

When he told Gann about Carol, the man cursed. "I was afraid she was going to get in trouble one day."

"Why do you say that?"

"She wasn't satisfied just covering small stories. She was intrigued with murder. She was relentless and pushed people until she got what she was looking for."

Except if she'd uncovered something important, she'd taken it to the grave.

♦ ♦ ♦

Mona stopped in Cocoa's Café for coffee on the way to her office. "I'm enjoying your show, Miss Monroe," Cocoa said. "You got some interesting callers. Course most folks around here are freaked out about the possibility of another serial killer being in town."

"I know. You've lived here a long time," Mona said. "The teenage girls who died used to come in here, didn't they?"

Cocoa's dark skin glistened with perspiration as she set a tray of hot sticky buns on the counter.

Mona couldn't resist snatching one as Cocoa handed her a steaming mug.

"I don't mean to speak ill, but they were spoiled rotten and cliquish," Cocoa said. "Still, they didn't deserve to be killed and thrown away in the woods like that."

Mona frowned. "They didn't let just anyone into their group?"

"No, they were kind of a threesome. I remember a couple of girls who wanted to be in the 'in crowd,' but they snubbed them."

"Do you remember the girls' names?"

Cocoa wiped the counter with a rag. "One of them was Felicity Hacker. She was pretty but not striking like the others. She used to hang around and try to fit in, but . . . she never quite did."

Rita Herron

Mona's instincts prickled. "I heard from someone that she got pregnant that year."

"Yeah." Cocoa sighed. "Poor thing. Think the baby was stillborn, although no one ever talked about it. Bernice at the hair salon said she thought she gave the kid away. Someone else said they thought she got rid of the baby."

"Got rid of the baby how?"

Cocoa shook her head. "I don't know. I don't like to gossip myself."

Mona frowned. No wonder Felicity hadn't wanted to talk to her.

"After that, she kept to herself. Owns that plant nursery outside town. Grows the prettiest roses. Her mama taught her to do that."

Roses? Mona's mind took a strange leap. If Felicity had been shunned by the girls, she could have killed them and framed Johnny Pike, and jammed the rose stems down their throats to teach them a lesson.

While she had Cocoa talking, though, Mona had to find out more about the students that year. "I'm sure Felicity wasn't the only girl in Graveyard Falls to get pregnant while she was in school."

Cocoa hesitated. "Like I said, I don't like to gossip."

Mona offered her a tentative smile. "I guess since I'm working with folks in town, I'm just curious about everyone."

Cocoa sighed. "Well, I did hear that a girl named Charlene got pregnant when she was a junior," she said. "Folks said her daddy was as mean as a snake, that he locked her up till that kid was born."

Mona swallowed hard. She hadn't found Charlene's name at the county office. Was it possible Charlene was her mother?

"What was her last name?" Mona asked. "Did she have a boy or a girl?"

"I don't remember her last name, but I think she had a boy."

Mona's hopes deflated. Although it might be helpful to talk to Charlene anyway. Perhaps she and Mona's mother had bonded over their teenage pregnancies. "Where does Charlene live?"

194

"No idea. People said her daddy was so ashamed of her he moved them up in the mountains far away from anyone in this town. Other rumors spread that he killed Charlene and the baby and buried them in the hills."

Mona fiddled with her purse strap, uneasy. "What about Kay Marlin?"

Cocoa's brows rose. "You are curious, girl." She spoke in a conspiratorial whisper. "Word is that Kay didn't even know who the daddy was. I think her aunt or some other relative took the baby up north to raise it."

Mona thanked her and drove to her office, contemplating what she'd learned.

When she arrived at her desk, Anna DuKane was waiting, looking upset, her complexion pasty.

"Come on in, Anna," Mona said. "Can I get you some coffee or water?"

"Coffee would be good." Anna rubbed her hands up and down her arms. "I can't seem to get warmed up."

Mona gestured for the older woman to get comfortable on the love seat while she went to the corner side table and poured Anna a cup of coffee.

"Sweetener or cream?"

Anna shook her head. "Just black."

She poured herself a cup as well, stalling, giving Anna time to settle down.

When Mona handed her the mug, Anna took a quick sip, closed her eyes, and sighed as if she'd desperately needed the caffeine, then looked into her cup as if she were a million miles away.

"Tell me what happened," Mona said.

"I found Carol Little dead at Graveyard Falls."

Mona bit back her surprise "You went to the falls?"

Anna traced a finger along the rim of her cup. "Yes. I know it sounds crazy, but I . . . had to see the place again."

"Did you know Ms. Little?" Mona asked.

A flicker of guilt in her eyes. "No, not really," Anna said a little too quickly. "But she came to my father's house for an interview. I didn't want to rehash the past, so I refused to let her in."

Anna jiggled her leg nervously, and Mona reached out and laid a hand on her knee. "Why didn't you want to talk to her?"

"Because I was dating Johnny Pike back then. Everyone thought I knew he was a killer!" Anna cried. "They even thought I covered up for him."

Mona couldn't help but wonder the same thing.

CHAPTER
TWENTY-FOUR

Cal was still contemplating Carol's death as he entered the Boar's Head.

The decor consisted of animals that had been preserved by a taxidermist, the faces and eyes so real that he felt like they were following him as he crossed to the bar.

It was obviously a common decorating scheme in this part of Tennessee.

Rustic wood floors, booths, battered wood tables, and cane-back chairs added to the primitive country look. A few people were eating lunch, and three men in jeans and overalls drank beer at the bar.

He spotted a waitress with reddish-brown hair leaving one of the tables, carrying a tray of dirty dishes and walking toward a swinging door that led to the kitchen. He slid onto a barstool near the door.

The bartender, a young guy in his twenties with a sleeve of tattoos, slapped a napkin down in front of Cal. "What do you want?"

He wanted a beer but asked for coffee instead. Too much work to do. When the guy returned with the mug, he thanked him, then flashed his ID. "I'm investigating the murder of two women whose bodies were found at Graveyard Falls." He showed him pictures of Gwyneth and Constance. "Did you see either of them in here?"

"No." He gestured toward a picture of three fishermen showing off a huge catfish. "We mostly get hunters and fishermen."

A heavyset man in jeans and a wife-beater T-shirt pushed through the swinging door from the kitchen, sweat pouring down his ruddy neck. When he saw Cal, his eyes flickered with disdain.

A second later, he came over to Cal. "I'm the owner, Burrell Fergis. Why you bothering my people?"

"Because two women were murdered and left at Graveyard Falls, and now the reporter, Carol Little, who wrote about the story was found dead there as well."

Fergis's jaw tensed.

"I think Carol came to this bar to talk to Sara Levinson." Cal said.

Fergis looked away, wiping his forehead with the back of his arm.

"Shit. I was afraid something happened to that lady."

"Why do you say that?"

"That little Toyota she was driving. It was still in the parking lot when I got here this morning."

He hadn't seen it. "Where?"

"In the back lot," Fergis said.

Cal's pulse jumped. "Did you talk to Ms. Little?"

"No. She wanted to speak to Sara. Got her all tore up."

"What do you mean?"

"She asked all kinds of questions about Sara's daughter and that Pike boy."

He waved Sara over to join them.

Sara approached, her brows narrowed with worry. "What's going on?"

"They found that reporter dead," Fergis said.

Sara's eyes widened. "My God."

"What exactly did she say to you when you spoke?" Cal asked.

Sara twisted the rag tied at her waist. "She asked about my daughter." Her eyes grew moist and she swiped at them. "Even after all this time, I can't bear to talk about losing her. It was just so . . . senseless."

Compassion filled Cal. He couldn't imagine losing a child, especially in such a violent manner.

"What did you tell her?" he asked.

"There wasn't much to tell," Sara said. "The boy who killed my Tiffany was arrested and has been locked up for years."

Cal frowned. So Carol hadn't learned anything new from Sara? "You believe the right man went to jail?"

Sara's eyes flickered with turmoil. "At first I didn't. Tiffany loved that boy and had her heart set on going to the prom with him. But he used that against all the girls and lured them to the falls with a rose." She wiped at her eyes. "When the sheriff found all that evidence, I was shocked. But it all made sense then, that he did it."

Cal stood. "Thanks. I need to see Ms. Little's car." Maybe he'd find her computer and whatever she'd stumbled onto that had gotten her killed.

♦ ♦ ♦

Anna couldn't bear to look at Mona. She knew the questions in her eyes would be there. The same questions that had turned into bitter accusations when she'd lived in Graveyard Falls.

The questions her father had yelled at her the night before he'd arrested Johnny.

Although Johnny's lawyer had argued that not finding the jewelry meant Johnny was innocent, it hadn't been enough. Johnny had folded and accepted the plea.

"Anna, you know whatever you tell me is confidential," Mona said. "You might feel better if you talked about it. Did you know Johnny killed those girls?"

She shook her head emphatically. "No. I didn't believe it." At least she didn't want to believe it.

"But your father was the sheriff?"

"Yes, he hated Johnny because I was dating him. He told me that another girl said Johnny attacked her, and that she escaped."

Mona kept her face calm, a fact that was beginning to annoy Anna because she sensed Mona wanted to push her harder, wanted her to confess her deepest, darkest secrets.

There were some things she still never talked about. Things she never *would* share with anyone.

Pain so deep that she felt as if a knife was cutting her open from the inside out, splitting her in two.

"Let's talk more about Johnny. Did you sense he was dangerous?"

She'd been asked this a thousand times. "No. When they first questioned him, I was shocked because Johnny seemed like the kindest, most gentle boy in the world," she said and realized she still meant it. "After they arrested him, I replayed moments in my head over and over, and nothing Johnny ever did or said made me think he'd kill anyone."

"He didn't have a temper?" Mona asked.

Anna shook her head. "The only time I saw him get mad was when one of the wrestlers bullied a girl with Down syndrome. Johnny stuck up for her, and got in a fight with him."

Mona looked surprised. "That was nice of him."

Anna smiled sadly. "Before he hit a growth spurt in high school, he was small and got picked on. So he couldn't stand to see anyone else suffer." She couldn't help but wonder how much he'd suffered in the state pen.

"Have you visited him in prison?" Mona asked.

Anna cut her eyes away, the guilt and pain pressing on her chest so unbearable she could barely breathe. How could she visit him when she felt as if she'd abandoned him?

When she'd kept secrets from him. A secret nobody but her father knew . . .

A secret that had to stay buried to protect her daughter.

♦ ♦ ♦

Cal studied Sara. "Is there anything else you can tell me? Before Carol left, was she talking to anyone?"

Sara wrinkled her nose, her hands still twisting the rag. "Just Billy Linder. But they didn't talk long, and she jumped up and left. I thought she had a phone call or something."

Cal drummed his fingers on the bar. "Did you hear what they were talking about?"

"Not really."

"Tell me about this guy Billy."

"There's something off about him," Sara said. "I don't know if something happened to him when he was little, but he's odd. Sort of slow. He and his mother live way up in the mountains and don't socialize much." She gestured at the coyote on the wall above the jukebox. "In fact, he's the taxidermist who did all the animals in here for Burrell."

Cal startled at the mention of *taxidermist*. "You mean Doyle Yonkers didn't do all these?"

"No. It was Billy." She made a face. "Burrell likes them, but I think they're creepy."

"Do you think Billy is dangerous?"

"I can't say for sure. He likes hunting, that's all I know."

That wasn't much—a lot of men living around these mountains were hunters.

"I always thought his mama was strange too," Sara said. "She hovered over him like he was a baby even though he's probably in his twenties."

"So the mother is about your age?"

Sara nodded. "Her name's Charlene."

Alarm bells clanged in Cal's head. "The Charlene who claimed Pike attacked her?"

"Yeah. She dropped out of high school after that. I heard she got knocked up and her daddy was a mean drunk and nearly beat her to death when he found out she was pregnant. Maybe that's what's wrong with Billy. He has brain damage from that beating."

If he had brain damage, he probably wasn't smart enough to orchestrate a crime. Still, if he was the last person seen talking to Carol, Cal needed to talk to him.

He punched Peyton's number and asked her to find Billy Linder's address while he searched Carol's car.

♦ ♦ ♦

Anna was still keeping something from her, but Mona couldn't push her any more. The poor woman had obviously suffered guilt for years over her relationship with Johnny Pike and the teenagers' deaths.

Whether it was justified or not was the question.

"Anna, even if you suspected your boyfriend of murder and didn't come forward, you were young and in love. It's time you forgive yourself."

"I want to," she said. "But it's hard."

Mona patted her hand gently. "Is there another reason you feel guilty? Did you suspect someone else of the murders? Maybe another teenage friend?"

"No, it wasn't like that."

"What about your father? Did he have any other suspects?"

"No, I don't think so." Anna stood, her agitation mounting. "Thank you for listening, Ms. Monroe, but I have to go."

She practically sprinted out the door, leaving an air of secrecy and fear behind her.

What was Anna afraid of?

Mona stewed over the possibilities while she saw her next few clients.

She finished her paperwork, then realized it was time for her radio show, so she grabbed her coat and gloves and rushed outside to her car. Ten minutes later, she hurried into the radio station.

Chance looked different tonight, she thought, as she took her place at the mic. A scowl pulled at his face, and he was on the phone, his voice terse. When he saw her, he averted his eyes and covered the phone with his hand so she couldn't hear his conversation.

He quickly hung up, then started the segment and patched the first caller through.

The first five callers wanted to discuss the murders in town. The women were panicked, the men angry that their loved ones were in danger.

Mona had no answers, but she tried to reassure them that the police were doing everything they could to catch the Bride Killer.

"Why would the killer dress the girls in wedding gowns?" an elderly woman named Henrietta said. "That's just sick."

"I don't want to speculate on air." Mona pressed two fingers to her temple. A headache was beginning to pulse, her nerves fraying. She understood the panic.

"It's just like before," the next caller commented. "All the young women in town afraid to go outside. Looking at everyone they meet, even the ones they know, like they're the killer."

No wonder Anna had left Graveyard Falls years ago. It was hard to escape the gossip and accusing eyes in a town where everyone knew your business.

When she answered the next call, there was silence for a moment. Then a heavy breath.

"Hello, this is Mona, what's on your mind tonight?"

"You were supposed to help me, but you don't help anyone. Tell them to stop saying bad things about me."

Mona looked up at Chance to see if he was paying attention, and his eyes darkened with worry. She tried to comfort herself with the fact that the call was being traced.

She just needed to keep the man on the line. And maybe figure out if he was Doyle William Yonkers.

"Tell them to stop saying what?"

"That I'm sick," he said. "All I want is someone to love me, to have a family. It's all I've ever wanted."

Keep him talking. "We all start out with a family," Mona said, improvising. "What happened to yours?"

A sound like a cry echoed over the line. Then he cleared his throat. "My mama's sick. I wanted to give her grandbabies before she died."

Mona's pulse clamored. Yonkers had made a similar comment.

"Is there something I can do to help your mother?" Mona asked. "Does she need medical care?"

Another sob. "I take care of her," he said. "But I don't want to talk about her."

Yonkers had said he took care of his mother, too.

Was Will Candy's brother?

Did he already have his next victim picked out?

"Then what do you want to talk about? The women who let you down?"

A tense moment. "It's your fault the girls had to die."

She started to respond, but the line went dead. His last words disturbed her.

Tears of helplessness, anger, and fear blurred her vision, and Mona decided she'd taken all the calls she could for the day. She motioned to Chance that she had to end the show.

She wanted to go home and forget the horror in the town.

"Are you all right?" Chance asked as she grabbed her coat and gloves.

"Yes." Her voice cracked on the word, and she dashed out the door. She'd call Cal as soon as she got in the car.

Maybe he could trace the call back to Yonkers, and if he was the killer, he could pick him up before he hurt anyone else.

Fresh snowflakes blinded her, and she pressed the keypad to unlock her car as she neared it. The lights flickered on, but a noise behind her startled her, and she jerked her head around.

A shadow jumped her from behind. She struggled, but she inhaled the strong scent of chemicals, her eyes blurred, and the world spun into darkness.

CHAPTER
TWENTY-FIVE

Cal scanned the parking lot near Carol's car for evidence of an attack. He found a silver loop earring on the pavement by her door. She must have lost it when the killer abducted her.

He checked the car door, but it was locked, so he pulled a tool from the Jeep and used it to open the door. Inside, the car was fairly clean. A leather jacket lay on the backseat, and a stack of blank notepads was jammed in a plastic bin. He found a folder and removed it, then thumbed through the contents.

Several articles about the Thorn Ripper.

He popped the trunk. Inside lay a pair of snow boots and another coat, then Carol's laptop.

Adrenaline pumped through him.

He checked the time as he hurried back to the Jeep. Mona's show would be over by now. Worry for her made him reach for the phone.

He punched her cell number, but the phone rang and rang. He tried her home number and the voice mail kicked in. Nerves on edge, he called the radio station.

No answer there either.

Dammit. Where was she?

His phone buzzed, and he checked the ID, praying it was Mona. Deputy Kimball instead. "Yeah?"

"I found that white van that ran you and Ms. Monroe off the road."

"Where is it?"

"It went over the side of the mountain. A sightseer spotted it when he and his wife stopped at the overhang to look at the view."

Shit. "Get a crew there to go down and examine it. Let me know what they find. I need the name of the owner."

"I'm on it." The line clicked to silence just as a text dinged from Agent Hamrick.

Yonkers visited graveyard where his sister is buried. I'm on his tail.

Maybe he'd make a mistake and they'd catch him doing something incriminating.

Cal punched Peyton's number. "Find everything you can on Carol Little. I have her laptop and need her password."

"Copy that." Peyton ended the call, and Cal decided to check the radio station for Mona.

Mona twisted and turned in the darkness, terrified when she realized she was in a trunk. Her head throbbed from whatever her abductor had used to knock her out and her mouth felt like cotton. She racked her brain to remember what had happened—one minute she'd been talking to that disturbing caller and he'd blamed her for the young women's deaths, then she'd hurried to her car and someone had attacked her.

Could it have been Will? Had he phoned from the parking lot at the station? He might have been waiting for her to leave and she'd been in such a hurry and so upset that she hadn't paid attention to her surroundings.

Her stomach roiled as the vehicle jerked to the right and screeched to a stop. She twisted her hands, trying to untie them, but they were bound too tightly. So were her feet. And he'd gagged her mouth.

Terror shot through her as the trunk opened.

◆ ◆ ◆

The counseling session with Mona confused Sylvia. She wasn't what she'd expected. Not a slutty woman who'd tricked Brent into marriage. Instead, she'd seemed . . . kind. Sympathetic. She'd certainly understood her grief and seemed like she genuinely cared about her.

Although her brother didn't believe it.

She was trembling after talking to him. Dear God, he sounded mad . . . as if he'd lost all touch with reality.

He'd always been protective of her.

And he loved her baby and hated that she was raising him alone.

But she'd never thought he would do anything about it . . .

Although their phone conversation scared her. He'd talked about Mona as if he might hurt her.

She tried phoning him again, but he didn't answer. "Please call me back. We need to talk." Her heart tripped overtime as she drove to his cabin in the mountains.

She buttoned her coat, threw her scarf around her neck, climbed out, and slogged through the slush to the porch. Debris from the trees pelted her as the wind shook it down. She knocked and called her brother's name, but no answer.

Was her mother here? She didn't want to see her.

But she had to talk to her brother.

Heart pounding, she eased open the door. A fire burned low in the fireplace, but the den was empty. She tiptoed across the den and looked inside her brother's room.

He wasn't there.

Her breath caught at the sight of his desk. Articles about the recent murders in Graveyard Falls covered it, along with photographs of each of the victims. A picture of the reporter Carol Little and the article she'd written about the Bride Killer was also there.

The other pictures disturbed her even more . . . candid shots of Mona at her home, at the radio station, at her office . . . one of Mona wearing a wedding dress that he must have used some computer program to create.

Sylvia grabbed the edge of the desk to keep from collapsing in horror.

◆ ◆ ◆

Cal screeched up to the radio station, frantic to find Mona and make sure she was safe. Her car was in the parking lot. A good sign.

But there were no other cars around.

Praying she was still inside, he jogged up to the station but it was locked.

Heart racing, he pounded on the door and yelled Mona's name. "Mona, if you're in there, open up!"

Nothing.

Stomach knotting, he ran to the windows and peered inside. No lights. Nothing moving. No one inside.

But her car was still here . . .

He ran over to it and looked in the interior. It was locked. He shined his flashlight through the window and saw nothing amiss. No phone or purse.

So where the hell was she?

Fear clogged his throat, and he sprinted back to his Jeep, hightailed it from the parking lot, and sped toward Mona's house. Maybe she'd had car trouble and Chance had given her a ride home.

Five minutes later, he barreled down her street, his tires churning on the ice. As soon as he cut the engine, he ran to the front door and banged on it. The lights were off, too, and when he looked in the windows, he didn't see anyone inside.

His phone buzzed, and he yanked it from his pocket. He didn't recognize the number, but he'd asked the police station to direct important calls about the case to his cell. "Agent Coulter."

"Agent Coulter, my name is Sylvia Wales. I . . . I might know who the Bride Killer is. I think he took Mona Monroe."

Sylvia Wales—that was the name of the woman whose prints they'd found at Mona's.

Cal closed his eyes, battling terror. "Who is he and where would he take her?"

"He's my brother," Sylvia said, her voice cracking. "I'm at his cabin and I found pictures of the dead girls and that reporter. And of Mona Monroe."

"I'll be right there."

◆ ◆ ◆

Mona still couldn't believe her eyes. Chance, the man who'd coaxed her into doing his radio show on relationships, had abducted her.

Her thoughts raced as he dragged her from the trunk. She glanced around with a sick feeling. They were in the woods near the falls.

"Why are you doing this?" Mona cried as he ripped the gag from her mouth.

"Just shut up and put on the dress."

Cold terror bled through Mona. The wedding dress . . . he was going to kill her just like he had the others.

Chance was the Bride Killer.

He yanked at her clothes, but Mona shook her head. "Don't touch me."

He shoved her backward. "Either you do it or I will."

Tears of rage burned the backs of her eyelids, but Mona blinked them back. She would not give him the satisfaction of seeing her cry.

He loosened the ropes around her wrists and tossed the gown at her. She glared at him, reminding herself to stall, that Cal needed time to find her.

But a hopelessness welled inside her, threatening her with panic. Cal might not even know she was missing . . .

Chance reached for her, but Mona shoved his hands away. "I'll do it, you sick bastard." She pulled her sweater over her head and tossed it to the ground. Desperate to keep him from touching her, she forced her head through the neckline of the dress. The lace felt scratchy, the thick bodice crinkling and wadding up around her as she tried to tug off her jeans and straighten it.

"Why are you doing this? I thought you were my friend."

"Friend?" His eyes flared with rage, his voice shrill and sinister. She'd thought Chance was a free spirit. She'd never imagined he had this dark side to him.

"You came into town and thought you knew everything about marriage. You had it all, didn't you? But you're a liar and you hurt people. You know nothing about love."

Mona's heart pounded as confusion swirled in her brain. "I'm not a liar," she said. "I believe the things I tell people. I try to help—"

"Help?" He yanked her arm and dragged her deeper into the woods. "You destroy families, that's what you do."

"Then why'd you give me the show?"

"So I could get close to you, watch you, hear what you had to say."

Tree branches slapped her face, the limbs clawing at her as he hauled her toward the falls.

Dear God, he was going to kill her. And she'd never get to tell Cal that she loved him.

CHAPTER
TWENTY-SIX

Cal's blood ran cold at the pictures of Mona on the desk. Coupled with the articles about the recent murders, it was a scary sight.

Sylvia had explained that she'd resorted to using her mother's maiden name after Brent's death, and that she was Chance Dyer's sister.

She was also Brent's other woman. Actually, they had been married before he met Mona, and she'd had Brent's child.

Damn Brent.

"I'm sorry, Agent Coulter," Sylvia said, near hysteria. "I love my brother, but I never thought he was capable of this."

Cal studied her. "He told you he was going to take Mona?"

"He said he was going to fix things, and that she was the problem." She paced the room. "He knew I was upset about her, and he went with me to her house. We wanted to scare her into leaving town, so we trashed her place."

"You wrote those messages on her wall and mirror telling her to leave town?"

She nodded, although she looked miserable. "I'm not proud of what we did, but I was upset that Brent married her."

He forced a neutral expression. He didn't blame her for being mad, but she should have taken that hurt and anger out on Brent, not Mona.

"Your brother blamed Mona because she kept Brent from you?" Cal said.

"Yes. I . . . guess I did, too. Then I went to see her at her office and . . . she seemed really nice."

"But you trashed her place anyway," Cal said bluntly.

Sylvia wavered. "I know that was wrong. At the time I was just emotional and Chance convinced me she deserved it. But . . . she doesn't deserve to die."

"No, she doesn't," Cal said. "And Sylvia, she has no idea about you."

"I figured that out." Regret washed over Sylvia's face. "He lied to us both, didn't he?"

Cal nodded. "I'm afraid so."

Sylvia touched his arm. "Please find her. Find him. And . . . don't hurt him." She gestured toward the wall. "He needs help."

He needs a cell, Cal thought. But he refrained from making that comment.

"I understand his motive where Mona is concerned, but why kill those other women?"

Sylvia touched one of the pictures. "I don't know. Chance was a geek when he was young. He had a hard time getting a girlfriend."

"Was he abused?"

"No. The opposite. My mother doted on him."

So he was looking for someone as doting as her?

Or maybe Mona was his end game, and he killed the other girls to throw off the police and make them think a serial killer was responsible.

"Do you have any idea where he'd take her? Does he have another cabin or place he'd go?"

"Not that I know of."

"Does he have a white van?"

"My mother does. Why?"

"He ran me and Mona off the road," Cal said, then saw her face blanch. "What kind of vehicle does Chance own?"

"A black Land Rover."

"Give me your mother's address."

She jotted down the address, and Cal raced back to his car.

Despair threatened as he sped away and maneuvered the switchbacks. Apparently Chance's mother lived in a cabin not too far from the one he'd rented, but cut deep into the woods, so far back that if Chance wanted to hurt someone there, no one would hear the woman scream.

The Jeep bounced over ruts, skidding on the icy roads, but thankfully the four-wheel drive gave him traction and he plowed down the narrow dirt road.

By the time he reached the cabin, he could hardly breathe for the fear squeezing his lungs.

He scanned the woods and clearing for a vehicle or signs of Chance, but didn't see anything. Perspiration beaded on his neck as he jumped out and hurried up to the porch.

The cabin looked dark, but a dim light burned low in the room to the right. He eased up to the window and looked in and saw a middle-aged woman sitting at a table hunched over, an afghan draped around her shoulders.

He leaned toward the glass, searching for Dyer and Mona, but didn't detect any other sounds.

He had to make sure, so he eased to the front and knocked on the door. Several seconds later, he heard footsteps shuffling, then the lock turning.

"What'd you do, forget your key?" the woman called.

When she opened the door, she looked startled. "You're not my son."

Cal flashed his badge. "No, ma'am, I'm Agent Coulter. But I do need to speak to Chance. Is he here?"

She shook her head. "I haven't seen him today. Why? What's going on?"

"It's about a case I'm working on. I need to ask him some questions." He eased past her. "Mind if I take a look around?"

"What for?" the woman asked, her eyes widening.

Cal didn't answer, though. He moved past her and walked through the small house searching for Mona.

But there was no sign of her anywhere. No sign of a wedding dress or sewing machine either.

"What is going on?" Mrs. Dyer demanded.

Cal handed her his business card. "Please call me if you hear from him, no matter what time of day or night."

She gripped the card, her face strained with worry. He'd ignored her question. It was either that or tell her that he suspected her son was a killer.

He raced back to the Jeep, his heart pounding as he headed toward the falls. It was the only other place he knew to look.

He had to find Mona.

♦ ♦ ♦

Mona frowned. He was making no sense. "What are you talking about, Chance?"

"Brent loved my Sylvia, not you. But then you turned up pregnant and he married you, too."

"What? Sylvia?" The Sylvia she'd met at her office? Mona dug her heels in the snow to stall as he pushed her into the woods.

"Yes, you took him from my sister. Because of you, her little boy doesn't have a daddy."

Mona tugged at his arm. "Chance, I don't understand." She racked her brain. "The only Sylvia I know is a client. She came to see me because she lost her husband." And she had a baby. Mona had seen him that day at the housing project. But they had nothing to do with *her*.

"See, you're lying again! They were married, but then you went and got knocked up, so he married you, too."

Mona gasped. What was he talking about? Brent was already married when he exchanged vows with her?

"I told Sylvia not to meet you, that you'd try to make it seem like it wasn't your fault, that you didn't trick him, but she insisted on going to your office. Said she had to know what Brent saw in you."

The truth sank in. "Sylvia and Brent were married before I met him?"

"Don't act like you don't know!" Chance shouted. "She and Brent and Rodney were a family until you came along." He gripped her arm so tightly that pain shot up her shoulder and her legs buckled. "You're a whore and a liar and a home wrecker," he hissed. "That's what you should be telling people on the radio."

Mona's heart splintered with the pain of betrayal. Brent had lied to her from the moment they met.

And he had a son.

No wonder he'd balked at the idea of them trying to get pregnant again after she lost the baby.

Another painful truth followed. If Brent was a bigamist, their marriage had never been real . . .

♦ ♦ ♦

Cal careened down the mountain road to the falls, then threw the Jeep into park beneath some trees and hit the ground running.

His boots dug into the snow as he used his flashlight to illuminate the path leading to the base of the falls.

Every minute counted.

Leaves swirled around him, trees shaking violently in the winter wind. His face stung as sleet pelted him. Somewhere the sound of animals foraging for food echoed, then the sound of a cry.

His heart jumped to his throat, and he took off running, maneuvering through the forest. He checked the base where the first victims were left, but no one was there, so he raced to another section. The deputies were supposed to be watching the falls, but there were miles of woods. No wonder they hadn't caught this guy in the act—there were too many places to hide.

Then through the branches, he spotted something white. Dear God.

Mona was kneeling on the ground in a wedding dress, Chance squeezing her throat with his hands. A rose stem lay in the snow beside them.

Cal lifted his gun and aimed, easing through the brambles and over an ice-covered tree stump. "Let her go, it's over."

The man's head jerked toward the woods in search of Cal, but Cal remained hidden in the shadows of the trees.

"She has to die, she wrecked my sister's home!" Chance shouted.

Cal eased behind another tree, inching closer. "She didn't know," Cal said in a deep voice. "Brent lied to her just like he lied to Sylvia."

Chance's hands still gripped Mona's throat, a weak, choked sound coming from her.

"No, she stole Sylvia's husband."

"Brent was the liar," Cal said, tightening his grip on his gun. "He lied to both of them. He was good at that. Mona had no idea he had another wife."

Her eyes widened in horror as she spotted him.

"He was a cheater!" Chance yelled. "That's the reason he had to die." He shook Mona, her cry of terror barely discernible as he squeezed her neck harder.

"So you killed Brent?" Cal asked.

"He deserved it for hurting my sister, and so does she." Suddenly realizing Cal was behind him, Chance spun around and jerked Mona in front of him.

Cal had a split second to make a decision. It didn't take him that long.

He fired a single shot into the man's temple. Chance's head jerked back, blood flying. His body bounced against a tree, then he sank to the ground.

Mona collapsed on her hands and knees, gasping for air.

Cal quickly checked Chance's pulse. He was dead, so he hurried to Mona. He dragged her into his arms, cradling her against him, the fear he'd felt when he thought he was going to lose her still racking his body.

Mona's lungs strained for air, and her throat was so raw—she tried to speak but couldn't. She felt dizzy, weak, and . . . confused.

Chance . . . Sylvia . . . Brent's wife . . .

Brent had a son. No wonder he hadn't wanted another baby with her. And Cal . . . had he known?

Pain wrenched her heart, betrayal and humiliation cutting so deeply that she tried to push away from Cal, but she was too weak.

"God, Mona, I'm so glad you're okay." He searched her face. "You are okay, aren't you?"

Tears blurred her eyes, and she managed a nod, but she wasn't okay and she sensed he knew it.

He scooped her up, and she laid her head against him and closed her eyes, giving in to exhaustion as he carried her through the woods.

The next hour was a blur. Cal called an ambulance and insisted they transport her to the hospital for observation while he waited for the crime team and medical examiner to arrive.

By the time the ambulance drove away with her, the realization that Cal had covered for Brent had hit her, and she felt sick to her stomach.

She had loved both of them, but they had both betrayed her.

♦ ♦ ♦

The medical examiner hunkered down to examine Chance, although Cal knew what the autopsy would reveal. Still, they had to go by the book.

He watched the ambulance drive away with Mona, a sick feeling in the pit of his stomach. He'd figured Mona would find out about Brent's deception, but he hadn't wanted it to be this way.

But they had found the Bride Killer. That was the good news.

Doubt niggled at the back of his mind, though. He had to make sure, had to find the evidence and process it. He hadn't seen any roses or garters at Chance's.

He also needed to find that jewelry . . .

That was one key piece of evidence missing from the Thorn Ripper case. It was also important to the Bride Killer . . .

"We'll take him to the morgue. Does he have family?" Dr. Wheeland asked.

Cal nodded grimly. "A sister and mother. I'll make the notification." Then he'd have a team search and process Chance's cabin.

Deputy Kimball arrived, and Cal asked him to supervise the crime scene. He left Wheeland to take care of transporting the body, then drove back to the man's cabin. Sylvia met him at the front door, her face lined with worry and fear.

"I'm sorry," Cal said quietly. "I . . . I had to shoot him . . . He was strangling Mona Monroe, he wouldn't let go."

"Oh, God, no . . ."

Cal caught her around the waist and helped her back inside, then ushered her to a chair.

"I don't understand," she wailed. "I never wanted any of this . . ."

When he'd first suspected that Brent was unfaithful, he'd assumed the other woman was someone who had seduced Brent. But Sylvia appeared to be a nice woman. And she had a son.

Except she had helped Chance trash Mona's house.

Still, she'd been as much a victim as Mona.

Self-loathing assaulted Cal. Why the hell had he kept Brent's dirty little secrets?

Mona had deserved better. And he intended to tell her that as soon as he could.

"I called a crime team to search the cabin," Cal said.

Sylvia made a strangled sound. "I still can't believe he killed those women."

Cal gritted his teeth. "He killed Brent, too, Sylvia. Did you know that?"

Sylvia dropped her face into her hands on another sob. "What? No!"

"He blamed Mona for your son not having a father. But he's the one who stole the baby's father from him."

Mona tolerated the poking and prodding of the nurses and doctor, all the time insisting she was fine. She just wanted to go home.

Thankfully one of them had given her scrubs to change into, but she knew Cal would want the wedding gown for evidence, so she had them bag it to give to him.

"You should stay overnight for observation," the young doctor told her. "And we can arrange for you to speak to a counselor."

Mona bit back a laugh. "I am a counselor." Although she knew that fact didn't preclude her from needing help herself. She had been kidnapped and nearly strangled to death. That was traumatic.

But even worse was learning Brent had lied to her, had been married to another woman, and that he had a son.

She closed her eyes, battling more tears. If she fell apart, the doctors would never let her go home.

"Please, I'll rest better in my own house," Mona said, although the memory of the intruder haunted her. Now she understood the shredded and torn photographs. Chance had blamed her for hurting his sister.

The nurse asked her to sign release papers, and she called a cab for a ride home. She certainly didn't want to call Cal.

The driver didn't ask questions, just looked at her with sympathy and drove in silence. Snowflakes fluttered down, adding to the blanket of white on the ground.

When they reached her house, she ran inside for money, then paid the driver, and hurried back up the steps.

The scent of Chance's hands on her made her stomach roil. She climbed into the shower, leaned her head back, and let the hot water sluice over her. Then the tears began to fall.

Deep, agonizing sobs racked her body, but she didn't fight them. She needed to purge her emotions so she could move on.

Because she would move on. There was no way she'd let Brent's lies destroy her.

Except it wasn't Brent's face that taunted her. Or the memory of his loving hands or body that made her double over with grief.

It was Cal's.

She was in love with him. Maybe she always had been. Maybe Brent had even known that all along.

But Cal had lied to her about Brent, had known that he was unfaithful.

He couldn't have done that if he cared about her.

She scrubbed her face and finally dried her tears. She wouldn't waste another tear over either man.

As soon as she stepped from the shower and dragged on her robe, the doorbell dinged. She had a bad feeling she knew who it was.

Gathering her courage, she dragged a comb through her damp hair, then tightened the belt on her robe and headed down the steps.

A knock sounded, then Cal's deep voice. "Mona, it's Cal. Let me in."

She couldn't look at him tonight. Not after all that had happened. Not when she still wanted him.

"Go away, Cal," she said through the door. "I don't want to see you right now."

Silence, thick and tense, stretched for a full minute, then Cal said, "Please, Mona—"

"I said go away." She flipped off the downstairs light and hurried back up the steps. When she reached her bedroom, she slammed the door and crawled into bed, pulling up the covers and burying her head in her pillow.

◆ ◆ ◆

Josie stared at the picture of Johnny Pike in her mother's yearbook, studying his features. He had been a handsome young man, popular, and the star football player.

And her mother had been in love with him.

That much she'd learned from the diary. Her mother hadn't done a great job of hiding it, so she dug it out from its recent spot under the mattress, knowing her mother would be furious. But she'd come this far and she had to know everything.

Her pulse pounded as she quickly skimmed the pages.

Johnny Pike had been arrested as the Thorn Ripper and had been given a life sentence in prison.

She then flipped through several more pages, shocked at the contents. Her mother had . . . been pregnant.

With Johnny Pike's baby.

Josie's breath caught and she did the math. Thirty years ago—Josie was twenty-nine . . . Was it possible she was Johnny Pike's daughter?

Had her mother lied to her about her father all these years? Invented a story about some man she'd met who'd died in the service because her father was a serial killer?

The door swung open, and Josie startled. Her mother stood in the doorway, her eyes wide, her face red with anger. "I told you not to read that. It's private."

"You lied to me," Josie said, her own anger spiraling. "All these years." She swung the yearbook around and stabbed a finger at Johnny Pike's picture. "You were in love with him, and you were pregnant. But he went to jail for murder, so you made up a story—"

"I told you not to screw around with that boy!" Josie's grandfather stumbled in, his look of confusion mingling with rage.

Anna gave her father a harsh look. "Daddy, that was a long time ago."

"You little whore. You got knocked up. I told you he was good for nothing." He swung a finger at Josie. "I told you to get rid of that kid, too. You should have listened."

Josie gasped, the truth dawning.

Her grandfather had wanted her mother to get rid of her because the Thorn Ripper was her father.

Her mother tried to take her father's arm, but he jerked back and glared at her. "You little liar. You were covering for a killer."

"Daddy, stop!" Anna shouted. "Johnny said he didn't kill those girls."

"But he did," her grandfather hissed. "And I locked him up."

Josie's eyes blurred with tears. Now she understood the chasm between her mother and grandfather. He'd arrested her mother's lover for murder.

Fighting a sob, she ran past both of them, desperate to get away.

He saw the girl Josie again. She looked so sad as she entered the church.

She must be lonely, too. Maybe she needed a friend just like him.

Mama had been getting sicker every day. Last night when he'd curled up beside her, she'd been so cold and still. And her bones were sticking through her skin.

He ducked into the church behind Josie and watched as she shook snow from her beautiful hair with her fingers. The long strands made him want to tangle his hands through it.

Damn that Carol Little for writing about him like he was a monster.

He was somebody. He had skills. He wanted a family, and by God, he was going to get one.

Mama would be proud. And she would like Josie. Josie was a church girl.

He'd take her back to Mama tonight and start her lessons on how to be a proper wife.

He wondered what she'd look like pregnant, her belly round with his baby.

CHAPTER TWENTY-SEVEN

Cal leaned against Mona's door, his chest aching.

Mona hated him.

He could hardly blame her. He'd kept secrets from her. Had covered for Brent's deception.

And he'd never told her how he felt about her.

He inhaled a deep breath, disgusted with himself. He had owed Brent his life.

But Brent had taken advantage of his loyalty, and he'd taken advantage of Mona.

Cal should have stood up to his friend, should have fought for Mona. Should have confessed that he loved her.

But if he told her now, she'd never believe him.

Maybe if he gave her time, she'd listen to him. Forgive him.

Yeah, fat chance of that.

Still, there was nothing he could do tonight. And he still had details to follow up on to close this case.

Then he could leave Graveyard Falls.

Except he didn't want to leave. Not without Mona.

A weariness crept over him as he walked back to the Jeep, but he forced his feelings to the back burner as he remembered he still needed to search Carol's computer.

He stopped by the diner and ordered a plate of food to go, then drove back to his cabin and carried the food and laptop inside.

Peyton had texted with several suggestions for the reporter's password, one of which had worked. A cold beer helped take the edge off his nerves, and he ate the chicken fried steak as he searched Carol's files.

One entry summarized her conversation with Deputy Kimball where she'd learned about the victims being dressed in wedding gowns. Another folder contained notes on the original Thorn Ripper murders. She had obtained a copy of the file of the investigation led by the former Sheriff Buckley.

Buckley had been convinced that Johnny Pike was a cold-blooded killer.

His daughter had also been dating the young man.

Nothing new.

Cal frowned as he skimmed the details about the evidence against Pike. Photos of each of the girls after they'd been killed were discovered in a shoebox beneath his bed.

But the jewelry he'd taken had never been found.

Carol had written a question mark by Pike's name as if she suspected he might not have been guilty.

Earlier, Cal had questioned the sheriff's possible involvement . . .

And Agent Hamrick was still watching Yonkers.

He glanced at the names of the other boys who'd been interviewed in the case. Two seniors, but they had alibis for the time of the murders. Females who'd been questioned included the mothers of the three victims, other classmates, and a girl named Charlene Linder.

Linder? Where had he heard that name before?

He rubbed his temple, then it hit him. Billy Linder was the name of the taxidermist who'd preserved the animals for the Boar's Head.

He searched further but found no other notes on the investigation, so Carol must have just started asking questions.

His phone buzzed, and he stabbed the Connect button.

"Agent Coulter."

"Cal, it's Peyton. I examined that wedding gown that Ms. Monroe was forced to wear. It was store bought, not homemade like the others."

Cal's detective instincts snapped to alert. "You're sure?"

"Absolutely. There's a label inside. It's a designer imitation. I checked around, and it was purchased from a bridal store."

"He didn't make any other purchases?"

"No. And the CSI team didn't find any garters or other dresses in his house." She hesitated. "There's more. The white van that deputy found—it belonged to Dyer."

So he had tried to run them off the road.

But he'd used his bare hands to try and strangle Mona, not a garter. Although he had had a rose.

"The day he bought this dress was the same day the second victim died," Peyton continued. "I spoke with a hotel clerk who confirms he spent the night in Knoxville that evening. So he couldn't have killed Constance Gilroy."

Cal cursed. Dyer had taken photos from the Internet for his wall and studied them so he could replicate the crime scene, and forced Mona into that wedding dress to throw off the cops. To make them believe that the Bride Killer had murdered her so no one would suspect him.

If Chance Dyer wasn't the Bride Killer, that meant the bastard was still out there.

♦ ♦ ♦

Unable to sleep for thinking about Cal, Mona went to her dresser and picked up the baby bootie charm.

Cal might have found the Bride Killer, but she still needed answers about her past.

She'd studied human behavior and counseling enough to know she had trust issues because her adopted parents hadn't told her the truth, and she hadn't learned it until they were gone. And now Brent and Cal had both lied to her.

Her phone buzzed, and she glanced at the caller ID. Cal.

Her chest tightened. Part of her wanted to answer it. But what could he say that would possibly justify his lies?

If you didn't have trust, you had nothing.

The phone rolled over to voice mail and she listened. "Mona, I know you don't want to talk to me, but please listen. Chance was not the Bride Killer. I have reason to believe the killer's still at large, so be careful." A hesitation. "I'm sorry," he said, this time his voice gruffer than normal. "I didn't mean to hurt you. Please call me. We need to talk."

Mona squeezed her eyes shut to stem more tears, his words echoing in her head. Chance wasn't the Bride Killer.

Did his sister, Sylvia, know that?

She remembered the anguish in the woman's eyes when they'd met. Sylvia had known who she was at the time.

Another person who'd lied to her . . .

Yet Sylvia had been a victim of Brent's lies as well. Mona couldn't let her continue thinking her brother was a serial killer.

She hurriedly dressed, grabbed her purse, and threw on her coat, then rushed outside. Ten minutes later, she debated the wisdom of her decision to visit Sylvia. But the first time she'd seen her at the project housing, she'd sensed a troubled soul. And then the session when she'd visited Mona had connected them.

Sylvia had just lost her brother. She might blame *her*.

Still, she had to tell her the truth anyway.

Sylvia didn't deserve to think Chance had murdered all those women.

Before she even knocked on the door, it opened, and Sylvia stood on the other side.

For a moment, the two of them simply stood there, too full of pain and anger to speak. Then the baby in her arms cooed, and as Sylvia rocked him back and forth, Mona's anger evaporated. This child was innocent.

And now he would grow up without a father.

"I was going to come and see you," Sylvia said, her voice raw with tears.

Mona twisted her hands together. "I didn't know about you or . . . your son."

Sylvia cradled the baby closer. "I know that now. And . . . I'm so sorry about Chance. He was always overprotective, but I never dreamed he'd try to hurt you."

"I'm sorry he was shot," Mona said, her eyes still glued to Sylvia's baby. Brent's son.

The wind whipped up leaves and made the wind chimes on the porch clang. Sylvia smoothed the blanket around the infant. "Do you want to come in?"

Mona shook her head, then remembered the reason she'd come "I received a message from C—Agent Coulter. He doesn't believe Chance killed those other women. I . . . thought you'd want to know."

Sylvia's lower lip quivered, fresh tears pricking her eyes. "Thank you for that."

Mona nodded. She didn't know what else to say. She turned to leave, but Sylvia called her name, and she turned to face her. "I see why he fell in love with you," she said in a quiet voice.

Mona tensed, suddenly despising Brent for what he'd done to both of them. "And I see why he loved you." She smiled at the woman, and Sylvia smiled back.

If they'd met under different circumstances they might have been friends. It was possible they still could be.

But right now they both needed time to heal, so she walked back to her car.

She'd made peace with Brent's real wife. Now she had to make peace with herself for being foolish enough to fall for his lies.

♦ ♦ ♦

Anna was frantic. She had to find Josie.

She ran outside to her car, started the engine, and drove away from the house she hated and the father she despised.

She couldn't even blame his hateful attitude and cruel words on the brain tumor. He might have been sheriff and thought his job was to protect the citizens, but he'd always been a bastard to her.

And now he'd hurt her daughter.

Poor Josie. She'd misunderstood everything.

And now she'd run off. She probably felt alone and confused and betrayed.

It was a mistake to have come back.

She drove down the mountain road into town, searching the side roads, the stores, and businesses for her daughter's car. Not at the coffee shop. Or the bookstore.

Damn.

Her father had torn her and Johnny apart, locked Johnny up, and made sure he went to prison. He'd also made her doubt his innocence.

She hated him most of all for that. She hated herself even more.

But she'd been pregnant and scared, and traumatized by Johnny's arrest. The town gossip had made it worse. All those accusations.

Then that Charlene girl had come forward and claimed Johnny had tried to strangle her, and Anna had relented to her father's demands and gone away.

She had to explain the truth to Josie. Make her understand.

Beg her forgiveness.

She checked the library parking lot, the diner, the bar. Not that Josie frequented bars, but she had been upset, and she might have decided to have a drink.

But she wasn't in any of those places.

Good heavens. Where was she? They hadn't been in Graveyard Falls long enough for her to have made friends. Anna called the numbers of two of Josie's friends back home, but neither one had heard from her.

Anna turned down a side street, once again searching the businesses and streets for Josie's car. But she didn't see it anywhere.

Where could she be?

The truth hit her, hard and unsettling. She'd probably read Anna's heartfelt entries about Johnny's prison sentence in the diary.

If Josie thought that Johnny was her father, maybe she'd gone to meet him.

Nerves knotted her shoulders.

If Josie went to see Johnny, Anna needed to be there to explain things to both of them. And she'd finally be forced to tell Johnny the truth.

♦ ♦ ♦

He carried Josie inside the cabin, his heart beating so fast it was roaring in his ears.

"Look, Mama. I found her. The woman I'm going to marry." He traced a finger over Josie's cheek, memorizing her soft features. Her skin felt so delicate and soft. Her eyelashes fluttered as she tried to open her eyes. The stun gun had knocked her out so quickly that she'd fallen into his arms.

"She's perfect, isn't she?" he asked his mother.

"Yes, she might be." The brunt of her illness strained her voice. "But she has to pass the tests."

"I know. You can start the lessons right away." He gently laid her on the sofa so he could look at her while she slept.

A second later, though, Josie opened her eyes and saw him. She looked confused and disoriented, then she tried to sit up and realized her hands and feet were bound, and she began to scream.

CHAPTER TWENTY-EIGHT

Cal gripped the phone with clammy hands as Deputy Kimball filled him in. "I got a lead on those wedding dresses. I spoke to a woman who does alterations out of her home, and she said a lady who lives out on Deer Park Road might know who made them. I'm on my way there now to speak to her."

"Let me know what you find out."

Cal's phone was buzzing that he had another call, and he connected it. "Agent Coulter."

"This is Pastor Hopwood at the First Baptist Church in Graveyard Falls."

Cal frowned. "What can I do for you?"

A hesitation. "Well, I'm not certain about this, but I think a woman may have been abducted outside the church a few minutes ago."

Cal's pulse kicked up a notch. "Go on."

"There's a young lady, Josie DuKane. She's Sheriff Buckley's grand-daughter. She came in once before asking about the memorial service for the victims of the Thorn Ripper. She drives a blue Jetta and it's in the parking lot. But it's empty and she's not in the church."

"What makes you think she was kidnapped?"

"I heard a noise, and when I looked out back I saw a man carrying a woman to a pickup."

Cal cursed. "Did you recognize him?"

"No, he was wearing a dark coat and ski cap." He hesitated. "Although I thought it might be the young man who sometimes volunteers to clean the church. His name is Billy."

Cal's pulse clamored. Billy the taxidermist. He was waiting on an address. "Do you know where he lives?"

"No, somewhere in the mountains."

"Describe the truck for me."

"Black. Rusted. Old. I don't know the license plate."

"I'm on my way." Cal rushed to his vehicle, then headed to the little church. "You said the man was carrying the woman?"

"Yes, it looked as if she was unconscious."

He barreled around the corner, tires screeching, and pulled into the parking lot. The pastor was waiting by the Jetta.

Cal yanked on gloves, then glanced inside the car to search for clues.

The preacher gestured toward the ground by the driver's door. "I found her keys and purse in the dirt."

The scene was reading like an abduction, all right. Cal checked inside the purse and found her cell phone, then scrolled through until he spotted a contact she'd named Mom.

He punched the number, hating to alarm a family member, but he needed to know if this was an emergency.

A female voice answered. "Hello, Josie, where are you?"

"I'm sorry, Anna, but this is Agent Cal Coulter."

"Oh, God," the woman said, panic in her voice. "What's wrong? Why are you calling on my daughter's phone?"

Cal gritted his teeth. "Ma'am, I don't want to scare you, but I'm at the First Baptist Church. Your daughter's car was found here abandoned, her purse and keys still here."

"Oh, God . . ." Anna's voice broke.

"I thought you might know where she is."

"No, she left the house upset. We had an argument. I'm out driving around looking for her."

"Does she have a friend in town, someone she might meet up with?"

"No, we're just here temporarily."

"So she doesn't have any male friends? One who drives a truck?"

"No," Anna cried. "What's this about a truck?"

Cal inhaled sharply. "I . . . the pastor thinks she was abducted."

A sob caught in her throat. "My God, you don't think that crazy killer got her, do you?"

Unfortunately, that's exactly what he thought.

Mona was relieved she'd made peace with Sylvia and her son. Forgiveness and acceptance were part of the healing process. Holding on to hatred and bitterness would only hold her back.

She steered her car toward her house, but her cell phone buzzed, startling her. Cal.

She clenched her jaw, still furious with him, and let it go to voice mail. A second later, she listened to the message, her chest clenching at the sound of his worried voice. "Mona, I think the Bride Killer has another victim. Her name is Josie DuKane. She's the sheriff's granddaughter."

Mona swerved and nearly ran off the road. Josie—Anna's daughter. Anna, who'd confessed she'd been in love with the Thorn Ripper.

Anna, who must be crazy with fear now.

She steered the vehicle toward the radio station. If Chance wasn't the Bride Killer, and the man who'd called in was, maybe she could convince him to talk to her.

It might be Josie's only chance.

Josie tried to recall tips she'd heard from news stories about how women had survived abduction. But fear clogged her thoughts.

She'd heard the man's mother call him Billy.

He was crazy. Delusional.

Worse, the house smelled like rotting eggs and body waste and . . . death.

Her eye caught something in the corner, and bile rose to her throat. A wedding dress. Ivory lace, pearl buttons, taffeta skirt . . .

He was the Bride Killer.

"Mama says you have to cook something for me." He scrubbed his hand through his hair, sending the dull brown ends sticking out. "That's your first test. Then we'll see how good you are at cleaning."

Josie swallowed revulsion as she looked at Billy's mother in that wheelchair. The poor woman—

"Did you hear me?" Billy dragged Josie up to stand, but her feet and hands were bound, and she stumbled. He caught her, then cradled her face between his hands. "It's all right now, Josie. I love you. I want to make you my wife." He frowned and turned to his mother.

"What, Mama?"

"Billy, please," Josie said in a choked voice. "This is not the way to win my love. Why don't we go out on a date? We could go to dinner—"

His eyes clouded over for a moment as if he was considering her idea, but then he jerked his head back toward his mother. "No, Mama says I need a wife who can cook for me."

Hysteria threatened to immobilize Josie, but she forced herself to remain calm. Maybe if she stalled long enough, her mother would realize she was missing and come looking for her.

God . . . she'd been so angry with her. What if she died and never got to tell her she was sorry? That she loved her no matter what? That even if her mother had lied to her, she'd forgive her because that's what families did.

Her mind raced. He wanted her to cook. "All right, Billy, let me make you an apple pie. I have a recipe I'm sure you and your mother will love." If he gave her a knife to chop the apples, she could use it on him.

"I do like apple pie," Billy said. He leaned over to talk to his mother. "What, Mama? You're right. She should make biscuits and gravy. Anyone can make an apple pie."

"But mine is special," Josie said quickly. "I add a little bourbon to it."

Billy's nostrils flared. "Mama said good girls don't drink whiskey. I thought you went to church."

Tears of fear clogged her throat. "I'm sorry, I didn't mean to offend your mother. I do go to church and I pray every day." She was praying now, praying she'd survive.

Billy grabbed her arm and ushered her over to the kitchen counter. She struggled with the ropes. "I can't cook with my feet and hands tied."

"Yes, you can." Billy dragged a bag of flour from the cabinet below, then a rolling pin from the drawer, and set a carton of buttermilk on the counter. "These better be good," Billy said. "Mama loves biscuits." He turned on the radio. "I hope you like church music. Mama used to sing in church before she got so sick."

"I like to sing, too," Josie said, desperate to befriend him.

But instead of music, the radio counselor's voice echoed from the speaker.

"This is Mona Monroe talking to you live."

Billy tensed. He looked panicked at the sound of Mona's voice, as if he thought the police might be onto him.

Maybe they were.

Josie had to stay alive long enough for them to find her.

He moved up behind Josie, sweat trickling down his neck. "Show me you're the one, Josie."

"I will." Josie began to hum "I'll Fly Away" beneath her breath as she scooped flour into the bowl. She'd play along for now. If she could get close to a kitchen knife, she might be able to free herself and fight back.

◆ ◆ ◆

"The last time we talked, many of you expressed concern over the recent murders in Graveyard Falls," Mona began. "I understand your concerns, and if anyone has information regarding those deaths, please call the police." She took a deep breath. "I just learned another woman may have been abducted. Her name is Josie DuKane. Her mother, Anna, is terrified that something bad has happened to her, so if you've seen this young woman or know anything about her disappearance, please call the police. I also want to make a plea to the man who phoned before. He calls himself Will. If you're listening, please call me."

The phones started buzzing, the switchboard lighting up. Mona gritted her teeth. Chance should be here to handle this, but he was dead.

That meant no screening of calls.

She connected the first caller. "Hello, this is Mona."

"Are you talking about Anna Buckley, Sheriff Buckley's daughter?"

Mona tightened her fingers around the phone. "Yes."

"Anna dated that awful boy Johnny Pike who killed those girls at the falls."

Mona sighed. "Do you have information that might help locate her daughter?"

"Maybe she should ask Johnny. She covered for him years ago. Maybe he has a protégé trying to copycat his crimes."

They had already considered that theory.

The caller hung up, and she connected the next call. "This is Mona Monroe."

"Perhaps Anna Buckley turned into a killer herself. I always thought she might have helped that Pike boy."

Mona gritted her teeth again. No wonder Anna had had to leave town and change her name. "I'm sure the police questioned her and eliminated her as a suspect."

"The police?" A sardonic chuckle followed. "Hell, Anna's daddy was the law back then. He arrested the Pike boy and could easily have covered for his daughter. No way he'd let his precious girl go to jail."

"Thanks for your thoughts," Mona said. "I have someone else on the line." She connected the next caller. "This is Mona."

"I never believed Johnny killed those girls," the caller said.

"Why do you say that?" Mona asked.

"Cause he was tenderhearted. I taught him biology and he got upset when we killed the frogs we had to dissect."

She wasn't sure that meant he couldn't have killed the girls. "If you think he didn't do it, do you have any idea who did?"

"Not really. I just thought he got railroaded, that's all. I don't think the sheriff ever looked at anyone else."

The woman ended the call, and Mona clicked to answer another one. "This is Mona."

"I was friends with Johnny back then," a man said. "I didn't think he was guilty. Everyone liked Johnny. He wasn't cocky or stuck up like some of the other popular kids."

"Was he involved with the girls who were killed?"

"Not really. He dated them a couple of times, but then he dropped them and started seeing Anna Buckley." The man made a low sound in his throat. "He was in love with her. Told me he planned to marry her someday."

Instead he'd gone to prison for life.

"I always thought the sheriff framed him," the man said.

"Why would he do that?" Mona asked.

"Because he was real protective of his daughter. He didn't want her dating anyone, and all the guys at school knew it."

Mona massaged her temple. If the sheriff had framed Johnny, and Johnny was innocent, who had killed those teenagers?

◆ ◆ ◆

Sheriff Buckley cursed as he listened to that damn radio show. Some folks still thought Pike was innocent.

And his daughter . . . Anna . . . she'd torn out of here like a bat out of hell.

But that woman Mona's voice reverberated in his ears. She'd said Josie was missing.

That was what had Anna so upset.

Josie was his granddaughter, only he couldn't look at her for thinking about what had happened back then.

About those girls' faces staring up at him in death.

About those roses and the thorns that had ripped at their tongues and throats when they'd cried for help.

About her father . . .

He might have crossed the line, but he'd done what he had to do. And he couldn't turn back now.

◆　◆　◆

Johnny paced his cell, his shoulders and body knotted with agitation.

The moment he'd seen the article about the Bride Killer, he'd had a bad feeling it would somehow all lead back to him. That fingers would point at him again even though he'd been locked up for nearly three decades.

And it had. Already that one Fed had come to see him.

If it was up to Sheriff Buckley, he'd do whatever he could to tie the two together and use this to tack on the death penalty to his sentence.

He needed to tell his side of the story.

But who would listen to him? They hadn't believed him years ago when he'd denied pushing those girls off the falls. Even Anna had doubted him in the end.

That had hurt the most.

He leaned his head against the bars and fought back a guttural howl at the injustice. God, he'd loved her.

Hell, he still did. Of course he was stuck in time because he'd been trapped in this damn hellhole.

But she'd moved on. She'd married. Had a daughter.

But now that daughter was missing.

He'd heard the guards talking about it. Anna must be terrified.

If only there was something he could do . . .

He gripped the bars with clammy hands and stared at his bruised and battered knuckles. He'd learned how to fight hard in here. Had resorted to acts he wasn't proud of.

Had become the animal they'd said he was.

But . . . none of that mattered. Only saving Anna's daughter did . . .

The reporter had written that this damned lunatic dressed his first victim in a wedding gown. A homemade one. And the guards had been talking about a second victim. They were calling the case the Bride Killer.

A memory nagged at him, distant. Disturbing.

Was it possible the same person who'd framed him was killing again? If so, he had a good idea who it was. He'd wanted to tell the police years ago, but he'd remained silent, caught in a vicious trap. All to protect Anna.

"Guard!" he shouted. "I need to make a phone call."

The guard strode over, one hand stroking his baton. "Ain't your time."

Johnny balled his hands into fists. "It's important I talk to that FBI agent who came to see me. Agent Coulter."

A nasty chuckle reverberated from the guard, his eyes sneering at Johnny. "You know who this Bride Killer is?"

"Maybe," Johnny said. He was finally going to tell the truth. The whole truth.

It was something he should have done years ago.

But he'd kept his mouth shut to keep Anna safe.

Now at least three other women might have died because of it.

CHAPTER
TWENTY-NINE

Cal tried to banish the image of Josie DuKane lying dead at Graveyard Falls as he drove to Anna's. He had to stop this maniac before he killed her. If he wasn't already too late . . .

He parked and hurried to the door. When she let him in, Anna wrapped her arms around her waist as if to hold herself together, but he sensed she was teetering on the edge of hysterical panic.

His phone buzzed. He was surprised to see the number for the state penitentiary and answered immediately. "Agent Coulter."

"This is Warden Brisbin at the state pen. One of our prisoners says he needs to talk to you right away."

Cal's pulse jumped. "Let me guess. Johnny Pike?"

"Yes. He claims he has information about the Bride Killer."

"Did he give you a name?"

"No." The warden grunted. "He doesn't trust anyone here. He says he'll only speak with you."

Cal raked a hand through his hair. "Do you think this is some kind of stunt to get attention?"

"I don't know," Warden Brisbin said. "But in all the years Pike's been here, he still claims he was framed."

Cal considered that possibility. If so, the person who'd framed him might be killing again. But why would he have lain low all these years, then started up again now?

"I'll be there as soon as possible to talk to him." Cal hung up and turned to Anna. "Johnny Pike wants to talk to me about these murders."

Pain and hope mingled on Anna's face. "I'm going with you."

"I'm not sure that's a good idea."

Anna gripped his arm. "I don't care what you think. My daughter is missing, and if Johnny knows something about who took her, then I have to see him."

Cal didn't have time to argue.

The Bride Killer hadn't held his victims long before he'd strangled them. Josie might already be dead.

He watched Josie lift the biscuit pan from the oven, his heart pounding with hope. He'd untied her feet so she could move around and make the meal, and she surprised him. She actually knew how to cook.

The biscuits were golden brown and fluffy, and she'd even fried chicken. Fried chicken was his favorite. Besides the stews.

"Watch out for her," his mama said in a frail voice. "She looks like a sly one."

Why was Mama always finding fault with the girls he brought home? Just like she'd found fault with him all these years.

Sure, she'd loved him and cuddled him, but she hadn't spared the rod either. She'd beaten him plenty of times for disrespecting her, and if she wasn't so damn weak she'd do it again.

But he wouldn't disrespect her. He loved her.

Tears nearly choked his throat. He couldn't believe she was dying and going to leave him all alone.

You're not alone. You have Josie now.

Josie stirred the gravy, and his mouth watered at the smell. "Look, Mama, Josie made my favorite meal."

Josie looked over at his mother, nerves flickering in her eyes. "Yes, I did. I hope you'll like it. Can I bring you a plate?"

His heart soared again. She was so nice to his mama. Yes, she was the one.

"Mama will eat with us at the table," Billy said.

Josie's fingers curled around the handle of the cast-iron skillet. "Of course, dear, whatever you say."

He smiled and wheeled his mother over to the table. Gently, he laid one hand on her bony shoulder. "Smells delicious, doesn't it, Mama?"

She sniffed. "I suppose so. But I don't have much of an appetite."

"Maybe you'll feel stronger when you eat a little bit," Josie said.

"She's right, Mama." He unfolded her napkin and spread it across her lap. "Maybe you'll even get well."

Josie started toward the table with the biscuits, but he took the pan from her and set them on the stove. His hand brushed her soft skin, and his body hardened.

Yes, Josie would feed his belly and his other needs, too. He couldn't wait to run his fingers through those long strands of hair and pump himself inside her.

He felt a drop of semen leaking from the tip of his penis and dampening his jeans at the thought.

"What would you like to drink, Mama? Tea?"

She murmured, "Of course," and Josie took the pitcher and poured a jelly jar half full, then set it in front of his mother. "You want me to serve you now?"

"My son can do that," his mama said.

He wanted to shake his mama for the way she was talking to Josie. He really liked this girl.

But he couldn't hurt his mother, especially when she was already suffering so much. He had to hold on to every minute they had left.

He stepped over to the stove and filled a plate with a chicken breast, mashed potatoes, and two biscuits, then spooned gravy over the potatoes. He was just about to carry it to his mother when Josie picked up the frying pan.

A second later, he jumped back with a howl. Hot gravy flew all over him, scalding his face and arms, and he dropped his mama's plate.

Josie threw the pan at him, turned, and ran toward the door. He bellowed her name and lunged for her just as she reached the doorknob. Her hands were still bound, but she swung them at him and jabbed his face with her fingernails.

He yelled in pain, snatched her hair, and flung her back across the room. Her head hit the hearth, and she fell to the floor, her head lolling to the side.

"I told you not to trust her," Mama murmured.

He reached his hand back and slapped his mama, something he'd never done. Her head whipped backward, shock widening her eyes.

An instant later, he crawled over to her and tugged at her hand. "I'm so sorry, Mama. Please forgive me." Sometimes his rage got out of control, and he couldn't stop himself.

Her bones creaked as she laid one hand on the back of his head and looked into his eyes. "You're a bad boy, son. You have to be punished."

"It was her fault," he cried. "I loved her but she tried to get away."

"You know what you have to do now."

He nodded mutely. Josie wasn't the one after all.

It was time to take her to the falls.

Cal pushed the speed limit as he and Anna drove toward the state pen. She'd phoned her father twice to ask him if Josie had come home, but he hadn't answered.

Cal was tempted to put an APB out on the former sheriff. But he had a feeling Pike knew something that would help. And Josie's life might depend on what that was. Had he been in contact with the Bride Killer? Maybe the unsub had sent him photos or written to him.

Although, if so, Peyton would have found something by now . . .

"What if Johnny really was innocent?" Anna asked. "I abandoned him just like everyone else."

"I'm sure you did what you thought was right," Cal said.

Anna bit her lip and turned to look out the window at the passing scenery. "I did what my father told me to do," she said in a bitter voice. "Not what I thought was right. If I'd done that, I would have stuck by Johnny and . . ."

"And what?"

Anna wiped at a tear. "And I would have stood up to my father."

"But the evidence was damning," Cal said.

"Johnny insisted someone planted it."

Cal considered everything he knew so far and the people involved.

Her father had hated Johnny. And he was the one person who had the knowledge and skill to frame Johnny.

Sheriff Buckley may have sent the wrong man to prison to keep his daughter from running off. Or to protect someone else.

Like himself.

Josie's ears rang from where her head had hit the brick, but she blinked rapidly to try to focus. She couldn't just lie here. She had to get away.

She struggled to get to her feet, but she was so dizzy the room spun around like a merry-go-round.

"I thought you were different," Billy wailed. "That you were kind and good and would treat me and Mama right."

Billy had his head on his mother's shoulder now, soaking in her comfort.

Josie blinked again and scanned the room in search of a weapon. Maybe if she could reach that fire poker on the other side of the hearth . . .

But her gaze caught sight of a framed photograph on the table, and her heart tripped a beat. The man in the photo looked young, high school age, and was wearing a football uniform. He had short dark hair and was smiling, a football tucked beneath his arm.

It was Johnny Pike.

The same boy she'd seen in her mother's yearbook, the same boy her mother had been in love with years ago.

The same boy she thought could be her father.

Confusion clouded her brain. Why would Billy's mother have a picture of Johnny when he was in high school? Had they been friends?

He wiped at his tears and kissed his mother's cheek. "I know, Mama, I'll take care of her."

Cold terror seized Josie. She had to do something.

Desperate, she pointed to the picture. "Who is this, Billy?"

He wiped his nose on the back of his sleeve. For a moment he looked disoriented, as if she'd caught him off guard or his mind had drifted to another place.

Josie tried to soften her voice to keep him calm. "Do you know him?"

Billy's big chubby face softened, and he took the framed picture, then traced his fingers over the boy's face. "That's my daddy."

Josie's throat closed. "Johnny Pike is your father?"

He bobbed his head up and down. "He's kind of famous around these parts. But he had to go away before I was born."

Nausea flooded Josie. Yeah, he'd gone away because he was a serial killer.

And now his son was following in his footsteps.

CHAPTER THIRTY

Sweat trickled down Billy's neck. He so wanted Josie to be the one. He needed her. He wanted her.

He didn't want to be alone.

Josie was looking at him oddly, her face pale, her eyes big. "You're sure Johnny Pike was your father?"

He thought he saw blood in her pretty hair and hated that. But she had tried to run.

"Is he your father?" Josie asked again.

"Yes, just ask Mama." Why did Josie care who his father was? He whipped his head toward his mother. "Tell her about him, Mama."

But his mother had clammed up. Her head was slumped over, her face mottled with dark-purple blotches.

When she didn't answer him, panic bubbled in his chest. "Mama, tell her about Daddy!"

"Billy, listen to me," Josie said, her voice shaking. "That man Johnny Pike—he's in prison for the Thorn Ripper murders."

He narrowed his eyes. "I know that. Mama told me all about him. And she told me all about those girls, the whores who wanted Johnny."

He angled his head toward his mother, but she remained silent, her lips pinched and cracked like leather, eyes bulging in their sockets the way animals' did in death.

Terrified, he ran over to her wheelchair and touched her hand. Ice cold. Her skin felt cracked, dry, brittle.

No! She couldn't have died and left him yet. He hadn't gotten his bride. She was supposed to stay until then.

"Mama, please talk to me," he pleaded as he grabbed her shoulders and shook her. "You can't leave me alone."

Her head tilted back, but a tiny bit of air puffed out. She was breathing.

Fear and helplessness engulfed him, and he cried out an animal sound that echoed through the room. A sound that wasn't human, the sound of his heart being ripped out.

It wouldn't be long. He was going to lose her.

He spun toward Josie, hissing his rage. "You did this. You're killing Mama!"

Josie started to shake her head, but he lunged toward her.

"You're killing her, and I don't want to be alone."

"No," Josie said in a choked voice. "You can't kill me, Billy."

His fingers tightened, digging into her larynx. "Yes, I can, you have to die just like the others."

"But you won't be alone, Billy. Not anymore. Johnny Pike was my father, too." She gasped. "I'm your sister."

Billy gaped at her in shock. Sister? He had a sister?

How was that possible? Why hadn't Mama told him?

Cal and Anna relinquished their cell phones to the officer at the visitors' desk and made their way through security. Anna kept fidgeting, twisting her hands together, obviously nervous.

Cal wanted to offer her comfort, but at this point, he had no idea if her daughter was alive or dead.

Due to the seriousness of the situation and the fact that Pike had asked them here to discuss the Bride Killer, the warden arranged a private room for them to talk.

Of course a guard stayed in the room, and Johnny remained handcuffed and shackled. Anna's face paled at the sight of the man in the orange jumpsuit.

And the way he looked at her—any fool could see Pike was still in love with Anna. Emotions darkened his face as he soaked in her features. "Anna, you came," he said brokenly.

Anna's expression mirrored Pike's. Pain, grief, and the love they'd once shared mingled in the tense silence.

Cal gave them a moment to absorb the shock of seeing each other after all these years. But just a minute.

Every second counted. Josie could be fighting for her last breath that very moment.

"My daughter, Josie, he has her," Anna whispered. "I can't lose her, Johnny."

A muscle ticked in Johnny's jaw, but he sank into the chair, his handcuffs clinking against the table.

Anna stared at them, a tear trickling down her cheek.

Cal cleared his throat. "You said you have information regarding the Bride Killer?"

"Do you know who he is?" Anna said in a raw whisper.

Johnny rubbed at a scar above his eye. "I don't know for sure. But . . . I have an idea."

Irritation knotted Cal's shoulders. "Look, Pike, don't waste our time. Have you been in communication with him?" His voice hardened. "Did you mentor him?"

Pike's eyes turned stormy. "No, and no."

Cal stood abruptly. "Then what the hell did you call me for?"

"Because . . . I . . ." He rubbed the scar again, his voice cracking. "I have my suspicions."

"Please, Johnny." Anna reached out to touch his hand. The guard shook his head, but Cal flashed him a look. They needed to use everything in their power to persuade Pike to talk.

"Tell me."

Johnny's cold mask faded. "It goes back to the murders I was accused of."

"You mean the ones you were convicted of," Cal pointed out.

Johnny nodded again. "I didn't kill those girls. I . . . swear I didn't."

"I never believed you did," Anna whispered.

"God," Johnny muttered.

Cal didn't know whether he believed him, but he had to play along. "If you didn't kill them, who did?"

Johnny made a guttural sound in his throat. "I don't have proof. She set me up good."

Anna gasped. "*She?* Who are you talking about?"

"There was this girl back then, she was homely. Her father abused her. She had a crush on me, and one night I saw her on the side of the road, stranded. I felt sorry for her and gave her a ride home. She said she was scared of her old man, and begged me to come in, and I did. But she must have drugged me because the next morning I woke up and . . . I didn't remember what happened."

Cal cleared his throat. "What did happen?"

Johnny's jaw clenched. "We must have had sex," he said. "I . . . was ashamed that it happened. I felt like a fool and I . . . was too embarrassed to tell anyone." He raised his gaze to Anna. "My father was pressuring me to get that scholarship, and I knew he'd go off the deep end. Pikes didn't go around getting drugged and raped by women."

Cal heaved a breath. "Then what happened?"

"I thought it was done. I tried to put it behind me and I avoided her. But then all that business about prom came up, and the guys were supposed to buy a rose for the girl they wanted to ask."

"You sent notes to each of the victims inviting them to the falls under the pretense of giving them that rose," Cal pointed out.

Johnny flattened his scarred hands on the table. "I didn't send any notes."

Cal considered the possibility. Three decades ago, handwriting and DNA analysis were practically nonexistent. But if Buckley had kept those notes in evidence, Cal could have them compared to Pike's handwriting.

Johnny swiped his handcuffed hands across his forehead with a sigh of despair. "Then the murders started, and it made me nervous. I'd dated each of the girls at one time." He looked at Anna. "Before you." He swallowed hard. "I loved you so much, Anna. I was afraid she'd hurt you, too."

Anna made a strangled sound in her throat. "That's the reason you sent me away when I came to visit you. You said that I would be safer if I never saw you again."

Johnny's eyes flickered with desperation. "She would have killed you, too. I couldn't take a chance on that."

Anna gripped his hands, tears glittering on her eyelashes.

"What made you think this girl was the killer?" Cal asked.

"Little things she said when no one else was listening."

"Like what?" Cal asked.

"'You're mine, Johnny. No one can have you but me.' Shit like that." He sighed. "And then some of my stuff went missing. At first, it was just a hunch, a kind of sick feeling. I thought maybe I was wrong, and I felt sorry for her."

Cal's brows shot up. "You felt sorry for the girl who drugged you and supposedly raped you?"

Johnny shot Cal a sharp look. "I know that sounds weird, but when I met her father, he was a big, mean, drunk bully who abused her."

Anna made an anguished sound. "But when they arrested you, why didn't you mention her? At least you might have convinced the jury of reasonable doubt."

Johnny clung to Anna's hands. "Because she told me she was pregnant with my baby."

Anna choked out a shocked gasp. "Maybe she was lying . . ."

"She sent me pictures later in prison. She had a little boy." He coughed. "I . . . thought about telling someone, trying to get the kid away from her, but what could I do in here? My parents deserted me. They wouldn't have wanted a child they thought came out of all this." He looked into her eyes. "And then she threatened to hurt you, Anna."

"I would have been fine," Anna argued.

"Maybe. But she'd already killed three people, Anna. I couldn't take the chance."

"What was the girl's name?" Cal asked.

"Charlene Linder," Johnny said.

Anna sighed. "I remember her. She was odd, a little off mentally."

"I know. I should have done something to save the little boy from her, but when I saw the picture, I just didn't see myself in him. Then I started doubting everything she'd said, except for the threat against you."

"Oh, Johnny," Anna whispered.

Johnny scrubbed his hand over his face. "I told your father all this, but he accused me of lying, and when my attorney asked him about it, he said he'd questioned Charlene and she claimed I tried to strangle her. Of course your father believed her. He said some other girl named Felicity Hacker also claimed that I attacked her."

"Felicity Hacker?" Anna said.

Johnny muttered a frustrated sound. "I don't really even remember her, but she was friends with Tiffany, Brittany, and Candy."

"He said, she said," Cal commented.

Johnny nodded. "There was so much evidence stacked against me that no one believed me." A muscle ticked in his jaw as he looked at Anna. "Even you started to doubt me."

Regret and sorrow flashed in Anna's eyes. "Oh, Johnny . . . I never really thought you did it. It was just my father . . . and . . . I was so scared. He was so sure you were guilty, and everyone thought I covered for you."

Cal drummed his fingers on the table. "So what does this have to do with the current murders and the Bride Killer?"

Johnny lifted his eyes to Cal, but his look was tortured. "Charlene's mother was a seamstress. She sewed wedding dresses, and Charlene used to help her. That night I was there she showed me a dress, and said she was working on her own dress, the one she intended to wear when she married me."

♦ ♦ ♦

Shock filled Anna. Johnny had a son with another woman. With Charlene Linder, the girl he suspected of murder.

The girl who'd framed him and stolen his life.

Stolen both their lives.

"You think Charlene is the Bride Killer?" Cal asked. "But why would she start killing again after all this time? She can't be strong enough to have carried the victims to the falls by herself."

Johnny made a low sound in his throat. "I don't know. But when I saw the article about the Toyton woman being found in a wedding dress and heard the guards talking about another victim it made me think about Charlene. She was abused, emotionally unstable. What if she abused the boy? He would be thirty now."

"He could be following in his mother's footsteps. There are similarities in the MOs." Cal reached for his cell phone, then remembered they'd turned them in at security. "I'll get a warrant and find out where she lives. If she and her son have Josie, we'll find them."

He hurried from the room, and Anna laid her hands over Johnny's. She'd waited so long to see him, had yearned for him forever. And now here he was, offering a suspect who could clear him and set him free.

And hopefully help them find Josie.

"Johnny, I . . . I'm sorry I left town and didn't come to see you. I . . . didn't want to go."

Johnny shrugged. "I understand. I mean, back then I was angry and hurt, but you had your life ahead of you and I couldn't blame you for not wanting to be saddled with a felon."

Tears clogged her throat as the painful memories bombarded her. "That's not why I left," Anna said softly.

Confusion clouded Johnny's eyes as he looked at her. He had aged, and so had she. But he was still the boy she loved.

The only man she'd ever loved.

"I know how your father was," he said.

"That was hard, and he tried every way possible to make me hate you," she admitted. "But that wasn't the real reason I left." She took a deep breath for courage. "You see, Johnny, I was pregnant, too."

Johnny paled. "What?"

A sob escaped Anna. "I was pregnant. When my father found out, he forced me to leave town so no one would know I was carrying your baby."

Mona had ended her show and was just about to leave the station when another call came in. She snatched it up, anxious for information that might help the police find Anna's daughter.

"This is Mona."

"Mona, you have to help me." A heavy breath rattled over the line.

"Talk to me, then."

"Josie was supposed to be the one, but now everything's all wrong."

Mona forced her voice to be level. "Josie is with you now?"

"Yes, but it's all messed up. She says she's my sister."

"Your sister?"

"Yes," he said brokenly. "Johnny Pike is my daddy, and she says he's her daddy, too!"

Mona's heart raced. "Let me come to you. Please just tell me where you are, and I'll help you."

"No, I'm scared."

"It'll be all right. Tell me where to meet you."

Tension vibrated between them, his breathing unsteady. Then he finally mumbled an address.

"Hang on, Will, I'll be right there. Just don't hurt Josie."

But a second later, a female scream pierced the air.

CHAPTER THIRTY-ONE

Mona punched Cal's number. As much as she didn't want to talk to him or see him, it was foolish to meet this killer on her own.

She couldn't ignore his plea for help or the fact that he was unbalanced and could kill Josie any minute. If there was a chance she could save her, she had to try.

Cal's phone buzzed but rolled over to voice mail. She made the turn off the main highway onto the mountain road that, according to her GPS, would lead her to the Bride Killer.

"Cal, it's Mona. I got a call from that man Will. He has Josie. He was distraught and said Josie told him that Johnny Pike is her father. He also said Pike is his father. I convinced him to let me come to him." She hesitated, her tires screeching over black ice as she maneuvered a switchback. "I wanted to wait for you, but I heard Josie scream, and I had to leave. I'm texting you the address."

A beep on his machine cut her off, and she ended the call. Hopefully Cal would get the message soon and be right behind her. She called the sheriff's office as well, but the phone cut out as she lost service ascending into the mountains.

All the Beautiful Brides

The car skidded, and she gripped the steering wheel to maintain control, then veered toward the right onto a gravel road. One hand slid to the gun inside her coat pocket. If she needed it, she'd use it.

The car bounced over potholes as she drove deeper into the woods. Gravel spun behind her tires, spitting into the icy slush. She shifted into low gear to climb the ridge and saw a cabin sitting on a hill in a thicket of trees.

A detached garage held a sign for a taxidermist office, and she swallowed hard as she slowed and parked. The wind caught the handmade wooden sign and swung it wildly, banging it against the side of the building. The office looked closed, though.

She wrapped her coat around her and checked her gun, praying she didn't need it.

Battling nerves, she made her way up the path to the door. Lights burned low inside the cabin. Smoke curled from the chimney into the sky, and wind shook snow from the trees to the ground as she climbed the porch.

She peeked inside the window. A shadow moved, and she heard crying inside.

Josie?

Suddenly a cold, hard hand clamped over her mouth from behind, and she felt something jab her in the back. A gun? A knife?

"Please, don't hurt me, I'm here to help," she said in a muffled whisper.

He shoved the door open and pushed her inside. The first thing she saw was a multitude of dead animals, all preserved, their wide eyes staring at her in the bleak light.

She held her breath as she scanned the room for Josie, then spotted her on the floor tied to the bed next to a pale woman slumped in a wheelchair.

The horrible stench of sickness and decay swirled around her. But it was the shiny jewelry adorning the woman's skeletal frame that made a shudder course up her spine.

They were the souvenirs taken from his victims, and he'd given them to his mother.

♦ ♦ ♦

Cal's blood ran cold when he heard the message from Mona.

Jesus God. She was on her way to meet Charlene's son. Johnny Pike's son.

The man Pike believed was a serial killer just as Charlene was.

He explained to the guard that he needed to get back to the room with Pike, and he escorted him down the hall. When the guard opened the door, Cal saw Anna enclosed in Johnny's arms.

He didn't have time to question what was going on. "Anna, I need to go. Mona is on her way to Charlene's. Her son has Josie."

Pike paled and stepped back from Anna, his handcuffs rattling as he absorbed the news. "Maybe if I went . . ."

Cal shook his head. "Sorry, Pike, but I don't have time to wait for you to get cleared." Besides, he had no proof the man was telling the truth. Although his gut told him Pike had been framed as a kid.

"I'm going with you." Anna stepped toward Cal. "I'm sorry, Johnny. About everything."

"Me too," Pike said. "Just go, save Josie."

Cal reached for the door and Anna followed, both of them silent as the guard led them through the prison to the exit.

They had to hurry.

♦ ♦ ♦

The older woman cried out her son's name, and the man holding Mona choked on a sob. "It's okay, Mama. Everything's gonna be all right."

"Billy," Mona said in a soothing voice, calling him by the name his mother used. "You don't want to hurt me. I'm here to help."

She met Josie's eyes, a silent understanding passing between them. They had to stay calm, keep him calm.

Help was on the way.

At least she prayed it was on the way, that Cal had received her message and was flying toward this place.

"But I wanted to show Mama my bride before she died. She doesn't want me to be alone."

"You're not alone," Josie said. "Remember what I told you. We're sister and brother, Billy. That means we have to take care of each other."

Mona had no idea if what Josie was saying was true, but she admired her courage.

Billy pushed Mona to the floor beside Josie.

Obviously his mother's illness had triggered a psychotic break. He was lost somewhere between reality and his delusions.

"But Mama never told me I had a sister. Why wouldn't she tell me that?"

Billy ran his hands through his hair and began to pull at it, yanking strands from the roots. He seemed oblivious, though. He'd also done it before. Tufts of his hair lay scattered on the floor beside his mother's wheelchair.

"That's because she didn't know," Josie said hurriedly. "My mother was pregnant when Johnny was arrested. Her father, my grandfather, was sheriff back then, and he arrested Johnny. Then he forced her to leave Graveyard Falls to have me so no one in town would know that I was Johnny Pike's illegitimate daughter."

Mona struggled not to gag at the smell and grisly sight of the woman in the wheelchair's deteriorated condition. She should have been in a hospital.

"Tell us about your mother, Billy," Mona said softly. "You obviously love her very much. Did she make the wedding gowns?"

Billy touched the wedding dress hanging on the hook of the bedroom door, then gave her a predatory look. "Yes, she used to sew for other people just like my grandma did."

Billy ran his finger over the sequins lining the bodice of the gown. "She was alone all her life—well, except for me—and she wanted me to have the family she never had."

He removed the hanger holding the gown and turned to Mona, a gleam in his eyes. "I can't marry Josie 'cause she's my sister, but you can be my wife, Mona." He leaned over and kissed the skeletal jaw of his mother's face. "She'll do, Mama. She can be my wife and give me babies. And you and Josie can celebrate with us after we say our vows."

Mona trembled inside as he reached for her hand and pulled her toward the bedroom to change into the dress.

♦ ♦ ♦

Cold fear gripped Cal as he maneuvered down the icy mountain road toward Charlene Linder's cabin.

Once he had this lunatic in custody, he wanted to talk to Felicity Hacker. If she'd lied about Pike's attack it could help Johnny get released.

And the sheriff . . . he'd deal with him, too. He'd railroaded a young man and ruined his life.

Anna clutched the seat with a white-knuckle grip, obviously terrified for her daughter's life and still shaken from her meeting with Pike.

"We'll get to them in time," he said, reassuring himself as much as her.

She nodded mutely, but the tight set of her mouth and her strained face suggested she was desperately praying he was right.

He was praying the same thing.

He'd phoned the deputy and left a message filling him in, and asking for backup. His phone buzzed. Kimball.

"I just talked to a woman from that church sewing circle. She said Charlene specialized in wedding dresses. But Charlene hasn't been to church in weeks. She also mentioned that the son has mental problems.

She suspects abuse in the family running back generations. Thinks Charlene's daddy molested her. He died suddenly. Then she had this baby boy, but there was something weird about their relationship."

Unwanted images played through Cal's head. "So if this man's mother is near death, it could have triggered him to have a breakdown."

"That's what she thought. Said the kid was obsessed with animals when he was little. He's a taxidermist now."

"I saw some of his work at the Boar's Head," Cal said.

"That's his?"

"Yes. I'm almost to the Linder house now."

"I'm on my way."

Cal hung up and veered onto the side road leading to the mountain cabin where Charlene and Billy lived.

"I can't lose Josie," Anna whispered into the darkness. "She's all I've got."

He gave her a sympathetic look. "I have a feeling she's not all—Pike still loves you."

She made a strangled sound. "But how could he ever forgive me for what I did back then? For deserting him?"

He had no answer for that. He wanted Mona's forgiveness more than anything in the world.

But first he had to make sure this madman didn't kill her. Then he'd beg her to give him a chance.

To let him love her the way he'd always loved her in his heart.

He chugged up the winding road past the Boar's Head, then climbed the hill toward the cabin. When he spotted the glow of a lamp in the house and saw smoke curling from the chimney, he cut the lights and shifted to low gear, coasting the rest of the way so he wouldn't alert anyone to his arrival. Mona's Honda was parked by the house.

God, he hoped he was in time.

Anna's breath echoed in the silence as he parked between some trees. "Stay here," he said as he removed his gun and slipped his car door open.

"No way." Anna eased her door open and was sliding out. "This is my daughter we're talking about. I'll do whatever's necessary to save her life."

"I understand," Cal said. "But this man is dangerous, and you have to stay behind me, Anna. I can't be worrying about you if I'm going to take him down."

Anna nodded and fell in step behind him as they inched their way through the sludge to the front porch. Cal raised his finger to warn her to be quiet as he crept up the steps.

When he looked through the curtains in the front window, fear threatened to immobilize him.

Mona was dressed in a wedding gown as she stood beside a big, burly man in front of the glowing fire. Josie was chained to the bed by a skeletal-looking woman obviously near death. He couldn't tell if Josie was hurt, but she appeared to be alive.

And Mona . . . Billy was about to marry her. At least his version of marriage.

But the other women he'd brought home to marry had ended up dead.

Cal reached for the door handle. He didn't intend to let the sick bastard take Mona's life.

CHAPTER THIRTY-TWO

"There's Josie," Anna whispered.

"Shh. We don't want him to know we're here."

Anna stooped behind him. "What are we going to do?"

"Save them. Stay behind me and don't do anything rash," Cal told Anna. "We don't know if he's armed."

She gave a slight nod, and he removed his gun from his holster, motioned for her to wait, then glanced through the window again.

Billy pushed Mona in front of the fireplace, fixed the veil around her head, fluffed out the skirt of her wedding dress, then stepped back and snapped a picture.

Cal gritted his teeth. Had he taken photographs of all his victims dressed in their wedding dresses as part of his signature? He'd kept a piece of jewelry from each of them—just like the Thorn Ripper had.

If this man's mother had killed the teenagers thirty years ago, would they find the girls' missing jewelry inside?

Every muscle in Cal's body quivered with anger as Billy lowered the camera and clasped Mona's hand. She looked frightened, but unharmed at the moment.

But if she crossed Billy or didn't please him, he might crack.

Cal squinted in search of a weapon, but didn't see a gun. He slowly tried the door, trying to keep it from making a noise, but it was locked. He raised his fingers in a count of one, two, three to signal to Anna what he intended to do, then kicked the wood door open and burst in, his gun aimed.

Billy jerked around and dragged Mona in front of him, then wrapped his arm around her throat in a choke hold.

Mona gasped, her eyes widening as she spotted Cal and Anna, while Josie yanked at the chains holding her to the metal bed.

"Let her go, it's over," Cal said between clenched teeth.

"No, she's going to be my wife!" Billy shouted.

He sounded almost childlike, and a deep psychosis glinted in his eyes.

"We know who you are now," Cal said.

Cal grimaced at the sight of the jewelry on the woman's sickly frame. He recognized the jewelry from the descriptions given by the victims' families.

"Billy, listen to him," Mona said softly. "I care about you. Now let me go, and we'll get you the help you need."

"You're just saying that 'cause you're scared," Billy snarled. "You tell everyone how important marriage is and how we should love each other. That's all I want. Someone to love me like that."

Cal saw red. "It's over, man. Let her go."

Josie inched forward as far as she could with the chains, trying to get the sick man's attention. "I told you you're not alone. I'm your sister, Billy. We're family now."

◆ ◆ ◆

Anna's heart was racing. She had to save Josie.

And she had to tell her the truth.

She suddenly stepped inside behind the agent. "No, Josie, honey, you misunderstood."

Billy jerked his head toward her. "Stay out of here! Just leave us alone!"

"I'm Josie's mother, and I can't do that," Anna said. "Just like your mother always wanted to protect you, I want to protect my daughter."

"But Mama . . ." Billy's voice cracked. "Mama isn't supposed to die . . ."

"No, and I'm sorry she's sick," Anna said. "But Mona is a kind person. She wants to help you. And my daughter Josie is just an innocent young woman."

"I do want to help you," Mona said. "Just release me, Billy, and it'll be all right. I promise."

"But what about Mama?" Billy said brokenly.

"Your mother killed three teenagers thirty years ago," Cal said. "She'll have to answer to that."

"They deserved it," Charlene screeched, suddenly stirring back to life. "Those girls acted like Goody Two-shoes, but they were nothing but liars and whores. They made a pact that all of them were going to sleep with Johnny before prom. And they all had dates with him, but he ignored me."

Anna gasped. "That's why you framed him." She faced Billy. "Your mother killed those girls and then stole their jewelry. Is that why you took Gwyneth's and Constance's jewelry, too? So you could give it to your mother?"

"Mama likes pretty things," Billy
said in a childlike voice.

"Release Mona and you can meet your father," Cal said, trying to distract Billy. "In fact, I just talked to him."

"You did?" Billy's voice held almost a hint of wonder.

Josie looked at her mother. "You talked to Johnny Pike?"

"Yes. I thought you might have gone to see him." Anna gave Josie an imploring look. "I'm sorry, honey, that you read my diary. But Johnny is not your father."

Cal crept forward. "Billy, listen to me. Your mother sent your father to jail when he was an innocent man. She kept him from you."

"No!" Billy shouted. But he turned to his mother with an angry glint in his eyes. "That's not true, is it, Mama?"

"He didn't deserve to be with you!" Charlene cried. "Not the way he treated me."

"See, your mother is the liar, Billy. She lied and murdered those girls, and now she's turned you into a killer just like her."

"Shut up!" Billy released Mona and lunged toward Cal.

Billy was a big guy and full of rage, but Cal fired and the bullet struck him in the stomach. He bellowed in pain and shock, then rocked back and collapsed.

Mona stumbled and fell to the floor, gasping for air. Anna ran toward Josie and dragged her into her arms, rocking her back and forth. "I'm so sorry, baby, I'm so sorry. This is all my fault."

"No, Mama," Josie whispered. "It's all right."

Anna looked into her daughter's eyes and saw the man who'd fathered her. But it wasn't Johnny. She hadn't lied about that.

"It's time I told you everything, Josie."

Even though Billy was bleeding, Cal unchained Josie, then dragged Billy over to the bed and handcuffed him to the metal frame. Then he raced over to Mona while Charlene collapsed into hysterical tears in her wheelchair.

◆ ◆ ◆

"Are you okay?" Cal searched Mona's face and ran his hands over her arms and shoulders. "Are you hurt?"

"I'm all right," Mona said. "Call an ambulance for Billy and his mother."

Cal checked Billy's pulse as he made the call. Cell phone service was spotty in the mountains, but he got a connection.

Anna lifted a chain from around her neck, indicating a charm of a baby bootie on the end. "Josie, honey, I did have a baby by Johnny," Anna said. "Another little girl. Not you, Josie, but you do have a sister."

"What happened to her?" Josie asked.

"I gave her up for adoption."

Mona frowned, Anna's words sinking in as her head began to clear.

"Daddy was sure Johnny was the Thorn Ripper, and he insisted I give the baby up for adoption. He made me leave town until the baby was born."

"That's the reason you and my granddaddy don't get along," Josie said.

Anna nodded. "I hated him for making me give her up." She rubbed her fingers over the charm. "I was so distraught that a few weeks after that, I met this other man, your father. I got pregnant right away . . . I guess I felt so guilty I had to replace one child with another."

"So my father really did die?" Josie said.

"Yes, honey, I'm afraid so."

Mona made another sound in her throat. "Anna, you gave up a baby . . ." Her gaze latched onto the baby bootie charm.

"Yes, a few months after Johnny's arrest," she said. "Daddy said my baby would be better off with a stable married couple, that if I kept her everyone would know she was a serial killer's child."

Mona's heart pounded. "What happened to that baby?"

Josie frowned. "Yes, Mom, where is she?"

"I don't know," Anna said. "My father arranged for her to be adopted. He used the lawyer in town." Anna's voice cracked, and she stroked the charm frantically. "I held her for a minute after she was born, and I gave her a charm just like this one, so she'd have something from me, something so she'd know I loved her."

Mona's chest ached with unshed tears as she lifted her own chain from beneath the wedding gown.

It was the same baby bootie charm Anna was wearing.

"My God," Anna gasped.

"My parents died, but they left a letter for me with their lawyer explaining that I was adopted, and that I was from Graveyard Falls. I've been looking for you for months."

Emotions wrenched Anna's face as she reached out for Mona.

Mona embraced Anna, tears clogging her throat. She had been looking for her mother, and now she'd finally found her.

♦ ♦ ♦

Deputy Kimball arrived with an ambulance a few minutes later. Cal made sure the medics examined Josie, then he ushered Mona, Anna, and Josie outside while the CSI team entered the cabin to process it for evidence.

He instructed the deputy to drive the women to the police station to give statements, and to phone Sheriff Buckley to meet them there. "After that, pick up Felicity Hacker. We still have some details to clear up."

Deputy Kimball agreed, and Cal phoned Agent Hamrick, filled him in, and told him he could stop the surveillance on Yonkers.

The similarities between Yonkers and Billy were eerie, but Cal had learned a long time ago that sometimes the most obvious suspect wasn't the killer. He knew one man who would agree wholeheartedly with that statement—Johnny Pike. Cal still wondered if Yonkers was dangerous, though.

Hamrick drove over to escort Billy and his mother via ambulance to the hospital, where they would be placed under strict guard and psychiatric care. Billy would also be treated for the gunshot wound, and his mother would receive medical care.

Before the deputy left, though, Cal stepped out to talk to Mona and Anna. "I don't want to go back to my father's," Anna said. "Not now."

"Come to my house," Mona said. "You and Josie."

Cal heard the emotion in Mona's voice and knew she had a lot to deal with. She had been searching for her mother for a long time, and now she'd found her and a half sister. She even knew her birth father's name and hopefully could meet him.

Anna folded her arms. "We have to talk to the judge and free Johnny, Agent Coulter."

"We will. The jewelry was the missing link before, and now we have it," Cal said. "And the crime team will search this place thoroughly. Charlene may have kept more evidence than we know. I'll also have those notes Johnny supposedly wrote analyzed. The handwriting should prove that Charlene wrote them."

"Billy took pictures of me," Mona said. "He probably took them of the other victims."

"Okay. We'll look for them." His eyes searched Mona's. "Are you okay?"

She nodded, although she averted her gaze. More than anything he wanted to hold her in his arms and console her.

But this wasn't the time or place to confess his feelings.

Anna wrapped her arm around Josie and then Mona. "Come on, girls. Let's ride with the deputy and give our statements, then we can go home together."

Deputy Kimball escorted the three of them to his squad car. As they left, Cal went to confer with the investigators.

One of the techs stepped from the mother's bedroom carrying a wooden box. "There are dozens of letters in here," he said. "Love letters written from Charlene to Johnny that she never sent." With a gloved hand, he dangled one of the letters in the air. "In this one, she writes about how she enticed the girls one by one to go to the falls with a rose and a fake love note from Johnny. The note claimed that he had chosen her over the others for his prom date. The girls went expecting a romantic rendezvous but fell to their death instead." He removed another letter and showed it to Cal. "This one has a list of the victims—she titled it 'All the Little Liars.'"

Cal sighed. "That and the victims' jewelry should be enough to get Pike's conviction overturned."

Anna would be thrilled. She obviously still loved the man.

And now Mona would get a chance to know both of her birth parents.

CHAPTER
THIRTY-THREE

Cal made certain the crime scene investigators searched every inch of the Linder house and roped it off as a crime scene before he drove to the station.

He carried the bagged evidence of the jewelry, the Bride Book, and Charlene's letters to present to Sheriff Buckley, but more importantly, to a judge.

By the time he arrived, Mona, Anna, and Josie were waiting in the back. "I had each of them write down their statements," Deputy Kimball said. "And I took them coffee."

"Thanks."

Felicity Hacker, a woman Anna's age, looked worried as she paced the front office.

"Thank you for coming," Cal said.

"I didn't think I had a choice," Felicity said, her voice cracking.

"It's important, Felicity." He started to explain, but Sheriff Buckley burst through the door.

He looked frazzled and confused. "What's going on? Is Anna okay?"

"Yes, Sheriff," Cal said.

Odd that he didn't ask about his granddaughter.

"I've made an arrest in the Bride Killer case and I wanted to fill you in."

Felicity looked panicked at the sight of the sheriff. Sheriff Buckley hitched his pants up and scowled, though, as if he didn't know her.

"I told Anna you didn't belong here. I don't want Johnny Pike's bastard kid in my town."

Cal frowned, but Felicity curved her arms around her waist as if she wanted to disappear.

Deputy Kimball hissed between his teeth. "Sheriff, this is Felicity Hacker, not your granddaughter."

Now Cal was beginning to understand the reason the man had retired. The brain tumor must be causing dementia.

"Let's all sit down in one of the rooms in back, and I'll explain."

Felicity glanced at the door as if she wanted to run, but the sheriff shrugged and followed the deputy to the back. When he opened the door and Buckley saw his daughter and granddaughter, his face paled.

Then he looked at Mona and an odd look crossed his face. "What are you doing here?"

"Just sit down, Daddy," Anna said. "We have a lot to talk about."

Buckley dragged out a wooden chair and straddled it. Felicity looked at Anna, then Mona, and started to tremble.

"Take a seat, Felicity," Cal said gently. Although he didn't know why he was being gentle. Her statement about Pike, which he now suspected was false, had helped send an innocent man to prison for half his life.

Felicity practically fell into the seat, then shut down.

Cal took the lead. "All right, Sheriff Buckley, Felicity, I'll tell you what we know so far, and then you can fill in the blanks or make any corrections that need to be made."

Felicity glanced at the sheriff for support, but he had a faraway look in his eyes.

Cal explained about tracking down and arresting Charlene Linder and her son, and the revelations he'd uncovered in Charlene's letters detailing her motive for the murders.

"So Johnny Pike was innocent," Felicity said, her expression stricken.

Anna gave her a look mixed with anger and grief. "Yes. Why did you lie about him attacking you?"

Felicity wiped at tears. "I was so shy and didn't have many friends, and I wanted to be in that group with Tiffany and Brittany and Candy. I thought if they liked me, everyone else would." She hesitated, twisting her hands together.

"Go on," Cal said.

She sighed. "I heard them talking about that pact, that they were all going to sleep with Johnny. Then he went out with each of them, but he paid no attention to me."

"So you claimed he attacked you?" Cal asked.

She glanced at the sheriff, but he looked at her as if she were a stranger.

"Felicity, it's time to tell the truth," Cal said. "About everything."

She nodded, then looked down at her hands. "I was so upset about everything that I slept with this other guy one night, my cousin's friend, and I got pregnant. My father threw me out and I ran away. I was living in an old abandoned place and one night I . . . started bleeding and the baby came, but it was stillborn."

She gulped back tears. "I was all alone and scared, and then the sheriff showed up, and I thought he was going to arrest me and say I killed my baby."

"What are you talking about?" Sheriff Buckley said.

Anna stood, her angry gaze on her father. "Dad, let her talk."

"He said I did something to the baby, and he was going to tell everyone and I'd go to jail for the rest of my life. Then he asked me who the father was, and I said Johnny, because I was just so mad and upset and I wanted it to be Johnny."

Anna whispered a soft sound of denial, and Josie and Mona each clasped her hand.

"I'm so sorry," Felicity said. "I didn't mean to get him in so much trouble, but when I said Johnny was the father—" She faced the former sheriff, who was glowering at her now like she was a madwoman. "The sheriff told me not to worry, that he'd help me take care of things. He helped me bury my baby." Tears streaked Felicity's face, an agonized cry escaping.

"So when the first murder occurred, the sheriff assumed it was Johnny," Cal said. "That he'd attacked the girl. Then Charlene framed Johnny and claimed he tried to strangle her, and the sheriff believed her because of your story."

Felicity nodded, her face tormented.

Sheriff Buckley's face contorted. "Who are you? What are you saying about me?"

Anna crossed her arms. "Dad, you turned on Johnny based on a lie, and then you railroaded him into jail."

"I'm so sorry," Felicity cried. "I . . . I'll testify to the truth if you need me to free Johnny."

"I think we have enough evidence to exonerate him," Cal said.

Mona stood and went to the woman. "I'm sorry for what you went through, Felicity, but thank you for telling us the truth now."

Sheriff Buckley made a blustery sound. "I got to go arrest that Pike boy. He's nothing but trouble."

Anna hugged Josie to her as her father shoved his chair away and strode from the room.

Cal gestured to the deputy to let him handle the situation. "Drive the ladies home. I'll take care of the sheriff."

"He needs to be hospitalized," Anna said, her voice bitter.

Cal nodded. Buckley had memory issues now that would play in his favor, but he had definitely run roughshod over a young man's life, and by focusing all his efforts on putting Pike away instead of finding the truth, he'd failed to do his job. Worse, he'd allowed his own personal feelings to cloud his judgment.

Because of that, Charlene Linder had escaped prison and raised a serial killer, who had started a murder spree of his own.

♦ ♦ ♦

Mona was still in shock as the deputy dropped off Anna, Josie, and her at her house. She'd stripped off that hideous wedding gown and dressed in her own clothes before they'd left. But she still felt dirty.

Anna had asked them to make a quick stop at her father's house, where she and Josie packed an overnight bag.

They had all just found each other, and none of them wanted to part. They had missed so much of each other's lives that they had to make up for it.

Still, Mona was worried about Josie and the trauma, but Josie insisted she didn't want to go to the hospital or see a psychiatrist.

"I have to shower," Mona said, still feeling the touch of Billy's hands on her.

Josie shuddered. "Me too."

Mona showed Anna and Josie to the guest room and bath, and she disappeared into her own bathroom.

She closed her eyes as she stepped into the shower, hoping to erase the memory as the dirty stench from Billy's house swirled down the drain.

But the dead girls' faces would haunt her for a long time.

So would Billy's. He was related to her—she still didn't know how to wrap her head around that fact.

They shared a father—Johnny Pike.

Yet Billy was psychotic.

Because of his mother, she reminded herself. An abusive mother, *not* because of their father.

Their father was an innocent man who'd served the majority of his life in prison because he'd been framed.

She scrubbed herself, washed and dried her hair, and yanked on a pair of sweats and a T-shirt, then went downstairs. Suddenly jittery with excitement and relief that she'd finally found her birth mother, and that she had a half sister, she hurried to join them.

A minute later, Anna and Josie both appeared, also showered and dressed in pajamas, and looking as shell-shocked as she felt.

"I can't believe you're here," Mona said as she looked at Anna. "I dreamed about finding you for so long."

Tears filled Anna's eyes. "No more than I dreamed about finding you."

Mona glanced at Josie. She could understand if Josie had reservations—she had been an only child all her life. But understanding and excitement glittered in Josie's eyes.

"I always wanted a sister," Josie whispered.

The three of them hugged and cried for several minutes, emotions overwhelming them.

"I know you have questions," Anna said. "And that you may have felt abandoned when you discovered you were adopted."

Mona didn't respond. She had felt those things, natural emotions for an adopted child. "I had a good family, though," she said. "I loved my parents, and they loved me. They took good care of me, Anna."

A mixture of sadness and relief lined Anna's face. "I'm glad they were good to you and loved you. I prayed for that every day." She tucked a strand of Mona's hair behind her ear. "There wasn't a moment that went by that I didn't think of you and wonder what you were doing, what you looked like, how big you were." She wiped at a tear, and Josie squeezed her mother's arm. "I wrote you letters all the time. And I bought a card for every birthday and holiday and wrote in it. I . . . just never sent them."

Mona's heart tugged painfully, and they hugged again.

When they pulled away this time, Anna smiled. "Now, tell us about your life, where you grew up, how you liked school." She clasped Mona's hand in one of hers and Josie's in the other. "I want to know everything."

"I want to know everything about you, too." Mona smiled. "And about you, Josie."

Mona poured them each a glass of wine, turned on the gas logs in the fireplace, then retrieved the photo albums she'd kept from her childhood and set them on the coffee table.

Then the three of them huddled by the fire and traded stories long into the night, replacing the horror of the evening with new memories of becoming a family.

CHAPTER
THIRTY-FOUR

TWO DAYS LATER

Mona, Anna, and Josie sat in the courtroom, tense but a unified front, their bond obvious as they watched Cal produce the evidence they'd uncovered.

"Charlene's love letters are filled with her obsession over Johnny. We also found notes she kept detailing her father's abuse and her plans to make Johnny suffer for rejecting her. She lured her victims to the falls by sending them notes supposedly from Johnny, saying he wanted a romantic rendezvous. In the original trial, these notes helped convict Pike, but handwriting analysis proves that Charlene Linder wrote them." Cal paused. "She admitted this in her letters, then described how each girl cried and begged for her life just before she killed them."

Johnny Pike sat stone still, his shoulders square, yet Cal noticed the twitch in his jaw. He still didn't believe he was going to be freed.

"The photos in the box found beneath Pike's bed were also planted. We found identical copies of those pictures, along with the camera used to take them, in Charlene's house. Her fingerprints were the only ones on the camera. There were additional photographs of the girls there as well, graphic ones showing them on their knees begging to be saved." Disgust knotted Cal's stomach, but at least now justice was done. "Charlene was also in possession of the jewelry she kept from the victims as souvenirs. We have tagged and identified each piece and submitted it all into evidence."

The judge nodded, his expression grave.

"She also lied to the police about Pike attacking her. That false report was crucial in convincing the sheriff that Pike was guilty."

The judge clutched his gavel. "Is that it?"

"Not quite," Cal said, then turned to Johnny. "After Mr. Pike's arrest, Charlene told him she was pregnant with his child and she threatened Anna. When the evidence became stacked against Pike, he finally gave in to a plea bargain to avoid the death penalty and to protect Anna."

Pike fidgeted and looked down at his scarred hands.

"Charlene Linder was extremely devious and manipulative, and Pike was a victim." Cal addressed the judge directly. "There's something else. Apparently her father molested her. He forced her to bite down on a rose when he was assaulting her so no one would hear her cries."

He paused. "Charlene's mother blamed Charlene for the abuse. She hacked off her daughter's hair in an attempt to make her look less attractive to her father. In turn, Charlene cut her victims' hair to make them look less attractive to Johnny. We also have conclusive evidence confirming that she lied to Pike about the baby." He glanced at Mona, Anna, and Josie. "Charlene was pregnant, but the child was not Johnny Pike's. DNA proves the baby was her father's."

A shocked, hushed whisper reverberated from everyone present.

Pike swung his gaze toward Anna, his look full of sorrow and regret.

The judge pounded his gavel. "Under the circumstances and in light of the new evidence presented today, I am officially overturning the murder conviction against you, Mr. Pike. On behalf of the court and legal system, I apologize for your false incarceration. All charges against you will be expunged. While I realize you have a right to be angry, and there's no possible way to make up for the time you've lost,

I hope you'll try to look forward to the future." He pounded the gavel again. "You are free to go."

Johnny stood in shock, but Anna shrieked, ran toward him, and threw her arms around him.

"You're free, Johnny," she whispered.

"I can't believe it." Johnny turned to Cal. "I'm really free?"

"Yes, you are." Cal extended his hand. "Your name is cleared, and you can walk out of here today."

Anna kissed him, then eased away as Mona approached. "Now there's someone I want you to meet."

Cal stepped back to give Mona and Anna some space. Anna clasped Mona's hand and coaxed her forward. The moment Johnny and Mona looked at each other, emotions clouded both of their faces.

"Johnny, this is Mona," Anna said softly. "She's your daughter."

"I'm so sorry," Johnny said in a hoarse voice. "I . . . we missed so much."

A tear trickled down Mona's cheek as Johnny opened his arms and she hugged him.

◆ ◆ ◆

Mona couldn't believe all that had happened in the past two days. The previous night Anna had retrieved the letters and cards she'd written Mona over the years and given them to Mona.

As she'd read them, she'd realized how much her mother had loved her, and how difficult it had been for Anna to give her up.

She also knew how much Anna loved Johnny.

Mona's father.

"I didn't know," Johnny said, his voice thick.

"I didn't either." Mona wiped at a tear.

"I'm so sorry," Johnny said. "If I'd known—"

"That's my fault," Anna said. "I shouldn't have listened to my father. I should have told you about the baby."

Mona took Anna's hand, then Johnny's, and smiled. "At least we're together now."

Johnny looked at Mona and then Josie, his face riddled with emotion. "I don't have much to offer, but I love your mother with all my heart. I always have. And I hope you'll both let me try to be a father to you. Or at least, a friend."

"I'd like that," Josie said without hesitation.

"I'd like that, too," Mona said softly.

Anna and Johnny hugged and drew Mona and Josie into their arms. Mona's heart soared with happiness. Cal had done this—he'd protected her and solved the Bride Killer and the Thorn Ripper cases, and brought her family back to her.

Only when she turned to thank him, he was gone.

CHAPTER THIRTY-FIVE

THREE WEEKS LATER

Mona and her new family had spent almost every minute together for the last three weeks, sharing stories and getting to know each other.

Today it would be official. Anna and Johnny were getting married.

"It's time," Josie said as she clasped Mona's hand, and they rushed to the dressing room at the small church where Anna and Johnny had decided to exchange their vows.

The town had been shocked to learn Johnny had been framed, saddened at the miscarriage of justice, and relieved the Bride Killer had been caught. The residents of Graveyard Falls were safe again.

Johnny hopefully would be awarded some monetary compensation from the state, but that would take time. Mona had given up the radio talk show, needing time to process all that had happened.

She and Josie slipped into their places as bridesmaids.

Anna's father, Mona's grandfather, wasn't invited. He had moved into an assisted living home. Anna was still struggling to forgive her father for his likely part in Johnny's arrest and for shaming her into giving up Mona.

Mona smiled as the piano music began, and she and Josie walked down the aisle. When Anna and Johnny joined hands and exchanged vows, thirty years overdue, tears trickled down her face.

She'd never been as happy as she was at that moment.

Except one thing was missing from her life.

Cal.

She had fallen in love with him when she'd first met him, and they had wasted so much time. But she didn't know if he wanted her now. She hadn't heard from him since the court hearing to clear her father.

Just like she hadn't heard from him after Brent died.

"I pronounce you man and wife," the reverend said.

Johnny cradled Anna's face between his shaking hands and kissed her with all the love he'd harbored for her for years. Mona and Josie clapped and hugged and congratulated their mother and Johnny.

Mona's heart ached to have the kind of true love they had found.

♦ ♦ ♦

Cal watched the ceremony from the back of the church, his heart hammering. He had left Graveyard Falls to give Mona and her new family time to assimilate and adjust to everything that had happened.

All he wanted was for Mona to be happy.

Liar.

He wanted Mona.

He wanted to hold her and love her for the rest of his life.

He wanted to make her his wife.

But . . . did she love him? Could she forgive him for keeping Brent's dirty secret?

Should he give her more time?

The kiss ended, and Mona pivoted to face the rear of the church. When she saw him, surprise lit her eyes, and a small smile tugged at her lips.

Enough to give him hope.

He forced himself to wait while she and Josie exited, then Anna and Johnny strolled down the aisle, grinning and kissing, their joy contagious.

The few friends who'd shown up followed, and Cal took a deep breath and stepped from the church.

The moment he saw Mona, though, his heart started beating so fast he could hardly breathe. Once, he'd stepped away because of Brent, but that had been a mistake.

He loved Mona. He always had. He should have fought for her.

He would now.

The wind shook snow from the branches of the trees, the mountains postcard perfect with the ridges dotted in white. Although the snow was starting to melt and the trees were budding. Spring was finally coming.

But it was Mona who looked ethereal as he strode toward her. Anna and Johnny hurried toward their limo, and Cal jogged down the steps to Mona, afraid she might leave before he had a chance to finally confess that he loved her.

◆ ◆ ◆

Mona felt a snowflake dampen her cheek, or maybe it was her tears from seeing how happy Anna and Johnny were. They were finally getting to start a life together, the life they'd been robbed of by a cold-blooded killer.

Then suddenly she felt a light touch on her arm and Cal was there. He looked so handsome in his black suit jacket that her heart stuttered.

"I thought you'd left town," she said, her voice quivering slightly.

"I had, but Anna sent me an invitation."

"They wouldn't be together if it weren't for you."

"I was just doing my job."

Mona tensed. "Is that all you were doing?"

Cal's eyes glittered with emotions she couldn't quite define. He was always so intense. Had been devoted to Brent. Had made love to her and held her and comforted her when she needed him.

"No." Cal took her hands. "I'm in love with you, Mona. I always have been. I just . . . I thought I owed Brent. He saved my life more than once when we were in foster care together."

Mona's look softened.

"But I paid my debt a long time ago. And I . . . I was wrong to not tell you how I felt." He inhaled sharply. "I'm sorry for that, for keeping things from you. If you'll give me a chance to love you, I'll never let you down again."

Mona's heart raced. "I love you, too, Cal. I always will."

A sultry smile curved his mouth, and he pulled her into his arms. "Good, because I'm never letting you go."

Her heart shouted with happiness as he closed his mouth over hers and kissed her.

Anna and Johnny had wasted so much time by keeping secrets, just as she and Cal had.

Now they wouldn't waste another minute because nothing would ever keep them apart again.

ACKNOWLEDGMENTS

A big thank-you to my developmental editor, Lindsay Guzzardo, who always knows how to take my rough draft and turn it into a better book. Also thanks to the Montlake author team and my editors Maria and Irene for their fabulous support. And to Diane for catching all my mistakes!

Also a big thank-you to my fantastic sister, Reba, who works as a counselor in a state prison, for answering all my questions!

A sneak peek at

ALL THE PRETTY FACES

The next book in the Graveyard Falls series

RITA HERRON

CHAPTER ONE

The dead girl stared up at Special Agent Dane Hamrick, her eyes wide with terror, her lips forming a cry for help that had probably gotten lost in the wind boomeranging off the sharp mountain ridges.

Her naked body lay in a tangle of weeds and brush in a ditch, one hand outstretched as if begging for help. The whites of her eyes bulged with broken vessels and had yellowed like an egg that had been cracked, the yolk spilling out.

Even more disturbing, tiny slits had been carved beneath her eyes, more tracking down her pale face like the claw marks of a bird of prey's talons etched in snow.

But it was the tears that got to him. They had dried, but stained with the blood, they created a crimson river down her cheeks.

Sheriff Kimball stooped to examine the body. "Special Agent Cal Coulter said I should call you. That you might have worked a similar case."

Dane shrugged. He worked with Cal at the Bureau. Cal knew Dane's history. "Maybe. Do you know who she is?"

The sheriff gestured toward the thick woods behind the motel. "Not yet. I didn't find any ID on her, but I haven't done a thorough search of the area yet. The janitor at the motel found her when he took out the trash, but the clerk at the front desk said she wasn't registered as a guest."

The stench of garbage suffused the air. The fact that this woman had been left near the Dumpster could be significant. They'd canvass the people registered at the motel. One of them could be the killer.

Or hell, the motel was off the highway, so the killer could have been a stranger passing through.

"She probably died from the stab wound to her chest," Sheriff Kimball said. "The ME is on his way."

Betsy had died from a stab wound to the heart as well. For a moment, the woman's face faded, and in its place Dane saw his younger sister. Betsy at twelve with the freckles sprinkled across her nose and that infectious giggle and those green eyes that always twinkled. Betsy, who'd driven him crazy with her silly jokes and pleas to take her with him everywhere he went.

At nineteen, she'd been innocent and sweet and excited about her future.

She'd looked up to him and depended on him to protect her.

But he'd failed and some maniac had stolen that future from her.

Just like this woman's had been stolen from her.

Ten years without justice ate at him like a cancer destroying his soul.

Storm clouds darkened the sky, casting an ominous gray over the scene. Dead leaves swirled around the woman's feet, the wind whistling through the spiny trees. It had been storming the day Betsy died, too.

He rolled his hands into fists. Finding the truth forced him to drag his ass out of bed every day and go to work when some days he wanted to bury himself in a bottle—or in the ground beside his sister—because his heart had an aching, empty hole that could never be repaired.

Dane had joined the task force assigned to track down the most wanted criminals in the States along with Cal, hoping to have access to any case that might lead back to Betsy's killer.

This was the closest he'd seen yet. Cause of death appeared to be the same.

Still, there were differences. The cuts on this victim's face had been carved by a sharp instrument. Either a scalpel or some kind of sculpting tool. They were precise, detailed, as if the killer was experienced and knew exactly what he was doing.

In his sister's case, the cuts had been crude, emotional, angry. Personal. Almost a crime of passion.

And they'd been made by a common pocketknife.

The murders were probably not related.

Although in ten years, the killer could have evolved, perfected his technique. Learned to be patient.

Either way, this woman was someone's daughter, maybe sister. And friend. They would want answers. Closure.

To see the sick person who'd done this pay.

He'd find her killer and get justice for her.

He wouldn't stop until he got it for Betsy, too.

"Yes, I was held hostage by a serial killer." Josie DuKane still had nightmares about that horrible time. But she schooled her emotions as she addressed the crowd in front of the city hall in the small town of Graveyard Falls.

Sad to say that that terrifying experience had inspired her to write a true crime novel. And now, to her surprise, a production company had decided to film a movie about the town and the murders.

"Your book *All the Little Liars* is based on that case?" one of the reporters asked.

Josie nodded. "Yes. During the course of the police's investigation into the Bride Killer murders, Special Agent Cal Coulter uncovered the truth about the Thorn Ripper case that occurred thirty years ago."

"They were related?" another reporter asked.

Obviously these reporters hadn't read her book. "Yes. A woman named Charlene Linder killed the three teenagers in the Thorn Ripper case, but she framed local football star Johnny Pike because he'd rebuked her. At the time she was pregnant, and later delivered a son named Billy." She paused, still processing the fact that her mother, Anna, had been in love with Johnny at the time, and that she'd had Johnny's baby, a little girl her mother had given up for adoption.

Solving both cases had led to Johnny's conviction being overturned, and now her mother and Johnny had finally married. They'd also reconnected with the baby her mother had given up, and now Josie had a sister, Mona. She and Mona were not only close in age but had become good friends. She'd even studied criminology like Mona.

"Billy Linder was the Bride Killer?" the reporter asked.

"Yes. Charlene was abused by her father, and she repeated the cycle by abusing her son. Billy's bedtime stories consisted of tales about the teenagers she'd killed and left at the base of the waterfalls. She referred to the victims as *little liars.*"

Another reporter waved her hand. "Why did she call them that?"

Josie blinked as the flash of a camera nearly blinded her. The sky was darkening from the threatening storm, the trees shaking with its force. "Charlene was disturbed. Her victims were popular cheerleaders who shunned her. According to her journals, she saw them as Goody Two-shoes who lied about being virgins. Apparently the three victims had made a pact to sleep with Johnny Pike, and she was jealous because he paid attention to them and not her."

The crowd of locals who'd gathered for the press conference shifted and whispered, still in shock from the events that had transpired in their town.

Some residents were also upset about the movie. They felt as if her book and the negative publicity glorified the killers and would drive families to leave town out of fear.

But Josie had been so close to the case that she'd had to write it and share the sordid story. In some ways it was therapeutic for her to talk about the kidnapping, even more so for her to study Billy's background and understand the reasons he'd done what he'd done.

Getting into a killer's mind was something her sister, Mona, who worked as a counselor, had helped her with. That insight had added depth to the story.

A male reporter in the shadows raised a hand to get her attention. "Have you been to visit Billy in the psychiatric unit?"

Josie fought a shiver. "Yes, both my sister and I have. Billy is a very disturbed man."

"That doesn't justify the fact that he killed three of our local girls," someone shouted.

"He should be put to death like they were," another woman said.

A raindrop fell and plopped against the podium, lightning zigzagging across the sky. More whispers and rumblings of protest echoed through the group.

Josie lifted a hand to signal them to let her speak. "I didn't write this story to condone what Billy and his mother did. But I believe the citizens of Graveyard Falls should know the truth." She took a deep breath. "And I think that understanding what caused both of these individuals to commit these heinous crimes may help the victims and their families recover. Hopefully it will also raise awareness of the cycle of domestic abuse." And maybe teenage bullying. Although the mothers of the teenagers would balk at the idea that their children had treated Charlene unfairly.

"Nothing will bring back our daughters," one woman cried.

"You should let them rest in peace," another local added with disdain. "Not cause more pain to their families by making them relive the sadistic crimes over and over."

Sara Levinson, mother of one of the Thorn Ripper's victims, stepped to the front. "Every time I see your book and think about watching my daughter being murdered on screen, I feel sick."

Josie tensed. Sara had balked over doing interviews. But she had finally agreed.

Apparently she had regrets now.

"I'm sorry, Sara," Josie said softly. "I understand your grief and pain. I still have bad dreams about being held by Billy Linder myself. But I think this book honors those we lost, and I hope you will see it that way as well."

Tension broke out as a cluster of folks in the back shouted disagreement. Someone yelled at her to leave town.

Others called out support, excited that the filming would boost the town's fledgling economy. Already the inn had been refurbished, and a local builder had renovated cabins on the river for production crews and others involved in the filmmaking process.

"We don't care about the money." This voice from someone in the back of the crowd. "We want our nice quiet town back."

She wasn't sure Graveyard Falls had ever been a nice quiet town.

An argument broke out, and the mayor stepped up to try to defuse the situation.

Voices grew louder and more heated as he fielded questions, so she decided it was time for her to exit.

She scanned the group, searching for the sheriff, who was supposed to be on guard in case of problems. But he'd texted earlier that he was meeting Agent Dane Hamrick from the FBI, and she didn't spot him anywhere. She'd met the federal agent when she was interviewing people for the book. He worked on a special task force.

Had another crime occurred nearby?

The wind stirred again, and the hair on the back of her neck bristled as she started down the podium. She had the uneasy feeling that something bad was going to happen.

Or maybe it already had.

Last week she'd received hate mail accusing her of sensationalizing the tragic deaths of the women.

Was the person who sent that letter watching her now?

♦ ♦ ♦

He watched Josie DuKane through the crowd, amazed that she seemed humble when the true crime book she'd written had garnered so much attention.

With those sparkling green eyes, Josie was attractive, too. Not beautiful like the models and actresses or even the high-class women who paid to perfect their faces to magazine quality.

But pretty in a natural way. She mesmerized him because she seemed real, not superficial. She was also smart and used her brain, not just her looks, to get ahead in life.

Yes, Josie was the perfect one to tell his story.

The others, though—they were just pretty faces waiting to be carved by his hands.

Pretty faces that would look even more beautiful in death.

He lifted his phone and smiled at the photograph he'd taken of the woman, then traced his finger over her face. His pulse pounded as he studied the claw marks. So fitting that she be marked by claws when she'd tried to sink hers into men to get what she wanted.

He clicked on the text symbol and sent the picture to Josie.

She was just stepping down from the stage, about to dart away from the cameras, reporters, and locals when the message went through. She checked her phone, then hesitated on the steps, her eyes flaring with shock as she lifted her head and searched the crowd.

She was looking for him.

He smiled, blending into the shadows.

"This is just the beginning of our friendship, Josie," he murmured. *Just the beginning.*

ABOUT THE AUTHOR

USA Today best-selling author Rita Herron has written more than sixty romance novels and loves penning dark, romantic suspense tales, especially those set in small Southern towns. She earned an *RT Book Reviews* Career Achievement Award for her work in Series Romantic Suspense and has received rave reviews for the Slaughter Creek novels *Dying to Tell* and *Her Dying Breath*. She is a native of Milledgeville, Georgia, and a proud mother and grandmother.

Printed in Poland
by Amazon Fulfillment
Poland Sp. z o.o., Wrocław